AMERICAN GENES

AMERICAN GENES
A NOVEL

KIRBY NIELSEN

atmosphere press

Mistaken regard for what are believed to be divine laws and a sentimental belief in the sanctity of human life tend to prevent both the elimination of defective infants and the sterilization of such adults as are themselves of no value to the community. The laws of nature require the obliteration of the unfit and human life is valuable only when it is of use to the community or race.

Madison Grant

The Passing of The Great Race, Charles Scribner's Sons, 1916 and 1918

Chapter 1
IMMIGRANTS

HISTORY SHOWS THAT IT IS NOT ONLY SENSELESS AND CRUEL, BUT ALSO DIFFICULT TO STATE WHO IS A FOREIGNER.
CLAUDIO MAGRIS

1911

Lars and Bridget Olson were the only passengers to get off the train. It was 10:30 p.m. on November 18, 1911, when they stepped onto the deserted platform where a freezing wind blew through their clothes.

The weather reminded them of Norway's high country. The sting of it squeezed tiny tears from their eyes. The extra moisture temporarily caused some blurry vision. Blink and things were clear again. Moisture. Blink. Clear. Lars had to repeat the blinking routine several times before his eyes were clear enough to see. The little bit of inconvenience dissipated within a minute, but it kept them from moving in any direction. *My God, I'm as cold as I have ever been,* Lars thought.

Jolted out of their travel-induced fatigue, a wave of anxiety and a tinge of panic replaced weariness. From what others told them, this was typical of every immigrant's journey to their promised land. It was feeling lost and alone as in a childhood dream with neither mother nor father coming to rescue you. In it, you must go on, press through the fear to find your parents. For Lars and Bridget, their destination was at hand; their dream would soon be a reality.

The platform was pitch black except for a small arc of light cast by the single bulb hanging over the depot entrance. The dimly lit sign said, Grant Grove, assuring them they had arrived at the place of their dreams.

At last, they were at their new home, and they found themselves alone. Lars' uncle, Albert, was not there. Lars sent him a telegram from Philadelphia, where they finished the immigration process, and from Minneapolis earlier that morning. He noted the obvious with a heavy voice, "I can't believe he isn't here."

"I knew we couldn't count on him," Bridget snapped back.

Lars wanted to say more but was too tired to care what she thought. Too tired to defend his uncle.

The depot was straight ahead, about thirty feet from the tracks. Nodding toward a set of double doors, Lars led her inside the lobby. Two bulbs hung over oak benches, emitting barely enough light to chase away the blackness. The small waiting room was empty. A "Closed" sign hung on the door of the station manager's office. An iron bar and steel lock secured the double-wide steel door to the freight room.

Lars and Bridget set their small wooden locker and two large bags on the floor and stood motionless and silent. All they could hear was the clock above the ticket window. They were alone and nearly frozen in a place that was to be their new home.

"Something must have kept him. He's had an accident, or maybe he's sick," Lars rationalized.

There was no response from Bridget, now leaning over the coal-burning heater found on the far west wall of the depot. She was trying to capture as much heat as she could from the embers smoldering in the stove. Fortunately, Lars found coal in a bin next to the station. Soon a small bright fire caused heat to radiate from the heater. With the chill taken out of the air, a hungry and disappointed couple spent the night trying to sleep on the hard, oak benches.

The dawn brought the first glimpse of their destination, Grant Grove. Before them, a small farming town lay on the gently rolling plains of southwest Minnesota. They were neither elated nor disappointed by what they saw. Travel weariness had sapped them of all emotions.

Lars' uncle Albert never did come to welcome them to the new world. Instead, it was the kindly stationmaster who helped them on their way. He asked the mailman to take them to Ruth's Café and introduce them to Ruth Carlson.

~ ~ ~

On Sunday, November 25, 1911, Johanna Bridenbaugh sat ramrod-straight and motionless. She pulled her shoulder-length brown hair up into a tight bun on the back of her head, every bit of it held in place by a broach and pins.

Her dress was conservative, old-style, exposing only her face, fingers, and feet. It was the color of the fertile brown soil found on the surrounding farms. The dress looked cheap, although the delicate lace that rose off her shoulders to cover her neck and the quality of stitching belied that notion. She looked at least ten years older than her actual age of twenty-four, and that was fine with her.

"Are you ready?" William Bridenbaugh spoke with a crisp voice that didn't fit his eighty-seven-year-old frail body. It was more of a command than a question. She knew she had better be ready, or she would receive a scathing lecture on the importance of promptness.

"Yes, father. Shall I get your coat?"

"Don't bother. I'm old, not decrepit. I can still get my coat."

"Yes, father."

Johanna and her mother got their coats and went outside, where they found Mr. Bridenbaugh had pulled the buggy near the house. They pulled blankets over their shoulders to help ward off the cold. The thermometer on the side of the house read ten degrees.

Johanna's father had blanketed the old, dapple-gray Belgium mare before adding the harness. Keeping the horses warm was another one of his many rules. Johanna recalled her oldest brother, often making the snide remark that their father treated the horses better than people. Down the road they plodded, slow and steady toward Grant Grove and Redeemer Lutheran Church.

Johanna sat stoically during the sermon, and her face strained from concentrating extra hard, trying to hold onto every word. It was a practiced pose designed to please her father, who also had strict rules of conduct while in church. Any member of his family violated one of his commandments at their own risk. When they were too old for a spanking or a few lashes with the willow switch, the boys had to spend extra hours cleaning out manure from the cattle barn. Johanna had to polish silverware and crystal for hours on end.

William Bridenbaugh came to Minnesota from Pennsylvania in 1883. He said his family immigrated to the US from Prussian Germany in 1860, so his father could fight with the North in the Civil War. He always reminded Joan about how "pure" his German bloodline was. Their ancestors were descendants of the early Germanic tribes. He was proud of the fact that no runts, imbeciles, or epileptics stained their pedigree.

Johanna had four older brothers: one killed in the Army during the charge up San Juan Hill, one was a minister in Duluth, Iowa, and two who took up ranching in Colorado. All the boys moved far away from their overly strict and opinionated father. Johanna chose to stay and help her ailing mother. She understood her father, identified with his code of conduct, and copied many of his mannerisms. If that pleased him, he seldom showed it. Still, she knew he approved of her, loved her, and favored her. She was as close to being daddy's little girl as one could ever get with William Bridenbaugh.

Her parents reluctantly recognized their age limits. Although he no longer farmed, William kept two cows for milk, a few hens for eggs, and the old Belgium mare for transportation. Martha Bridenbaugh had agreed to turn the garden over to Johanna. However, that didn't stop her from snipping at her if she wavered from the way she did things.

Anywhere between fifteen and thirty minutes after supper, old Mr. Bridenbaugh required everyone in the house to listen to him hold forth on some topic. Recently, one of these post-meal lectures dealt with a popular subject in the United States— eugenics.

"Johanna, did you read in today's paper that they are allowing more of those colored people from the Middle East and Africa into our fine country?"

"Yes, sir, I did. I know it's a terrible thing."

"And why is it so bad?" She knew he was testing her.

"It dilutes the bloodline making the white less pure. It's a fact; these races aren't as intelligent or hardworking as the rest of us."

"Exactly, and our country is being over-run by them. It's bad enough we are forced to tolerate those poor Irish bastards. These immigrants are crowding our cities, creating poverty and filth wherever they live. Then, they take jobs away from good people. It's terrible, a damn outrage."

Johanna didn't know much about "colored" races, immigrants, or the cities. She had never been to a big city. Other problems, such as deformed and defective people, had caught her attention, and Johanna had her own negative opinions of them. She and her father would talk for hours about what it meant to be an imbecile, idiot, moron, or crazy. And how feebleminded people were multiplying faster than "good" people could care for them. More of their kind meant increasingly more charity that would stretch the limits of what society could provide.

Johanna noticed some pamphlets at the librarian's desk about people wanting to form a new organization called the Southwest Minnesota Eugenics Society. She showed the flyer to her father, who immediately approved her attending the first information and organizational meeting of the society in Mankato. The organization was more than an opportunity to get out of the house and away from her parents. It was a chance to hear about ways to save the white northern European way of life.

Tapping the brochure as she read, she thought, *I'm going to become an expert in all of this. I am going to do something positive about all the mental and physical defectives. I'm going to learn about this new science of eugenics and save our way of life out here in tiny Grant Grove. Father will look down from heaven, and he'll be proud of me. Yes, sir, he will.*

CHAPTER 2
THE STORM

THERE IS NOTHING LIKE JUST INDIGNATION FOR FOSTERING UNREASONING HATE.
CHRISTIANA BRAND

1911

Lars and Bridget Olson were the first new immigrants to land in Grant Grove in over two years, making them the talk of the town. They were unsure of what to do next since an uncle named Albert left them stranded at the train station. Lars and Bridget quickly endeared themselves to several people. The first was Ruth Carlson, who owned Ruth's Café, a little diner on Main Street. She took the lost and beleaguered immigrants under her wing. Ruth served them their first meal in Grant Grove the morning after they arrived.

Wintry weather brought out the best in Ruth. She served up gallons of piping hot coffee, sweet cinnamon rolls, and oatmeal for breakfast. For lunch, there were extra-large portions of mashed potatoes and roast beef piled high on a slice of bread, both smothered with gravy. The windows fogged over when the hot steam from the grill and coffee pot met the bitter Minnesota cold.

"You two just got off the boat?" Ruth asked.

"No, ah . . . Philadelphia. One week, I don't remember, yeah one week—maybe."

"I mean, you're new to Grant Grove."

"We got here on the last train last night. My uncle, ah, Albert, do you know Albert Olson?"

"Sorry, I don't. Wait, I do know of an elderly Albert, but he's Albert Jensen. My parents might know Albert Olson. They know everyone within a ten-mile radius. I'll get my mom over here when things slow down a bit. She and my dad will get you set up. They love helping people. By the way, the first meal is on me. The only condition is that you come back." She left them with a smile and a coffee refill.

Ruth's parents, Olaf and Gorine Carlson, turned out to be like godparents to Lars and Bridget. They took the immigrants into their home and treated them like family. Gorine did laundry while Olaf took Lars on a tour of the small town, introducing him to everyone they met. People instantly liked Lars, and he seemed happy to meet them. Still, no one knew or ever heard of an Albert Olson. He was certainly not a resident nor even a regular visitor.

Grant Grove was typical small-town America— formed when close-knit families joined with ethnically similar ones by the universal need to survive. The town had two churches, a small bank, a grain exchange, a general store, a diner, and a farm machinery dealership. White was the color of choice for buildings and faded white was the standard indicator of a lack of money.

The first thing the townspeople learned about the newcomers were they had been married for ten months. Which explained why they held hands and often kissed— quick little pecks on the lips, cheeks, and neck whenever they thought no one was looking. Being Norwegian, white, fair-haired, and Lutheran meant they were hardly the kind of people that would be a threat. Plus, they were intent on joining his family in the area.

Lars was the responsible one, the decision-maker. He opened a bank account with quite a bit of money for an immigrant. By nature, he liked people, and strangers quickly warmed to his friendliness. Bridget was quiet and reserved. Lars spoke for them when they met people on the street or at church.

Bridget soon started to show that she was often moody and withdrawn. She was happy one minute, sullen the next. A few minutes later, Bridget would switch back to happy. There were times when she sat all by herself, staring out the window for hours on end. None of this was a surprise to Lars. She'd told him of her melancholy before they married, but that made no difference. He still loved her.

Within a week of their arrival in Grant Grove, the young couple took a room over Lindgren's General Store, where they shared a bathroom with three, sometimes four other guests. At least it was clean—and quiet, a place where they could sleep long hours. Their bodies and minds were still adjusting to a new rhythm of life. Unlike their ocean village, they had a chance to make love without the fear of someone coming through a door. They could have sex in the morning, sometimes in the afternoon, and every night. It was a wonderful time when love spilled over into passion at the mere hint of a smile.

They were resting on their bed when Bridget shared her dream of life in America with Lars. "I want a white house, neatly painted, with flowers all around."

"We can do that. For sure."

"The garden would be in the back, and trees would provide shade in the summer."

Lars was grinning. "We can do that."

"And, I want a white picket fence and green grass where our children can play."

One morning, with Lars standing guard outside the communal bathroom, Bridget soaked in the water, smiling at the notion of a real enamel bathtub. The bath helped her relax.

"Can I come in?" Lars asked with a newlywed desire in his voice. "I'll wash your back."

"No, you can't come in. You watch that door! Besides, what kind of thing is that a man watching his wife take a bath? Oofda."

"I think it would be a perfectly fine thing, a man enjoying the sight of his beautiful new bride. It would be entirely proper in my mind."

"Not in a public bathroom, it isn't. Besides, you see plenty of me in bed. That should be enough for you. There must be some decency left in this world." Bridget gave her response with a hint of cheeriness in her voice; perhaps his idea wasn't that bad after all, maybe he could wash her back another time.

Later that night, after making love, Lars wanted to discuss their dilemma. Where was Albert, and what would they do if they couldn't find him?

~ ~ ~

Lars did his best to explain to Olaf why they had come to Grant Grove. Back in Norway, his family was poor farmers. His father's brother Albert lived with them because he had no occupation nor land of his own. With nothing else available, he would go to Christiana to work in the factories. But he'd always end up back at the farm. He'd get fired because he was unable to leave alcohol alone.

"He and I felt we needed to come to America where we'd have a better future. I knew I was a good farmer, but like my uncle, I had no chance of owning a farm. When Albert was sober, we made big plans for what we could do here. We read brochures we found in the public library and laying around in restaurants. We learned about both free land and cheap land. All one had to do was come and farm it. We thought we would make money on our first farm and use that money to buy other farms. Then we could rent that land out, getting rich off the rents."

Lars went on to explain that with Albert being sober for over a year, he was sure his drinking problem was in his past. They decided he would come to America first and start to look for land and buy their first farm. He left Norway in July of 1908 and eventually came to Grant Grove.

Olaf smiled and shook his head as he tapped out the ashes from his pipe. "I hate to tell you, Lars, but someone told you a whopper of a lie. Yes, there are some farms for sale. But unless you came to America loaded with money, you'll have a hard time. The free land disappeared twenty to thirty years ago."

Later in the day, Olaf was drinking coffee with a group of older men gathered at his daughter's café. He told the group of the young immigrants' plans, causing them to howl with laughter. "Boy, someone sold him a real bill of goods."

As the laughter died down, another member of the coffee group simply smiled. "There's a sucker born every minute."

Three days later, someone recalled an Albert Olson poking around town a few years back. He soon disappeared, only to resurface from time to time, never establishing any kind of connection to anyone. They said his sole purpose in visiting Grant Grove was to buy groceries and alcohol. Another person mentioned his current location was probably out near Ruthven. He hired on as a farmhand for old John Peglar and was living across the road in the old Johansen place. Only later would Olaf tell Lars what some people said about Albert. He was not one of them, nor would he ever be. They saw Albert as a broken-down alcoholic, worthless trash.

After listening to Olaf's information, Lars said, "Please don't tell Bridget. I will do it later." For once, Lars had a somber look on his face as he turned away from Olaf. *God damn it, if he's drinking again, I'm sure all our plans are in ruins. No cheap land, no free land, no Albert whom I thought I could trust. How do I tell Bridget?*

On December 5, two weeks after their arrival in America, Olaf hitched his horse up to an old buggy. He gave Lars directions on where he thought they could find Albert. Gorine said it would be nice if Lars and Bridget took a little something good to eat to him. She packed a basket with sandwiches and cookies, a loaf of bread, and a small wedge of her homemade cheese. Finally, she tucked in a quart of fresh buttermilk: rich, creamy, and cold.

"Now, Lars, do you think you can make your way out there okay? Do you have the directions I gave you?" Olaf asked.

"Sure, not a problem." Lars grinned from ear to ear. He and Bridget were excited to get out into the country, to explore and to finally meet up with Albert, whom they assumed simply didn't get Lars' telegrams. Westward they went on the main road out of town, smiling and enjoying the sunshine and gentle breezes. The cold front that had gripped Grant Grove since they arrived finally moved on. The fatigue and tension of their journey had melted away, leaving behind a brighter, happier couple.

"Which of these farms will be ours, do you think?" Bridget asked Lars as she held onto his arm. Leaning her head on his shoulder, she smiled broadly.

"I don't know which farm Bridget. We don't even know where Albert is. We'll see what he has to say. Maybe he already bought one for us! That would be so great! He could teach me how to grow crops, and you could set up our house and have our first child." They were about two miles out of town when there was a hint cooler air was returning.

The horse trotted on over the bumps, up and down the gently rolling hills, past little rivers and streams. *Clip clop clip clop.* It kept a steady pace, not too fast for the road but enough to create a breeze on their faces. The landscape was stark with large patches of snow on the palate of deep brown soil. Trees planted by homesteaders many years ago looked like occasional afterthoughts. Farm buildings were all set back from the road.

"Did you see that? A snowflake!" Bridget observed.

"Yes."

Bridget smiled as she nudged him gently. "So, what do we name our first baby, Lars Olson? You are the head of our new household."

Lars laughed, "Ha, head of the household. Aren't we getting a little ahead of ourselves? This talk of a baby is probably not happening right now. Babies will come later when we get our farm."

"Well, yes, but you seem to be having your way with me quite a lot since we got here. You do know that is how babies are made, right?"

"Very funny," he pushed back at her with his right arm as they both smiled at her witty quip. "You don't seem to mind my advances all that much, Mrs. Lars Olson. You encourage them."

"What? Why never. A proper lady waits for the man to start the romance."

"That is old-fashioned, and you know it," beamed a blushing Lars.

They rode west, both noticing the ever-darkening skies. With the clouds came a few more snowflakes. As if to mirror the shift in the weather, their moods began to change, happy and carefree replaced by pensive and stoic. Westward the horse trotted, further out into the country. As directed, they took the first right after the big red barn. They rode north for a short while and slowed down when they reached a dip in the road and a small grove of cottonwood trees. Then came a left, which put them back on a westward course.

Lars read Olaf's instructions aloud. "There will be a farm on the left with stone pillars supporting a steel arch over the driveway. A sign on the arch should say Peglar Farms. Your uncle Albert should be on the farm directly across the road."

"There, the arch!" Bridget pointed to the sign.

Olaf's directions were perfect, Lars thought as they pulled into the first driveway on the right. Rundown was too kind of a phrase for this tired old farmstead, broken was more accurate. As they stopped the horse, they noticed once again the cold and wind. Suddenly, it was as cold as that night at the train depot.

Soon, the sky filled with giant flakes of wet snow. They stuck to anything they hit and began to cover the ground, the horse, and themselves with a coat of pearl white.

Lars got down from the wagon and walked toward an old, run-down house: "Hello, Albert, we're here." Lars shouted from outside the front door. There was no answer, so Lars turned to yell in the direction of an aging barn. "Albert. . . Albert, yoo-hoo!" He waited a minute or two more before walking toward the barn, assuming Albert might be feeding or watering the animals. He called out a third time.

"Yah, yah, yah, hold yer britches. I'm coming."

"Albert, my dear uncle." He gasped when he saw him. Lars hardly recognized the thin, wild-looking man who squinted, even though it was cloudy and snowing. He was teetering and weaving a bit, and seemed to be having trouble slipping the left strap of his bib overalls over his shoulder.

"How did you get here? Why didn't you let me know you were coming?" he said as he continued to approach Lars. Lars noticed how Albert needed to pay attention to each step, each sentence. It was the way he acted back in Norway when he was drunk.

Lars replied in Norwegian, "I wrote to you from Christiana and telegraphed from Philadelphia and Minneapolis. I told you our arrival time in Grant Grove. I did as we'd planned."

"Sorry, not many people know me right about now since I just moved. I'm kind of out here in the middle of nowhere. I should've written to you about my new address." Albert hung his head and seemed to be talking to the ground. He stopped short of Lars, not coming close enough to shake his hand or even give him a welcoming hug.

Lars closed the distance between them. Reaching out to Albert with both arms, he hugged him and instantly wished he hadn't. Manure, dirt, food, and liquor covered his uncle's clothes. He was close to gagging, and he quickly backed away.

"What have you done to yourself?"

Albert shrugged, "I've been down on my luck here lately. Things are better than they seem, believe me, they are."

"Come meet my wife. Bridget is over here."

"You're married? I never thought about that. We only talked about you and me in America, no wife."

"I wrote to you about her in the letter, Albert."

Motionless and unsmiling, Bridget looked frozen to the wagon seat. It was clear she had no intention of getting down, and Lars surmised she was angry with the bleakness of the entire situation.

Finally, Albert reached up to Bridget, offering his hand, albeit calloused, scarred, and filthy. Bridget nodded at him. The blank, drawn-out look on her face said it all. Lars knew she was struggling to control her anger at finding the promised land polluted with a broken-down uncle living on a dilapidated farm.

"You . . . are pretty" was all Albert could say.

The snow came down faster, and it was getting hard to see, and it was slightly past noon. "Looks like maybe a huge storm today," announced Albert. I've been here enough to know that it can really snow to beat the band. Big, bad, windy storms, you know, like gales out on the North Sea. Then sometimes it piles up and lasts all winter."

"Is this your farm, the one you have been writing to me about?" asked Lars.

"The guy who owns this land, Peglar, he lives across the road. He says I have first dibs on buying it once I get my down payment together. You know, get a loan. I was waitin' 'til you got here to see if you maybe wanted to go in on it with me."

"You expect my wife and I to live out here in this shitty place? I imagine the soil's as bad as the buildings!"

"Well, it could be great with a little work. You know I'm sorry, I didn't know you would be married, have a wife to support."

"Lars," Bridget yelled. "Come help me down; I don't feel well."

Bridget spotted the barely standing cubicle of sun-bleached wood and assumed it was the outhouse. On her way back, she tripped on an old iron wheel hidden by the light blanket of snow. She nearly hit the ground, her reflexes saving her from the indignity. When she turned her face to Lars, it was set hard, like steel, "I'm ready to go back."

"I don't think we can do that now. It's snowing too hard. Why we can't see five meters, and with this wind, I think you would get too cold. It's sure to let up soon. We'll have to wait this out. We'll die for sure if we go out in weather like this."

"Come now, Lars, put that horse in the barn," Albert yelled out over the growing roar of the storm. "I'll take

Bridget to the house. I didn't get it cleaned up for you, sorry about that. But it'll keep you warm at least. Yes, sir, it will do that."

"I'm not leaving his side," Bridget announced, "I don't care to go inside. Lars, let's wait in the barn until it lets up."

The barn was full of hay, but no animals. *Odd,* Lars thought. Albert didn't even have a horse. There was evidence that animals lived here at one time. The edges of wood were rounded smooth in the places animals repeatedly rubbed it. Dirt in the feeding troughs meant they had been unused for a long time. The dusty, dry smell of alfalfa hay was pungent. Lars soon adjusted to the intense, moldy dry odor. He listened to the sound of the wind blowing through holes in the siding. The snow had covered the horse by the time they got it inside and unhitched from the buggy. Lars took the harness off, wiped her dry with an old feed sack, and scraped together some hay for her to eat.

Time passed, how much, Lars couldn't tell, but they were freezing standing there in that drafty barn, watching the snow continue to pile up. Lars guessed it was knee-deep in most places. Bridget leaned toward Lars and whispered into his ear. "What are we going to do? I don't like your uncle. He's sad and smells awful, even from a distance. I can't imagine going inside his house. It probably smells worse than him."

"Well, where else are we going to go?" He needn't have spoken.

The moment Lars entered the house, he realized his and Bridget's worst fears had materialized. Against the far wall, rancid lard sat in a crock, spewing out a putrid odor.

Her stomach turned, she ran to the old sink and threw up. The smell, the disorder, the trash, and the rotten, half-baked chicken sitting on an old plate, all contributed to her fainting. She fell straight back into Lar's arms.

"I didn't bring my wife from Norway for this mess. I thought you'd have a thriving farm, but this looks more like a slum."

Albert stood, gawking at Bridget, his eyes wide. Lars detected he was shaking ever so slightly from his anger, disappointment, and from the strain of holding Bridget's full weight.

When she came to, she turned on Lars, "You-you brought me here, to this pigpen. You expect me to stay here? You're no better than my father." She began pummeling him with her fists. "I hate this place, I hate you, I hate it all. You gave me false hope. Who do you think you are to make me come here? You've ruined my dreams."

She looked over at a stunned Albert. "You . . . you worthless son of a bitch, you bastard. You let your whole family down. You lied about how good things were here. You are a pig living like this!" She grabbed a poker standing by the small stove and lunged for Albert. Lars grabbed her from behind.

"Bridget, stop. We aren't going to live like this. We'll leave soon, and this isn't going to be our house. We aren't living here. Understand?"

Bridget continued to struggle until Lars wrested the poker from her grip. She looked for something else to hurt Albert with, but nothing was near. Lars was tightening his arms around her from behind, pinning her arms close to her side.

After letting Bridget burn out her rage, Lars found old curtains piled on the floor in the back bedroom. He covered the bed with one and had Bridget lay down fully clothed. He put the other on top of her. By now, she was catatonic, her face blank, eyes empty, and mouth closed tightly. Lars waited by Bridget's side until she closed her eyes and went to sleep.

Lars came out and set about to start a fire in the small living room stove. He made sure it was going well before he threw on some coal. There was not a lot of wood to start a fire, nor coal to keep them warm for long. As he stared into the small stove, his mind wandered. *He's too occupied with drinking to even think of the essentials, like keeping warm. With our dreams shattered, I wonder what's going to become of us? If we make it back to Grant Grove, what then?*

Lars' resourcefulness got them through. He instructed Albert to go outside the back door and scrounge for wood. Albert soon returned with enough wood to keep a small fire going through the night. "I forgot I had a little bit of coal piled up out there too. We can use that tomorrow."

With very little food and only water to drink, Lars took charge of their lives. Before it got dark, he remembered the basket of food still in the buggy and struggled mightily to get to the barn to fetch it. In the dust-covered pantry, he found some flour sealed tight in a large glass jar and two jars of canned green beans. All looked edible, so Lars and Albert ate the food from the basket along with biscuits and green beans to ride out the storm. When she was awake, Bridget ate only a small bit of Mrs. Carlson's cheese.

Bridget slept the whole time. The only time she got up

was to eat and relieve herself. When Bridget was up, Lars was always by her side. She spat at Albert and searched for objects to throw at him, but Lars was there to restrain her. Both men were amazed that her rage could go on for so long.

Lars and Albert scooped the snow away from the back door. They needed a place to pee on the ground near the house. It would be folly to try to get to the outhouse in whiteout conditions. The indignity of peeing in the snow inflamed Bridget and prolonged her anger.

The next thirty-six hours were hell for everyone as the storm whipped and roared across Minnesota. When it finally ended, the sun shone bright, but the temperatures stayed low. Lars sent Albert to the Peglars to ask for help. He told him to bring back some food and ask them if he could bring Bridget over there until the roads were passable. Albert returned with a loaf of bread, a pile of ham wrapped in brown butcher paper, and an affirmative to Lars' request.

Soon they had a plan. Lars crossed the road pulling Bridget behind him. In places, the snow was five feet high, and it was physically exhausting walking through it. Each step forward met with resistance making each step a mighty effort.

Mrs. Peglar recognized that Bridget needed help. She fed her soup, dressed her in a full-length flannel nightgown, and put her to bed. All the while, Mrs. Peglar soothed and calmed her, enticing her back into the present world. Over the next few days, she gave Bridget a hot bath, washed the foul smell of Albert's house out of her clothes, and encouraged her out of her melancholy.

It took five days for Lars and Bridget to make it back

to Grant Grove to the extreme relief of the Carlsons. Lars told them the story of Albert and his pitiful condition, leaving out most of Bridget's trauma. Bridget said nothing of the trip except to say she was disappointed in Lars' uncle.

Chapter 3
Growing Roots

FOR IMMIGRANT GENERATIONS ESPECIALLY, FAMILY IS THE FIRST STRUCTURE, OR SHELTER, FOR A PEOPLE WHO ARE IN EXILE.
ALICE MCDERMOTT

1912

Back in Grant Grove, safely out of the wind, snow, and filth of Albert's old house, Bridget continued to return to her normal self. In the back of Lars' mind, he wondered why she became so angry and out of control? *Was it something in her past, before he met her? Was it the fact she had a baby when she was a teenager and that she had to give it up for adoption?* Bridget never gave any details, nor did he ask for them, he'd always felt it was in the past and best left alone. Now he was not so sure. Maybe he should have found out more about her before he married her.

For several days, they stayed with the Carlsons so Gorine could help Bridget finish her recovery from her traumatic experience. Both Lars and Bridget slept long hours and soaked in the warmth of the Carlsons' kitchen stove. Slowly but surely, Bridget's anger began to dissolve, and when she smiled for the first time, Lars and Bridget knew it was time to move back to their apartment.

After making love, Bridget looked deep into Lars' eyes. "Now what do we do? Albert has failed us. We're on our own. I do know one thing: I'm never going back to

Norway, that's for sure."

Lars thought he could detect some of her anger in the tone of her question. "Is there any place else in America you want to live?"

"How would I know? I never thought of anywhere but here. All I heard about was your Albert. I trusted in you, Lars Olson."

There was a growing sharpness to her words that cut into Lar's layer of confidence. Sensing her mood swing, Lars had a fleeting concern about a repeat of an episode like the one at Albert's place. "From everything I read, we're in excellent farming country. The soil is rich and deep. A good farmer could make money here—if he knew what he was doing."

"How do you know all of this, from your worthless bastard uncle?"

Letting the snide comment slide, Lars answered, "I read books and studied the atlas at the library. Plus, I talked to a few people who'd been to America. They said to go to Minnesota or Iowa. That's where lots of people like us immigrate."

Exasperated at having to decide with so little to go on, Bridget was suddenly assertive. "I don't care, I don't care, I don't care. I told you what I want: no Norway, no Albert. What I want is to be with you." She paused a second, and with a smile, she added. "And to have your babies."

Lars blushed and smiled back. "I think there are good farms here and I can learn how to be a good farmer. That's for sure." He paused for additional thoughts to form. "Plus, we have the Carlsons and Ruth. They have been nice to us, and all the other folks seem like good people. At least their parents came from Norway or Sweden. I feel like we could fit in. Right?"

"I suppose so. There isn't much choice. We are both too tired to go anywhere else, and we don't know where else to go. I'll be happy being with you."

There was no more wondering, no more doubt. Grant Grove would be their new home.

~ ~ ~

Ruth Carlson fed Lars and Bridget during their first weeks in Grant Grove. Hers was the only restaurant in town. She knew how to run a business successfully. She served tasty food at a fair price and made sure everyone left her restaurant with a smile on their face. Sometimes it was a free piece of pie for the children when she knew money was tight. Other times, it was one more cup of coffee or one more dinner roll. She smiled, hugged, and laughed her way into the hearts of her customers. People came back often because they liked her food, and they loved her.

Ruth's restaurant also served as the unofficial town hall, where information bounced from person to person, changing with each retelling. Weather, planting, harvesting, rumors, and roads were fair game, as was gossip about an errant son or a young woman pregnant out of wedlock. Lars and Bridget Olson were a popular topic for speculation, gossip, and pity. Thanks to Olaf's information about Albert, there were now questions about Lars. Did he have a gene that made him prone to alcohol like his uncle?

One old resident of Grant Grove commented, "They say that sort of thing runs in the family. It leads to a no-good lout who gets to be a drunk, and the next thing you know, he's beggin' for a handout. Then, we gotta pay for his welfare, so he don't freeze in the street."

"John, you grumpy old bump on a log, what do you know about it? Your brother-in-law ain't no shining star, that's for sure. Ain't nobody that doesn't have some clunker in the clan. I say we give these young folks a chance. Let's see if they can make it. Odds are, they'll head into Minneapolis or Chicago and he'll end up getting a job in a flour mill or tractor factory."

~ ~ ~

During the weeks before they found a house to rent, Lars and Bridget became regular customers at Ruth's Café. She was kind to them in many ways, and both appreciated the language lessons Ruth provided. Pointing at a word on the menu, "See this word, Lars? It says potato. Po-ta-to. Sometimes, when there are several of them, we say po-ta-toes."

"But I thought toes were on your feet."

Ruth laughed. "English is hard to learn, and you have to keep practicing. We'll try to learn as many words as we can."

Lars noticed a group of men sitting at a round table in the rear of the dining room. Mostly they were older, and from what Lars could tell, they were friendly to each other. Lars wondered what they were talking about for so long, so he asked Ruth.

"What are they talk about?" nodding towards the table of men.

Ruth chuckled. "That there is a group of men who

think they know most everything. All they do is gossip and spread rumors. Do you understand?"

"No. I'm confused."

"I'll put it this way. They have a good time talking about everybody else's business."

~ ~ ~

There was a vast void in Johanna's life brought about by the death of her father in June of 1912. At his autocratic worst, he was still her father, and Johanna respected and listened to him. She adored him in some ways and hated him for his cold, detached demeanor.

Only her brother John, the pastor, came to the funeral, and she loved him for that. On the other hand, she was boiling with anger toward the two brothers who refused to attend.

On January 5, 1913, her mother died, deepening her sense of loss and loneliness. At their mother's funeral, all her older brothers were there. There were brief and cold exchanges between Johanna and two of her brothers. John provided the only solace and comfort she would be given.

"So, you're going to get it all, the house, the farm, everything." Her youngest brother had that steel-hard glare of their father. "I guess you earned it, staying here with our father. At least you were a help to poor mother."

"Yes. That's the way he wanted it." She tried to be as cool and removed as her brother. But emotionally, it was hard. Tears came often, and sorrow surrounded her like a blanket. She thought it would never leave.

Johanna used her inheritance to buy a two-bedroom house off Main Street in Grant Grove. She kept the farm because its rental income would pay her living expenses. The move also precipitated her changing her name. Nothing official, she asked people to begin shortening her name to Joan. To her, it felt modern, American, and less foreign-sounding.

Education filled her void. Weekdays, Joan took a room near Mankato State University, and for two years, she took classes in the social sciences. She went against the grain of the time, having no interest in being a homemaker or some old maid school-teacher. She felt destined to be somebody important. Damn the fact that women seldom went to college. Damn the idea they were supposed to get a teaching certificate or study home economics. She studied social work, psychology, genetics, and history, and she did well, earning a two-year degree in social work.

In her spare time, she attended meetings to learn more about eugenics. One of her eugenic highlights was attending a lecture by Dr. Dight, the man who introduced eugenics to Minnesota. He was the state's leading advocate of sterilization of people with epilepsy, insanity, and mental incompetence. He came to Mankato to officially charter the Southwest Chapter of the Minnesota Eugenics Society — one of the first such organizations in the United States, and Joan became a charter member. Back in Grant Grove, she practiced what she learned on her neighbor:

"We all know that farmers breed their best boars with their best sows. They get better pigs that way. They do the same with horses and cows. Why are people any different? We see it all the time. When good strong, healthy people mate, their children grow to be intelligent and strong. The kind that makes our society great. We certainly ought to encourage more of this type of thing. Don't you think?"

Her neighbor, Wilma Hanson, wasn't so sure. "You believe we should think of people behaving like animals? There is more to people than breeding the biggest bull with the cow that gives the most milk. People are different. They got a brain."

"To a certain degree. But most of it is genetic. If we want a better country, we must encourage good white folks to have more children. It will keep the germ line pure."

"I don't know about all of that. It sounds sort of strange to me. Treatin' people like cows. How people turn out in life is more than the 'germline' or whatever you call it. You must have parents to teach kids about God, morals, and how to live right. When you get a little older and have your own children, you'll understand better. That's what I think anyhow."

"Wilma, I think if you had some education in these things, you would understand better. I've been to college, you know."

~ ~ ~

The Olsons found their decision to stay in Grant Grove rewarded. On December 13, 1911, Ruth introduced Lars and Bridget to John Dowd. He was by himself in a booth hunched over the last of his eggs and pancakes. As they sat down, he raised his head and surveyed the strangers before he spoke:

"You two are those Norskis come to town to make your fortune?" His voice was rich, deep, and had a slight nasal quality. For some reason, the way he spoke made them feel relaxed. "I'm always looking for good help, and I assume you two don't have any jobs yet."

"No jobs," came the reply from Lars.

"I operate two businesses here in town. On the east end of Main Street, I own a grain business, on the west side a livestock exchange, you know, sales barn."

They looked back at him with blank expressions.

"Look, Mr. Olson, Lars, is it? You come with me now. Mrs. Olson, come to my house at five-thirty a.m. tomorrow. I'll have work for you as well."

They nodded after conferring with each other in Norwegian, "We . . . we come to see you tomorrow morning," Lars replied. Bridget gave Mr. Dowd a pleasant smile.

"Good, then off we go, Lars. Mrs. Olson, it was a pleasure. I will see you tomorrow morning."

As they walked toward his business, John Dowd began to explain. "Olson, my grain exchange is where I buy farmers' crops like corn, wheat, and oats, mostly, when harvest time comes. I store it until I feel the price is high enough, then I sell it to larger grain dealers in Minneapolis, Omaha, or Sioux City. You understand?"

"No."

"Never mind then. My cattle barn is where farmers come to sell their animals, mainly pigs, cows, and sheep. I don't buy these animals, other farmers do. If the animals are ready for slaughter, someone from one of the big butchering plants buys them. I make a small fee off each animal sold. You understand?"

"Not much." Still, Lars continued to smile and nod his head. Lars soon learned that his job was to do all the things no one else wanted to do: hard, menial, and sometimes dangerous tasks.

The morning after they met, John Dowd hired Bridget to work for his mother, Petra Dowd. Petra and John lived in an expansive house. John's two sisters married and moved away while he stayed behind to help run his father's business. When his father died, it was just he and his mother in the large house.

Petra explained what she needed Bridget to do after the men left. "I'm eighty-five, and I need help with a few things. I no longer do laundry, nor cook. My baths are hard, so I need help getting in and out of the tub. Even the stairs are a problem. John wants me to move downstairs, but I don't want that. I love my bedroom. It's where my husband and I spent almost fifty-five years together."

Bridget was the right person for the job. She enjoyed helping Petra, and with her as a tutor, quickly learned to cook, do laundry, even some light house cleaning. The job gave Bridget a sense of purpose, something to focus on besides being in a strange place. Plus, she had someone to help her with her English and to teach her about a woman's role in Grant Grove's society.

~ ~ ~

At the grain exchange, Lars' main job was shoveling. When farmers came with their wagons full of grain, he pushed it from the wagon into an auger, which lifted it to the top of enormous storage bins. Later, when John Dowd sold the grain, Lars shoveled it from the silos into another auger, which took the grain to the train cars.

Sometimes it was dangerous work. One day, Lars and a co-worker, Richard, were inside one of the large silos, a square tower, sixty feet high and two-thirds full of kernels of corn. Their job was to stand on top of the loose grain and keep it flowing evenly as it emptied from the bottom of the silo onto a railroad car. Lars stood near one wall of the silo, shoving the corn that had accumulated there towards the middle. Suddenly, he disappeared straight down into the corn.

Unbeknownst to Lars, an air pocket below him had collapsed, sucking Lars and the grain around him into the void. He had no air to breathe since he was four feet below the surface and completely immersed in the corn, unable to move. His world was black, time stopped, and the only thing he knew was he was about to die. With lungs bursting and hope fading, he tried to put together a prayer. But all he could think about was oxygen to fill his lungs. The fear that gripped him as the pressure in his lungs grew was worse than anything he could have ever imagined.

Pure panic took over as Lars sensed being pulled even further into the bin. Then, he soon became aware that that crown of his head had appeared from the deadly grasp of the corn. Lars first felt the air around his forehead, then he could see. Finally, he sucked air in through his nose. In what seemed to Lars like an eternity, his mouth came open, and he inhaled a great gasp of air mixed with corn dust. He coughed but continued to breathe the precious air.

Finally, a dusty and shaken Lars emerged from the corn, frightened but alive. The only thing Lars could think to say was obvious: "Damn, that was a close one. One minute I'm scooping corn, the next thing I'm gone."

Richard and John told Lars what happened next. Richard did his best to move the corn away from above him. Meanwhile, John, who barely heard the call for help, stopped the auger and scrambled up a ladder attached to the outside of the grain bin. At the halfway mark, he stopped and pulled open a two-foot square escape door. Out came the grain, pouring out onto the ground below.

Later, outside the silo, Lars sat on the pile of corn, covered in grain dust, trying to expel the last of it from his lungs. Silently, he said a simple prayer of thanks, then in broken English, thanked Richard and John. "I will always thank God for you two saving me."

~ ~ ~

John Dowd's livestock exchange wasn't much safer. The manager spoke slowly, hoping Lars would understand. "Olson, most of the farm animals that we sell here are harmless, except for the bulls and boars. Those critters can be mean if they get cornered, which they are, on account-a being in these little pens. So always, *always* stay behind them. Behind. Understand?" Lars nodded as if he understood, but the man had talked so fast, he caught only a few words.

One of Lar's jobs was to herd the animals from their holding pens to the small arena where they would be on display for potential buyers. When it came time to sell one large, black Angus bull, Lars assumed he could simply open the pen, the animal would come out, and he would drive it down the runway and into the arena. He was wrong.

The moment the gate to the pen came open, the bull charged at Lars, who started running for his life. Down the runway they went, in the opposite direction of the arena. In a few seconds, the big black bull had Lars cornered.

They stared at each other, Lars frozen with fear and panic, unable to think clearly. He believed he would soon be trampled to death.

Thwack! A large oak fork handle came cracking across the snout of the bull, and it took several steps backward, giving Lars a chance to scamper up and over the walls of the runway.

"You're one lucky dumb shit! Good thing for you I saw you got yourself on the wrong end of that bull. Didn't I tell you not to let that happen? Lucky for you, I was able to get over here before he trampled the life out of you. Next time be sure to *stay behind them.*" This time, he clearly understood what his manager said.

"You betcha," was all Lars could say.

Lars never shared the stories about his near-death experiences with Bridget. Anytime she asked about his cuts and bruises, he smiled and said, "It's okay. I'm fine."

~ ~ ~

As time moved on, Lars began to think of his uncle in a different light. He was family, and at one time back in Norway they had been close. Lars would occasionally borrow a horse and buggy from John Dowd or Olaf Carlson and drive out to see him. Little had changed. He lived in that filthy house and did menial farm work for neighbors, earning just enough for alcohol and food.

One day when he was on a visit to bring him some food, he asked Albert, "Do you ever think about changing your life around?"

Albert didn't look directly at Lars; instead, he stared off into someplace behind him. "Oh yeah, sure I do. I'd like to do that, but you know me, this alcohol seems to have a hold on me. I can't break loose from it. That's a fact."

"I've heard you can break loose from it. Some people have done it."

"But I'm not 'some people,' my dear nephew. No, not at all. I am what I am, and I'm gonna die being like this. I'm sorry I don't meet the high and mighty ideals you and your wife have. You're wasting your time with me, Lars."

"No, I'm not wasting my time. You're my uncle, and I still love you and will see you as often as I can."

~ ~ ~

One evening, Bridget was slicing bread for their evening meal, her back to Lars. "Lars, did you know the Dowds have a gas stove?" Without waiting for a reply, she continued. "All you do is turn a knob, strike a match, and it comes on. In a few minutes, the oven heats up, and you can look at the thermometer to see how hot it is. I've never heard of such a thing."

Silence. Lars was trying to stay awake, his mind on a farm somewhere far off into the distance. She turned toward him.

"You haven't heard a word of what I was saying, have you?"

"What? Stove?" His eyes were drooping.

Bridget was frustrated with Lars. She knew he worked so hard and that most nights he fell asleep after finishing his evening meal. She wanted his attention, his affection, his gentle stroke on her smooth white skin. "I bet you'll perk up if I take off my blouse right here in the kitchen."

Lars was wide awake and grinning. "Oh, yeah, go

ahead and do it. I'll be plenty awake."

"Ha, you wish. Why the very thought of doing that is not proper even if we are married." After they finished eating, Bridget took Lars by the hand. "Come, my sweet Lars. Let's go to bed, and I'll take my blouse off for you."

~ ~ ~

One warm May evening with a breeze moving gently over the prairie and into Grant Grove, Lars and Bridget sat on milk crates outside their front door. There was no porch for rockers, so the wooden boxes were the closest thing at hand for this poor immigrant couple.

"Lars, there is something special I think you might like to know."

"Oh, yeah? And what would that be?"

"Do you think you will be a good father someday?"

"I guess so. Why do you ask?"

"Can't you guess?" Bridget started to blush. "Because you're going to be one."

Lars jumped up from his crate, took both of Bridget's hands, held her at arms-length for a moment, then pulled her close. "This is fantastic, the best news I ever heard! After you said 'yes' to marrying me, of course."

"Petra said it was true. I have all the signs."

When Bridget was eight months pregnant, John invited her and Lars to a Sunday dinner at their home. As they were finishing their dessert and coffee, John made an announcement. "My mother and I've been talking, and we would like to propose something that I think will help us all. Bridget, after the baby's born, we'd like you and the baby to spend your days here. After a while, if you'd like to come back to work helping Petra, you could ease into it as soon as you're ready."

"What John is saying is I would be thrilled to have the sound of a baby fill the house. I missed the grandmother part of life. My girls live so far away."

Lars looked over at Bridget and nodded his head. Spending the day at the Dowds' home was a better alternative to their staying in the tiny, three-room house they now called home. Bridget nodded back.

"Thank you, Petra. I'd like to do that."

On December 2, 1912, Peter Anse Olson was born. Lars wanted the baby's middle name to be his beloved father's first name, and Bridget agreed. Peter and his mother spent their days at the Dowds' and each night in the cozy comfort of his parent's three-room house. And the community was happy to welcome a healthy new resident.

Petra soon started spoiling Peter by holding him in her lap at nap time. Even John grew to love having Peter around the house. He'd get down on the floor and play with him. Building blocks, a small fire-truck, and a few old boxes were all they needed for hours of fun.

The Dowds valued the work Bridget and Lars did, but beyond that, they enjoyed sharing their large home and dining room table with their gracious and appreciative immigrant friends.

Chapter 4
THE FARM

FARMING IS A PROFESSION OF HOPE.
BRIAN BRETT

1913

In 1913, Lars and Bridget found a farm they could afford. The owner injured his back and was unable to work the land. He had no sons to take it over, and his two daughters had married professional men and lived in Minneapolis.

Lars was in John Dowd's office when a late April thunderstorm was getting ready to let loose. Thunder echoed off the granary walls and down through the town, causing everyone to stop and listen for more. The booms did little to ease Lar's discomfort. He didn't know why beads of sweat were forming on his brow. It could have been there because he was anxious about what he was about to tell John or because of the pre-storm humidity.

"John, ah, I found a farm for sale that would be perfect for Bridget and me. It's the Schmidt place out west of town, about five miles. Maybe you know it. Anyhow, I thought it best to tell you about it now. If it works out, we can't stay on with you."

"You sure you're ready? Farming here isn't like Norway."

There was a brilliant flash of lightning, another crack, a few sporadic *booms*, then the rain. These were life-sustaining rains farmers needed to water the crops, and everyone needed to fill basement cisterns.

"I think I've learned enough this last year that I know what I want to plant. I know I can make the seeds grow tall. Yup, I'm a good farmer, and I know you will give me a reasonable price when it comes time to sell my crops."

John did not look happy. "How are you gonna pay for it?"

"I brought some money from Norway, about two thousand American dollars. We saved half of what Bridget and I made with you, so that is another two thousand. I'll have to get a loan for the rest."

"Tell you what. You negotiate with Schmidt, and if you get a deal, then find out what the bank will charge you for interest. After that, come to see me. Okay? Don't take the bank loan till you talk to me."

Lars nodded, and a smile began to emerge. "Thank you, John."

Lars waited in John's office for the rain to stop and listened in silence to the click-clack clicking of the teletype machine in the corner. John Dowd was the first to get one in Grant Grove. He bought it because it gave him up-to-the-minute commodity prices. Wheat, corn, barley, bacon, beef, and oats purchase prices came spewing out of the machine, flowing onto the floor, and accumulating there like a small mountain of snow.

Nodding at the machine, Lars said, "Pretty snazzy deal there, John."

"Yes. It sure helps me know what's going on right now. It beats getting grain prices a day later in the newspaper."

On May 15, 1913, Lars ended up buying the eighty-acre Harold Schmidt farm. He paid ten thousand four hundred dollars for the farm, four hundred dollars for the meager crops that were already in the field, and fifteen hundred dollars for the farm implements and livestock. Lars talked to the bank manager, took notes regarding a rate of interest and payment details. The manager told him newcomers had to pay a higher rate of interest since they were new to the community and had no record of credit nor, as in Lars' case, experience as a farmer.

Later, John listened carefully to Lars explain what he had agreed to in terms of the purchase price, as well as the bank's loan offer.

"Lars, I don't normally make loans. But you and Bridget have done an excellent job for my mother and me. I think you are a good, honest man. So, I'll loan you the money you need to buy the farm, and I'll charge you the best interest rate available to someone with proven creditworthiness. How about fifteen annual payments with the principle and interest due each December first?"

A stunned Lars said, "Thank you very much!"

It was customary for farmers to sit at a roundtable at Ruth's and share information and advice over coffee. Shortly after buying his farm Lars was able to join the group, so Lars' purchase was the topic of the day. "The god damn banks make out either way, bloodsuckers. You pay the loan—they make money. You don't pay the loan—they own the property." Paul Grundy nearly spat the words out, "Be careful of those greedy sons of bitches."

From the other side of the table: "Lars, wheat prices are heading up. Plant plenty of wheat, and as soon as you make a few bucks, buy more land."

Another commented, "But if you go buyin' too much land, then you gotta have motorized machines. And you're gonna need to borrow for that, too. Next thing you know, you're in debt up to your ears. Keep it simple, Lars. Learn how to farm in this part of the world, then pay cash for more land or machines. No one ain't ever predicted when prices will fall."

"Sure," Lars replied. He was careful not to say anything about where he got his loan.

~ ~ ~

The Olsons and Dowds finished their Christmas 1913 dinner and sat savoring their coffee and tea. John asked Lars and Bridget, "Do either of you have any relatives in Norway who would be interested in coming to America? You know, to replace Bridget? Petra and I are having a hard time getting good help, isn't that right, Mom?" Petra nodded her agreement.

Bridget was the first to speak. "I can't think of anyone. I didn't know anyone in my family because my father never spoke to any of his kin. He said they were all heathens. My mom's family disowned her for marrying him, so we were loners. Lars, you're the one with a big family."

"Sure, I'll ask my mother. You're happy with one Norwegian, so you're going to try another, huh John?" John thought for a moment, smiled, and nodded his head.

Lars corresponded with his mother and older brother. There was a woman with distant connections to the Olsons who wanted to come to the U.S. but didn't have the means. She hoped to immigrate so she could live closer to a sister in Minneapolis. Letters went back and forth with Lars reading them to John and Petra. John dictated letters to

Lars, answering questions, and providing details about the job. Finally, they reached an agreement with Erica Tomlinson. In addition to paying Erica's fare, John Dowd arranged and paid for her room at a nearby boarding house.

In June of 1914, Erica arrived in Grant Grove. After spending a few days with Lars and Bridget, she was ready to move to her room in Grant Grove and meet Petra and John. Within a week of her arrival in Grant Grove, Erica took over the job of caring for the Dowd home and its occupants.

She immediately adapted to life in the United States. She learned how to run the Dowd household and, like Bridget, grew close to Petra. Their home was always clean, and a grand garden once again flourished in the backyard. Petra would sit in her favorite wicker chair and smile as she watched Erica work with the plants that supplied a variety of foods for their table.

Erica became friends with Bridget, who was making her transition to America easier. She gave English lessons and tutored her on the workings of life in rural America.

It wasn't long before Lars overheard gossip at Ruth's Café. "Yeah, I betcha that there's more goin' on than cleanin' there at the Dowd house. Ol' John got himself a good little gal there with that Erica. She's a looker, all right."

"Harry, you come up with the dirtiest thoughts . . . but I was thinkin' the same thing." A peal of laughter followed.

Other people in the community were alarmed: "I wonder if Pastor Nygard has spoken to John about this. Why, they all three come to church and act like one big happy family. There isn't any telling when she goes home and when she comes to work. She may be spending all night there for all we know."

The rumors continued to swirl through the community. The day after Thanksgiving 1914, Lars felt he had to ask John about his relationship with Erica and was shocked by what he heard.

"I love her, Lars, and I'm sure she loves me. We hit it off from the very start." John's radiant smile lit up the room.

"There are rumors, you know. Have you, ah, you know you and Erica . . . ?" Lars's face was glowing red.

"Heavens no, Lars! I know they all talk like we are living in sin, but everything is proper. Don't worry about it and tell those busybodies to poke their noses into someone else's business."

Seven months later, the rumors and speculations ended. John Dowd and Erica Tomlinson rocked the little Grant Grove community with the news that they were married on August 8, 1915. Pastor Nygard presided over the private service held in the Dowd home. Lars was the best man and Bridget, the only bridesmaid. Erica's sister from Minneapolis, a rapidly failing Petra, and Mrs. Nygard were the only guests besides Peter, who played quietly during the ceremony. At the time of their marriage, Erica had been in the United States for thirteen months.

~ ~ ~

Grant Grove was in Redwood County, where surveyors divided the land into squares, a mile on each side. Each square mile had six hundred and forty acres divided into eighty, one hundred and sixty, or three hundred and twenty-acre farms. Lars and Bridget's eighty-acre farm was near the intersection of County Road 15 and Schoolhouse Road. It was three miles west and two miles north of Grant Grove.

A short gravel driveway led to the farmyard. The Olson house was near Schoolhouse Road with the barn and other outbuildings to the north and east of the house. Lars learned that this was typical of North American farms because the prevailing winds in this part of the country blew from the west to the east. The winds carried the smell of animal manure away from the house, solving a potentially noxious odor problem.

Lars could stand at the side door of his house and look out on his fields, which gradually sloped down towards a wet marshy area. The marsh had standing water in the spring but turned to mud in late summer and fall. Lars' neighbor pointed out something Lars had failed to notice. "If you look closely, our farms are in the middle of a four-mile circle of farms that all drained down toward that marsh."

They took a moment to survey the surrounding area, and Lars could see that the observation was accurate. Altogether, the farms formed a large bowl. His neighbor continued. "The marsh hasn't always been there. It began forming sometime in the 1870s when farmers plowed up the prairie grasses to make farm fields. You see, prairie grass caught and retained rainwater, but farm crops didn't, so when they plant crops, all the rainwater that doesn't seep into the soil runs off the land and right into that low spot. Look over at my farm; there's one more interesting thing. See that little lane that runs parallel to Schoolhouse Road. That lane used to be an old Indian trail that got flooded over when the marsh started to form."

In the spring, Lars looked to the east and watched his deep green fields of oats and wheat swaying back and forth in the breeze. Their movement reminded him of a calm ocean with gentle swells of blue-green water. Summertime began the process of ripening and a gradual transition to a golden fall. Lars believed that the growing crops were the wonders of nature. He felt a sense of complete contentment watching them grow.

He often missed the deep green forests of Norway and the deep blue fjords with rocky cliffs pointing to the heavens. Yet, he was growing to love the plains and found a new kind of beauty in the bounty it provided. He often wondered, *How could one look at this and not be thankful to God for blessings received?*

Everything came together for Lars and Bridget. Wheat prices were continually rising to meet the war-related needs of Europe. Three dollars per bushel of wheat was double what it had been three years before. As a result, Lars and Bridget did well financially. They paid off their loan from John Dowd five years early. Plus, Lars remodeled the house to add a large room that served as a laundry room and pantry. He also added modern conveniences of indoor plumbing and wiring for when electricity would become available in rural Minnesota.

Despite the aches and pains of their arduous work, Bridget and Lars grew to be happy in America. They earned the respect of the residents of Grant Grove. They had applied for and became citizens in December of 1913.

Chapter 5
DEFECTIVES

1913

Joan Bridenbaugh had lived in or near Grant Grove her entire life. Baptized as an infant and confirmed as a teenager, she belonged to the Redeemer Lutheran Church Dorcas ladies group. She willingly contributed financially and served on various committees.

As with most folks who lived in small towns, she did her best to buy things from Grant Grove stores. She believed the small-town way of life to be superior to any other. When she ate at Ruth's Café, she often traded jokes with the old men sitting at their usual table. Or, they would tease her:

"Joan, when you gonna find yourself a good man and settle down?" said an old man in a flannel shirt and a wide grin on his face. He had known Joan since she was an infant.

"I haven't found the right one yet, Mr. Sloan. You are already taken, and they're hard to come by in these parts." Joan smiled in return.

A more serious looking, cigar-smoking friend took his

turn. "You might have to lower your standards. You ain't gonna find anyone to live up to the standards of your old man."

"Okay, I'll work on it. But I have more important things than having a family right now."

"And that might be?" asked a third man.

"Cleaning out the riff-raff from our society. I'm gonna spend my life ridding this part of the world from deviant and genetically unfit people."

The man in the flannel shirt broke back in. "Well, I'll be. That's a pretty tall order for one woman."

"You wait . . . you'll see."

There was a growing demand for welfare services creating the need for more social workers, and Redwood County was no exception. When Joan heard of an opening, she applied and started work on October 12, 1914. She couldn't believe her good fortune. *Now I can do something about improving society.*

Rural social workers like Joan served many functions. She found help for the elderly who couldn't take care of themselves. The assistance sometimes involved moving them to the county home, which was both a nursing and retirement home. She got help for a mother who was unable to care for an unruly child. Joan soon proved herself as a caring, helpful person.

Among their many other duties, social workers referred people to institutions for the insane and Helmhurst. The latter institution was well known for having the only epileptic program run by the state. It was also the only place accepting feebleminded and physically disabled patients.

The Minnesota Department of Public Welfare and its

Director of Social Services, Edith Stinson, was trying to deal with the problem of growing waiting lists for admission to Minnesota-run institutions. On August 12, 1915, she set up the first annual joint meeting of county and institution social workers. This meeting had two goals — to introduce the social workers to their counterparts with the hope of establishing better working relationships and reducing the waiting lists.

The damp, oppressive late summer heat permeated an already thick sense of unhappiness at the meeting. County social workers wanted more people admitted. Institution-based social workers wanted more people discharged to make room for people on their waiting lists. Everyone agreed on one thing. If the state would allocate the necessary funds to build more dormitories and hire additional staff, they could admit more patients. The legislature, however, chose not to provide the money.

Miss Stinson stood at the podium. "Ladies and gentlemen, we are here to learn about the roles we each play in our common problems. I say we must face these problems together. I would like to get the county social workers to focus on visiting each institution to find those patients who can return to their community. Likewise, institution social workers should begin visiting their counterparts in the communities they serve."

Joan sat in her familiar ramrod-straight posture. Her face was expressionless, only her familiar narrowed eyes and crinkled forehead indicated that something else was going on inside her head. It was apparent that she wasn't happy since she never used the word discharge. With no shyness or reservations, she approached Miss Stinson during a break in the proceedings.

"I'm Joan Bridenbaugh, from Redwood County. I know I have a lot to learn, but I don't understand why they would discharge anyone from one of these institutions. Weren't these people defective when we put them there?"

"Miss Bridenbaugh, there are many situations and reasons. It could be circumstances have improved in their homes, a mother has recovered from a surgery, or a father returned from military service. Sometimes, the patient has learned to be useful in society. Or they have overcome a problem that led to their admission. We are getting quite good at learning how to stop seizures so that the epileptic may go back to their families in good health."

Joan responded, "There are two solutions. The first is the easiest, the mandatory sterilization of every person who is even remotely feebleminded or physically infirmed. The second is to build more dormitories. The idea of making these people useful is getting to be old-fashioned. That was what they thought back at the turn of the century. What I've learned is that we should keep defective people out of the general population where they can dilute the gene pool with more defective people. One has to understand that these people are a threat to our way of life."

"Young lady, we do not run this system based on this eugenic thinking you are espousing. Once you learn more and really get to know the people in your county, you'll change your tune."

Joan was as hot inside as she was on the outside. She was incensed at the notion that this person of authority didn't support eugenics. It was a modern, scientific approach to a better society. She was angry at the fact that someone questioned her beliefs. Even worse was that this ignorant person was her supervisor. "Perhaps you are right, Miss Stinson, but I doubt it." She quickly turned and walked away, not allowing a response. It was a bold and arrogant act, to snub a superior that way. It would have made her father proud.

Those who could stay an extra day were encouraged to take the forty-mile train trip to the Helmhurst State School for the Feebleminded and Colony for the Epileptic, located outside Helmhurst, Minnesota. The superintendent, Dr. Schofield, arranged for a morning presentation of what the institution had to offer, followed by a luncheon, then a tour of the expanding facility which at that time housed one thousand five hundred and fifty-two patients. Joan was one of the twenty-five social workers who took the trip. Despite the fact she had never been there, she was already putting people from her county on the institution's waiting list.

Joan was at the edge of her chair as she listened to the speakers. *They make it sound like they offer excellent services. It seems like the staff is overly optimistic when they talk about these patients' potential for learning.*

During lunch, she had a conversation with another social worker who expressed views Joan felt were close to her own. She said, "Certainly, the feebleminded and epileptic might be able to learn some things, but by no means does that mean they are capable of living independent lives. As for the idiots and imbeciles, there is no hope for learning, no cure, no reason to think they would ever improve or change. An institution is absolutely where they need to live. So then, Miss Joan, what is your opinion of this idea of sterilizing the defectives that is sweeping the country?"

"I think it's a great idea. I would only add that we should also sterilize every single female patient living here."

Before she could add more, a staff social worker standing at the front called out her name. It was time to join her group and take the tour. The tour was of the utmost interest to Joan. She wanted to see what type of misfits lived here. *What do "idiots, imbeciles, morons, and feebleminded" people look like?*

The tour guide proceeded to lead them through the administration building, with offices on the first floor. The second floor housed a medical ward as well as offices for the professional staff. The third floor housed several classrooms. Some of them looked like a classroom in any Minnesota community. In one, several of the students wore leather helmets. "They're the epileptics. We have special doctors who know how to control their seizures, at least some of the time," the tour guide said. The group stood at the back of the room for a moment, before exiting back into the hallway.

They moved on to another classroom. "The teacher you'll see next is known throughout the state for her ability to teach the physically and mentally infirm. Her name is Clara Chowder, although she goes by her middle name, Bea. Teachers come here during the summer to take the special classes she offers." Joan studied Clara Chowder and noticed she was intently busy with the students and paid no attention to the tour. *What a waste of time and talent. If she were such a good teacher, she should be working with students who can learn better and benefit more than these defective children.*

As they left the relative cool of the gothic

administration building, a wave of heat engulfed them. No shade filtered the sun's powerful rays as they briefly stood to wait for their tour guide to make her way to the front of the group.

"Now, ladies, there is no need for alarm, but there are some areas where I will ask you to be aware of what is happening around you. Most of the patients we have are harmless, but sometimes one might try to touch you or grab your purse. It's just them being curious or wanting to greet you."

"I heard they were all dangerous," came a comment from a short, heavy-set lady standing beside Joan. She was sweating profusely and out of breath before they even started. Joan wondered if she would make it through the tour.

"Oh, no, most of them are harmless. Only a few, and I add very few, are dangerous. We'll not be going anywhere near the dangerous patients. Are there any more questions before we begin?"

They moved to a building where nurses in white uniforms cared for grotesque looking babies in cribs that sometimes looked like cages. The sight of the babies shocked several women who took deep breaths and turned their heads.

The next stop was another building that housed the deformed adult men. They couldn't walk nor talk nor move their arms. All were dependent on someone for all their care. This ward was on the first floor, so the staff placed patients on gurneys or modified wheelchairs to move them in and out.

The men here laid on mats strewn across the floor like sticks thrown on the ground. They were gaunt, with limbs and torsos frozen and wore nothing but adult diapers. Some had heads permanently fixed, looking right or left. Others had arms stretched outward, muscles locked and stiff. The men were wet from sweat and urine. Those who had not had their diapers changed all day lay in sticky yellow pools of piss. Many of the ladies had to cover their noses to block the sharp acrid smell. Some quickly stepped back out the door and into the hall. Joan, however, did not flinch.

"This is terrible," Joan pronounced.

"It's so sad, isn't it? Some of these poor people live this way for years," the heavyset woman commented.

Joan asked, "Why were they even allowed to live after they were born? Wouldn't it have been kinder to these creatures and their parents to let them die? Wouldn't that have saved the state all the money it spends caring for them?"

"Why, Miss Bridenbaugh, what a terrible thought! God did not place us on this earth to willfully let others die. Our role is to be as merciful and kind as possible to those less fortunate than ourselves."

Joan watched flies buzz in and out of the room through screenless windows. They walked on the faces of the men, who were powerless to swat them away. Joan tried to imagine having a fly walk across her nose, and her not being able to respond. To her, this one small thing seemed like it would be hell on earth.

One man caught Joan's eye. His pelvis twisted to his left and his head frozen, pointing to the right. The man's eyes found Joans, and for a few seconds, they looked at each other. She turned to their tour guide, "Do you suppose that man has a brain inside his head? I mean, a brain that works?"

"I have no way of knowing. He's what we call a vegetable."

Turning to her companion, Joan pronounced, "A vegetable, there you have it, my friend. It's cruel to allow them to live like this. They deserve pity, and I have pity. I would have been merciful and ended it at the very beginning before this type of suffering had a chance to start. That's not being cruel, and I think God would approve of us saving them from all this suffering. Making him lay in his stinking piss in ninety-degree heat, *that's* cruel. His is not a life worth living."

She turned and caught a glimpse of her companion heading for the door. Joan never saw the woman again.

Growing hotter and weaker as they went, the tour moved on to see a group of twenty-five to thirty little girls playing with what few toys they had. Mostly, they sat on picnic benches inside a long, barren room.

Their final stop was a place mentioned earlier. "Now, ladies, I caution you, hold on tight to your purses and be alert. These women will not hurt you, but they do try to grab at people if they think they can get away with it." As with the first few stops, their tour guide always spoke of how hard the staff worked to make life better for the patients. Joan wondered if all those fantastic sounding services they heard about in the morning presentation actually took place. The patients certainly didn't look well kept or happy.

Joan saw Helmhurst as a place where these people would live out the rest of their lives. Here they got adequate care. After all, all they needed was a clean bed, some food, and shelter from the elements. It was all the care they deserved.

Finally, the tour returned to the administration building to await a bus that would take them back to the train station for their short trip back to Minneapolis. A woman appeared from Joan's left.

"Joan, I'm Gertrude Bingham, a social worker here at Helmhurst. My assignment is to work with your county on admissions and discharges. I would like to review all the cases from your county to see if there might be some who can return to your community."

"It's Miss Bridenbaugh, actually, and no, I don't think any further review is needed. I faithfully check to see if anything has changed that would allow their discharge. I'm sorry, but none will be able to come back to Redwood County at this time."

Joan left a thwarted Gertrude Bingham standing with an arm full of files.

~ ~ ~

Lars washed the dust and dirt off his face, arms, and hands in an enamel bowl Bridget set out beside the back-door stairs. It was part of the routine Bridget imposed to try to keep her house clean.

"Mr. Weatherby stopped by and left that note for you," Bridget said, pointing to the kitchen table.

"Yeah, so I wonder what that's about?"

"I didn't ask; you'll have to read it."

Lars read for a moment, stopped, took a deep breath, and told Bridget. "It's from Ruth. She says that old Mr. Peglar, the guy who Albert worked for, stopped by. He told her to tell me that Albert died and that they buried him out there in whatever township he lived in." Lars slumped to his chair, and his head bowed for a moment. Bridget came over to him, took his face in her hands, and looked deep into his eyes. "I'm sorry he's gone, Lars. I didn't like him, but he was your uncle, and I'm sorry that you lost your only family connection in the US."

On November 23, 1915, Lars and Bridget drove out to the Peglar farm with a bouquet of fall flowers Bridget made for the grave. When they arrived, they were invited in for coffee and sweets. Bridget helped a noticeably older Mrs. Peglar set the table while Lars talked to her husband. He learned that they buried Albert a mile further up the road, in the paupers' section. His grave marked only by a rock inscribed with his name. Lars asked when he died, but Mr. Peglar wasn't quite sure. Albert hadn't shown up for two days, and he went over to the old barn to look for him, finding him dead, his body cold, in a pile of hay. Neither Peglar nor the sheriff could be sure of the date of death, so they picked November 12, 1915, to put on the papers the sheriff turned in to the county recorder. Lars asked about the cost of the burial, and old Mr. Peglar shifted back and forth a bit, then said, "Normally, it's $25, but I feel kinda responsible for Albert since he worked for me. So I wasn't gonna say nothing about cost."

"He was my uncle, so I feel I should pay." With that, he sorted through his wallet and pockets then handed Mr. Peglar four five-dollar bills and five silver dollar coins. "Thank you for looking after him. I will always remember your kindness."

Bridget and Lars once again thanked the Peglars and drove on down the road until they found the little cemetery. There, toward the back, was a new grave with a stone marker that said, Albert Olson. Lars put their flowers on the stone and said a silent prayer as Bridget respectfully bowed her head. She reached for his hand as they walked back to the car and away from another dark part of Bridget's past.

~ ~ ~

Little did Bridget know that contrary to her walking away from her past, she was walking closer to it. Two weeks later, Bridget sat in the dining room and watched their car disappear down County Road 15. She knew she should have gone to Grant Grove with Lars and Peter, but she was too tired. For reasons she could not explain, the dark thoughts of her melancholy greeted her when she woke.

She knew she should stay busy while they were gone. "Idle hands are the devil's workshop," the passage from Proverbs said, and she knew what it meant. Doing nothing would allow her mind to stray off into the darkness, a place she both feared and loved. It had followed during her entire adult life, but for some reason, its pull was stronger today, making it harder to avoid. She wanted to find out about what it felt like when there was no holding back. What would happen to her if she surrendered and let the darkness swallow her? She could resist no more. She closed her eyes, and within seconds, she traveled back in time.

She was sixteen and pregnant. Neither she nor her friend Thomas knew what caused babies. All they were doing was experimenting, allowing themselves to have sex that followed too much touching.

Her father exploded; his anger poured out in a tirade of accusations. "Why you, sinful little slut. Didn't we tell you not to have carnal relations before marriage? Didn't the word of God sink in? Apparently not. Babies don't appear out of thin air. Why did you do this to us? Why bring this shame to our family?"

He removed his belt and came toward her, ready to do what he always did when she was a bad girl. Her mother stepped between them.

"No whippings! There is a new life inside her. You are not going to cause harm to that baby. Now go somewhere else until you can calm down." Her mother's face was red, and for once, she was assertive. But instead of backing off, he rained down blows on her mother's arms and face. He pulled her out of the way by her hair and moved toward Bridget. Her mother tried to restrain him, draw his attention away from her. Her plan worked, but her mother paid a steep price.

She watched her father drag her mother into the living room. All Bridget could hear was her mother whimpering as the slaps came until finally, the storm subsided, and he left. The women cried until there were no more tears.

"I'm sorry, mother. I am very, very sorry. I didn't know, and I didn't think."

"How it came about is in the past. We have to find a way to handle this going forward."

Bridget opened her eyes for a moment, and she stared out the dining room window at their fields, gently sloping down to the bog. Within seconds, she was back in her Norwegian home.

She watched her father talking to a stranger, a large, poorly dressed man. He then turned his attention to her.

"You have to go away to have your baby. I can't have the shame of your sinfulness be a stain on our family. If you repent of your wrongdoing and agree to become a devout and pious Christian, you can come back home after the baby is born."

She saw her mother crying, begging her father for another way to handle the pregnancy. The man then grabbed Bridget and threw her into the back of his old car, pinning her down until they were out of town. Another man drove them to a dock on a small fiord Bridget didn't recognize. Soon, a small fishing boat appeared around the mouth of the bay. When it docked, the man forced her onboard then shoved her into a small compartment below deck. It was dark, dirty, and reeked from years of holding fish. Another man handed her a bucket and closed the hatch.

There were two other girls in the hull with her. Both, like her, were pregnant. Their parents would say they were away at a boarding school or living with an aunt. The ocean voyage was rough. The little boat rode up and down the swells causing them to vomit into their buckets until their stomachs were empty and their mouths dry.

At dawn the next morning, they reached their destination. As she stepped out of the little boat, Bridget saw a sign on the side of the warehouse next to their pier, Copenhagen, Denmark. Another car and another calloused man met them. The terrified girls were each taken to a different house.

For Bridget, the next six and a half months were lonely but pleasant. Locked in a cozy room, she had books to read and an occasional newspaper. The food was good, her bed was comfortable, and she got some fresh air when she used the outhouse in the back of the house. As she neared the end of her pregnancy, a midwife came to examine her. "Your baby is due soon," she pronounced.

Bridget began living a nightmare with the birth of her baby.

She asked the midwife, "Where's my baby?"

"Shush now. Don't you worry, your baby will be fine."

"But where is it? Is it a boy or a girl?"

Silence. Bridget watched herself experience the horror the silence brought and how she broke it with screams and sobs. Eventually, they told her the baby was with good people who would raise it as their own. Her baby . . . gone without it laying on her breast, or kissing it or experiencing its tiny fist gripping a finger. She cursed and stormed and raged until the man of the house came into her room and beat her with a shortened broom handle.

Bridget believed that losing her first child had to be the source of her melancholy. Denied the joy of motherhood, she had to experience the grief of losing a child alone as a prisoner in a strange place. She was never able to completely rid herself of that trauma.

Still, things got worse when she learned she was to work for the man of this house for two years to repay her room and board, the voyages, and the midwife's fee. Eventually, she and the other women from the boat from Norway were reunited. There were also other women, like themselves, who came here against their will, to have their babies. They worked long hours packing crates full of foods destined for export to far-away markets. Their hands were raw, their minds numbed by harsh living and working conditions. The women lived in a barren room forced to sleep on dirty cots at the back of the warehouse. Beatings, food deprivation, and rapes were routine. Days and months became a blur.

After two years and one month had passed, Bridget was allowed to return home to a tearful reunion with her mother. She savored being in the comfort of her loving arms. Her father was still harsh and unkind. However, this time, he was up against a daughter hardened and scarred by pain and torture.

He began in his typical manner. "I hope these two years have taught you a lesson. Carnal relations belong within the bonds of holy matrimony. You're now a tainted woman. You need to be one with God who alone can save you from your sin."

Bridget burned with hatred and anger. Her now lean, muscular body was tense and ready to strike.

"Stop. I should kill you for what you did to me, you bastard! Yes, I know that and a lot of other curse words, my dear father." Her rage pushed her forward into his face. "You put me through hell. Do you know they raped, beat, and starved me? Did they tell you about that or did they say I'd go to some lovely home in the country? Maybe you knew all along what they would do to me and still went along with it." She paused a second, and when she spoke next, her voice was quiet but stern. "If you even think about touching Momma or me again, I will beat you to within an inch of your life. Don't think for a minute I can't do it, because I can."

Her father's face grew pale as he listened to his little girl rage on. He took a step back, turned, and walked out of the room. From then on, he became silent and withdrawn. He seldom spoke to Bridget and did his best to avoid her.

The visions of the past were gone now. Bridget laid her head on the dining room table, exhausted from the emotional strain. She knew she could never share any of this with anyone; instead, Bridget created a mental prison where she could lock away anger and sadness. It was these emotions which escaped from time to time. When they did, she could not ignore them.

Chapter 6
ANNA OLSON

1917

On March 14, 1917, Anna Olson became the joy of her parents' life. To them, she was the sweetest and prettiest baby in the world. Her pregnancy was difficult, even painful at times. It culminated with Bridget's spending the last two months of her pregnancy restricted to bed rest. Several women from their church helped the Olson family, making life a little better for Bridget, four-year-old Peter, and Lars. Her delivery was long and painful. Her cries, yelling, and loud breathing began to scare young Peter, prompting his father to take him for a walk around the farm for the duration of her delivery. The very moment of Anna's birth brought Bridget the joy only a mother understands.

To celebrate his daughter's birth, Lars went into Grant Grove and bought two bottles of schnapps from Ruth Carlson. In addition to running her restaurant, she sold a limited variety of wine and spirits. Small-time bootlegging was a way for her to supplement her restaurant income.

As he made his way around her restaurant, Lars proudly proclaimed, "I'd like to announce we have a new baby girl! Anna Olson was born on the fourteenth, and both baby and mom are doing well. How about a nip of the best peppermint schnapps in Grant Grove?"

Most of the men accepted a drink; all the women declined. The second bottle he tucked under the seat of his horse-drawn wagon and took home to put in his barn. Lars stored his liquor in the barn since he never drank in the house. Later that night, when everyone was asleep, Lars went to the barn and drank enough to start singing old Norwegian folk songs to himself.

Even before her baptism, Peter bragged to everyone he met about his new baby sister. Anna would look at him and smile and kick her legs and wave her arms all about like he had some mysterious connection to her.

~ ~ ~

When Peter started school, Anna received Bridget's full attention. As a toddler, she smiled as she followed her mother around the house. When corrected, she seldom repeated a naughty behavior. Her physical and mental development was average, and Dr. Phyllips always gave her a clean bill of health. She was timid, hiding behind her mother's skirt when someone she didn't know paid attention to her. At first, this made people think she couldn't speak, when, in fact, she knew words and could speak in simple sentences at an early age. To those who knew her, she was a little girl being a little girl. In short, she was an average child to everyone but Bridget and Lars, who believed she was a special gift from God.

From the time she could walk, she had fun playing in the garden while Bridget cared for the vegetables. When she was old enough, she liked to pull vegetables off the plants and put them in a basket. Inside the house, Anna's favorite toys were a little doll and enamelware pots. All she would need would be tablespoons, a wooden mixing spoon, and a measuring cup, and she could play for hours. Both enjoyed joint cooking, where Bridget would let Anna stand on a chair at the counter where she would mimic her mothers' actions.

Anna brought a sense of completeness and purpose to everyone's life. To Peter, Anna was someone to torment and tease. For Lars, she was the warm cuddly little girl who liked to sit on his lap on frigid winter evenings. For Bridget, Anna was someone to bond with and a person to share her love of needlecrafts.

~ ~ ~

Joan Bridenbaugh was excited when she read about the new Minnesota Children's Code. It provided for either the provisional or permanent commitment of feebleminded persons to the State of Minnesota. It set out clearly, the procedures for how Redwood County could rid itself of its most problematic residents.

"Just think," Joan told a small group who gathered around the office to discuss the new legislation. "Now, with this new law, we'll be able to put more of our feebleminded and other defectives, into institutions. They will no longer spread their disease and filth everywhere they go."

"Maybe." The comment earned the person a glaring, angry look from Joan.

"Heavens, I've never been able to figure out what the

classification of 'feebleminded' means," observed another.

"Are you sure this isn't going to violate individual liberties? The State of Minnesota already has so much power over parents and families," came the third observation. "My Stanley thinks Minnesota meddles in our lives too much already."

"None of that matters. You've got to see the big picture! These people are a threat to our way of life! Think of it as a war against those who threaten to make our entire society weak!"

~ ~ ~

In the fall of 1922, Anna began school in a one-room schoolhouse, two miles straight west of their farm. Anna joined Peter on the trek down Schoolhouse Road. At first, she had to run to keep up with him and the other older children whose strides were much longer.

"Peter, wait up!" Anna yelled from the back of the small group of children.

He turned around, "I'm not standin' around for any little kid. You keep up or walk by yourself."

Anna fought back the tears. Today was her first day of school, and she was afraid. There wasn't anything but corn and hayfields surrounding her, and she was scared someone would come out of the fields and steal her away. After all, to a little girl, being alone is reason enough to be afraid. So she ran to catch up, leaving little puffs of dirt that floated away in the dry September air.

As soon as Anna and Peter left their house, they joined with the kids from across the road. This small group joined up with the Weatherby children about a mile further down

Schoolhouse Road. As they neared the school, there were anywhere from nine to eleven children in their little group. They had mud on their shoes when it rained, and cold hands and feet in the winter. The children considered it a special event if one of their parents would give them a ride to school in a grain or hay wagon. A car ride was even better.

Anna was an average student who behaved well and did her lessons faithfully. She formed friendships with other children quickly. Like her mother, Anna was slow to warm up to adults she didn't know. She seldom spoke to anyone other than her friends and sometimes seemed aloof and distant.

When Anna was in the second grade, a new teacher, Miss Pratt, came to the school. Anna didn't like her from the very day she started.

"She's always picking on me," she told Bridget one day after school.

"What do you mean?"

"I'm the only one who has to do my work over again cuz she doesn't like it!"

"Oh come now, Anna, she has no reason to pick on you. Keep trying to do your best."

In the third-grade, Miss Pratt asked a question of the students in Anna's little group, and like the others, Anna kept her hand down.

"Who knows what twelve divided by two equals?"

No one answered.

"Anna?"

Anna was looking down at the floor when she gave her barely audible answer. "Six."

"A little louder, please, the others need to hear your

answer." Miss Pratt's tone was sharp. She sounded angry.

"Six?" Anna replied with a firm but soft voice, her head raised to better project sound.

"I swear girl if you can't learn to speak up, I'm going to sit you in the corner with a big ole' dunce hat on."

"Six!" Anna almost spat the word out.

"That's much better. A good student talks so others can hear the answer."

Each day Miss Pratt either scolded Anna or criticized her for little things. By the end of the third grade, Anna no longer paid any attention to Miss Pratt's constant picking.

Peter and Anna had both friends and best friends. Peter's group of buddies included farm boys as well as a few city kids, mostly from their church. He spent most of his free time either going to a friend's house or having them over. Peter and his buddies enjoyed talking, throwing knives at tree trunks, and sometimes sneaking cigarettes.

Anna's best friend was Margaret Petersen, another student in her class. They loved going to each other's houses to play with their baby dolls, pretending they were keeping house, or serving tea. In the summer, they would swing on the tree swing Anna's father initially put up for Peter. They loved climbing trees and going up in the hayloft, pretending they were exploring the wild jungles of Africa. It wasn't uncommon for them to come in after spending an afternoon outside with legs and knees scraped and bleeding. Things, like climbing trees and getting into the barn lofts were supposed to be boys' activities, but many farm girls did the same things as their brothers.

The girls whispered and giggled at every little thing

leaving their parents to wonder why. Many times, they pretended they were thieves in a big city by sneaking into the kitchen, grabbing cookies or pieces of cake from the pantry. Most of all, Anna and Margaret had secrets.

~ ~ ~

Farm life revolved around the position of the stars, moon, and sun. Within the margin of a few days or weeks, planting and harvesting always took place at the same time each year. Life on the farm was predictable, giving people a deep sense of security.

In Grant Grove, civic, religious, and school activities fit around the farmers' schedules. Life was predictable. Sunday school was at nine-thirty, worship at eleven. School started the day after Labor Day. Parents rose at dawn, often with a rooster crowing. Papa would stoke the furnace to start driving out the chill of the night. Mother would put wood or coal in the stove for water to make coffee or oatmeal.

Anna lived within these boundaries and thought nothing of it. Like all farm children, she worked hard, doing her part to make her family run successfully. She felt safe, secure, and loved. Without the distractions found in the city, life was simple. Reading, sewing, helping her mother, and learning how to do useful chores were the building blocks of her youth.

By the time she was eleven, Anna could sew almost everything her mother could sew, and perhaps a little more. She always won prizes at the Redwood County Fair for her needlework creations. Anna had grown to be a sweet-natured person. With a few exceptions, she had outgrown her shyness.

Anna spent a great deal of time with her family. Before they could afford a radio, their evenings were spent around the kitchen table because the kitchen was cozy, heated by the always-warm stove. She and Peter did homework, after which she learned sewing techniques from Bridget, while Peter read magazines. Lars would often insist on everyone playing board games, no excuses; he wanted everyone to do something "fun" together. As a cranky teenager, Peter often failed to see the fun in playing with his parents.

Anna and Peter started doing farm chores as soon as they were either old or big enough. Their first assignments were to gather eggs and feed the two cows they kept for milking. As with most farm children, they graduated into more demanding work as they became older and stronger. Peter loved tagging along with his dad. In July and August, they walked up and down the corn rows pulling weeds growing between the plants. He enjoyed standing near his dad as he did the milking, listening to stories about his life in Norway.

When she was a little girl, Anna loved to help her mother in the garden, sometimes holding a bowl while Bridget picked peas or green beans. Yet, even this simple task presented problems. It was hard to hold the bowl and swat away the flies that made their way up from the barn.

Anna was very good at helping her mom around the kitchen and did not object too much to helping with the dusting and sweeping the floors. Together they shelled peas and canned green beans. Onions, carrots, and potatoes, once removed from the ground, were stored in gunny sacks in an old root cellar.

Anna was slow to learn the basics of cooking. She tried to imitate how her mother stirred the warm water and yeast into flour to make bread, but she often spilled at least one of the ingredients. Cooking together worked best if Anna simply helped. Together they turned out delicious meals with the limited ingredients they had available. For birthdays and on holidays, they made Norwegian food such as Lefse, a thin potato pancake. For Christmas, they made Berlinerkranse cookies.

When Anna was old enough, she gathered the eggs and brought them into the laundry room where she would wash them and place them in crates designed to keep the eggs from breaking. Once a week, an egg buyer would stop by their farm to pick up their eggs. Selling eggs gave the family a small but steady income.

During tough times, every little bit of income helped since grain prices, in general, were going down. By the 1920s, wheat plunged to $1.50 a bushel, half of what it had been in 1917. Lars stopped planting wheat and concentrated on growing corn, oats, alfalfa, and soybeans. Unlike most American cities, Grant Grove was in a depression in the 1920s, and families worked hard to survive. Farm children often wore homemade or patched clothes and were unable to go to movies or buy ice cream as often as their city friends.

~ ~ ~

Hot and sticky summer evenings would find the entire Olson family sitting on the front porch. They looked straight ahead at the small line of trees that stood between them and Schoolhouse Road. To their left were the fields.

Sometimes Bridget would make popcorn or brownies. Other times, Lars would share from his paper bag full of penny candy.

One August evening in 1924, it was so hot that beads of sweat formed on their brows even though they sat still on the porch. It was seven p.m., and the thermometer read ninety degrees. The humidity was so high that water seemed to drip from the air onto any exposed skin. Mid-August in southern Minnesota could be brutally hot, and that summer had broken all heat records. Today was the fourteenth day with temperatures over ninety-five degrees—the high, one hundred and one degrees in the shade.

There seemed to be an evening breeze, as heard by the rustling sound of the trees. But the air on the porch was still and close. The yellow tones of the setting sun rays painted the crops with a coating of golden lacquer-like molasses poured over pancakes. Amber light covered the dusty trees. As the evening wore on, the remaining sunlight reflected off the bottom of the few clouds lingering lazily off to the west, producing splendid silver linings. It was the beauty of these summer evenings that provided the otherwise color deprived prairie dwellers with another reason to live in rural America.

Lars was telling Bridget about how the crops were coming along and that if the grain prices held steady, they would be able to save a little money. Bridget shared with Lars what she was making with her needlepoint and told him she heard an interesting thing from a lady at her church group. "Today I heard that the Johnston's were losing their farm. I guess he was a drinker, not a worker."

"Don't believe everything you hear," he snapped back.

"At least half the time things are completely wrong, and the other half of the time, there is only one little bit of truth to it. One little rumor starts, and soon the whole town knows something that in all likelihood isn't true. Be careful what information you pass on to others."

His sharp tone and superior attitude stung Bridget. "I know, dear. I was simply telling you. I haven't passed this on to anyone else. With so many people getting into money trouble, it seems like maybe it could be true." She remained quiet for the rest of the evening.

Anna sat on the swing beside her mom, gently swinging back and forth. A tiny squeak from some unknown place in the swing helped produce a soothing, almost hypnotic trance. She played with her paper dolls, did needlework, and practiced what her mom taught her about mending a tear. They were always a pair, each busy at their needlework while listening to what was going on around them. Bridget once told Anna, "Girl, it seems to me you were born with a needle in your hands."

"What do you mean by that?" Anna looked like she was ready to cry.

"I mean, you learn so quickly, and your sewing is so neat and pretty."

"I thought you meant I had a needle stuck in my hand when I was a newborn baby." Now, Anna was smiling from ear to ear.

"You're a silly girl sometimes."

That evening, like so many others, found Peter sitting on the top step, his back to the stair railing. He was trying to read the latest *Black Mask* magazine in the dim light of the evening. The magazine was hidden inside an old *Look* magazine because his parents weren't pleased with him reading the scary stories in *Black Mask*. No longer able to read, he took out his pocket knife and a long narrow block of wood and started to carefully whittle away at it, trying to make a perfectly shaped very sharp point.

"Say, dad, did you hear that they are going to make people in the movies talk?"

"No. I'm sure that is another example of a rumor. There's no way they can make a movie where people talk. What can they do, jump off the screen and say their words? Where in the world did you hear something like that?"

"I heard it from Johnny Miller while I was over to the Christensen's makin' hay. He said some guy who works over at the Mankato Palace Theater said that they have a few of these movies in Minneapolis. Pretty soon, they'll have them everywhere. It could be, you know, they are comin' out with all kinds of new things nowadays."

"Well, you're right about that. Do you know what I think? It won't be long before everyone has a radio. I saw one for thirty-four dollars in the new Sears catalog. The only thing is, it looked complicated to operate.

Lars was in the mood to lecture, "Another thing, how can all those town people afford electricity for all those sweepers, toasters, electric lamps, all kinds of things? We poor farmers are barely making ends meet while everyone else seems to be getting richer. What are they going to eat when one day there're no more farmers left to grow the wheat that makes their bread?" The pitch of Lars' voice rose. Every time he thought about all the farmers going broke while everyone else seemed to have money for movies, he became irritated.

"Prices will go back up someday soon, Papa," Peter

replied without looking up.

"I suppose."

After a few minutes of silence, Bridget stood up. "There are too many bugs out here."

The Olsons gradually disappeared into the house to continue what they had been doing. They could hear the crickets chirping louder and louder as the early evening faded into night. Off in the distance, two dogs were barking. At exactly 8:45 p.m., they could hear the train signal its arrival at the County Road 5 intersection, two miles to the north. *Woo woo -woo woo.* The forlorn sound of a train whistle in the distance drew attention to itself. It stirred some inner emotion, although what it was, always remained a mystery. Then, there was only the sound of the cricket chorus, a high-pitched screeching blanket of noise that eventually faded out of awareness.

Without saying a word, Lars went to the barn as was his custom two or three times a week. Bridget and the children knew what he was doing, although they never talked about it. Lars drank alcohol regularly, never in the house. Instead, like his father and grandfather, he would drink in the barn. Bridget didn't object to Lars' drinking. On the contrary, she tried to get him to bring the liquor inside where he could enjoy a drink while she did needlepoint. He would simply shake his head and say drinking belonged in the barn.

Shortly after Lars left, Bridget sent Peter and Anna to bed and put out the kerosene lamps. She left the back door unlocked, and the screen windows open in case a breeze came along.

Chapter 7
EUNICE WEATHERBY

TO DAMAGE THE SOVEREIGNTY OF THE INDIVIDUAL IS TO REPLACE A COMMUNITY INSPIRED BY LOVE, BENEVOLENCE, AND BEAUTY BY ANOTHER BASED SOLELY ON POWER.
ANWAR SADAT

1926

Joan Bridenbaugh walked the first-floor hall of the courthouse with her familiar patent leather shoes clopping at a crisp pace, their sound amplified by the plaster walls. She walked so erectly she looked funny. Joan heard the jokes. *"She walks so straight to keep her head in the clouds."*

Thomas Belkner called out her name. "Say, are you Miss Bridlebaugh?"

"It's Bride*n*baugh." Joan was instantly annoyed. Plus, he smelled like a farmer with a combination of manure, sweat, and grease floating off his stained clothes. Most farmers changed to clean clothes before coming to town, not Mr. Belkner.

"Whatever. Folks say I should talk to you about my imbecile son."

Joan's crisp pace slowed. "What about your son? Wait, don't answer that right now. I need to deliver these papers, and then you can have my full attention. If you wait in this conference room, I'll be right back." Joan ushered Thomas into a small conference room, sat him in a chair, and left to deliver the papers.

When she returned, Joan sat across the table from the man. She wanted a chance to study his face, his eyes especially. "Now, tell me about this son of yours."

"Yup. You see, he ain't quite right. He's slow at everything. He don't know no words or nothin' like that, and he's going on eight. He follows his mother around all day long makin' these funny sounds. He kinda like grunts or something like that. In any case, my family calls him a runt and a disgrace.

"So, my brother goes to some meetin' down in Grant Grove, over there at the library. He sez they put slow people like this in a special place and take good care of 'em. They call 'em imbeciles or idiots. Then, someone sez I got to talk to you about this. Are you in charge of these people? That's what they say. You're like their superintendent."

"Yes, I'm in charge of everyone who isn't normal. I make sure that deviants get the proper care. Tell me about your whole family, starting with your parents and your wife's parents. Are there any other imbeciles, or maybe people who are simpletons, you know, slow? Any problems with drinkers?"

Joan quizzed Thomas Belkner for the better part of a half-hour before summing things up. "I'll need to evaluate your son, Mr. Belkner. May I come out to your home this Friday? I need to see your son and talk to his mother."

"Oh, sure, we don't go nowhere. Got no money for that, you know."

"Good. Then I'll be by Friday afternoon. What's the boy's first name?"

"Ralphie. Ralph, I guess I should say."

"And where do you live?"

As soon as Joan returned to her desk, she took out a clean sheet of paper and wrote the date neatly at the top, April 15, 1926, and recorded all the information Thomas had given her. She started a new manila file and labeled it with the child's name. Finally, she retrieved her little book and smiled as she wrote, *One more imbecile to remove from society. One person closer to a pure race.*

~ ~ ~

Eunice knocked twice on the side door. It was her trademark knock. "Yoo-hoo, anyone home?" Silence.

Feeling at home in the Olson house, Eunice came into the kitchen, took off her feed-sack scarf with the small yellow flowers.

"*Bridget?*"

"I'll be right down."

Bridget could see that Eunice was upset the moment she laid eyes on her. Her worn and frayed cotton dress had the remnants of that morning's breakfast splattered in several places. It wasn't like Eunice to go anywhere looking so messy. Usually, her clothes were clean and ironed.

"What's wrong?"

"Do I look that bad?" snapped Eunice.

Bridget replied, "I know you, and I can tell when you are upset about something. Come here and sit down." Bridget patted a kitchen chair. She turned and went to the stove to put the tea kettle on a burner still hot from breakfast. After adding a piece of coal to the fire, she stopped to listen to Eunice.

"Oh, Bridget, I don't even know where to begin." She

slumped down over the table, her head in her hands.

"Is it with your children?"

"Oh, no. It's my sister Ruth, the one who lives north of Redwood Falls. She has Ralph, the backward idiot boy. The kids and I went up there last weekend because it was too wet to work in the fields. I found Ruth all worked up again. I swear, since she met and married into that god-awful family, it's been nothing but one problem after another.

"Her problem is Ralph. Well, wait, that's not quite right. It's about her husband and *his* ignorant, meddling family. In a lot of ways, they are more backward and trouble than that little boy, if you ask me. It's so confusing, and I can hardly sort it out."

Bridget nodded. "I remember you telling me about Ralph and those awful in-laws." The tea kettle hissed as she set the table. Cups, spoons, saucers, tea leaves in delicate tea baskets, were quickly put in their proper place. She poured enough boiling water into each cup to submerge the tea basket, then she set the sugar and milk in the middle of the table. Bridget sat down, took her tea strainer, and gently bobbed it in and out of the water. There was a short silence as the women watched the hot water gradually turn light brown as it flowed through the tiny holes in the basket.

Eunice teared up, then suddenly put out the crux of her pain. "Ruth's husband, Thomas, and his kin want to take that little boy away from her, put him away in some institution." Eunice paused, trying to regain her composure, but the words would not stop. "Ruth is very upset about this. She loves that boy and wants to keep him at home. Is that so bad?" By the time she had reached the end of the last sentence, she could barely speak.

"A mother wanting to raise her child is never wrong," Bridget replied softly, staring into her tea.

Eunice composed herself. She straightened her back and stared into her teacup as she spoke. "He didn't grow up right. When he was a few months old, they could see that he didn't pay attention to sounds and things, you know, as healthy babies do. Usually, babies try to see what's making a sound. Or, they smile when they hear their momma's voice. Instead, he stared off into space. At first, nobody paid much attention, since he ate and slept okay.

"As a little boy, he never did learn to speak but maybe a handful of words, and he's now about eight. He doesn't usually remember to go to the potty unless told, but Ruth knows when to take him, so he doesn't have an accident. There's a lot of other things Ralphie doesn't do that he should, like dress himself.

"On the other hand, he's such a sweet child. He is no trouble at all." Eunice took a deep breath. "She says that little Ralphie is the light of her life and a 'blessing.' I don't understand how having an idiot child could be a blessing, but she says he is.

"His family says that Ralphie is an embarrassment to them, that he is stupid and unnatural. Like *they* are so special." She paused for a drink of tea before continuing, "They don't want to be associated with no idiot. They say Ralphie is a stain on their family record.

"It's breaking her heart, Bridget. I know I'm getting way too worked up here. But when you see your sister hurting so bad, it hurts your heart too. We women feel for each other." Eunice broke down and started to cry.

Bridget got up and moved to stand beside Eunice. She

put her arms around her shoulders, and pulled her close, to comfort and assure her friend. They held that pose for a moment as Eunice started to regain her composure. She dried her eyes with her napkin and sat in silence, staring out the kitchen window, her eyes focused on something miles away. Patting Bridget's arm, she said, "I'm okay now."

After Bridget sat down, Eunice started talking again, this time in a slower, more deliberate manner.

"They want to send her little Ralphie to Helmhurst over near the Twin Cities. That place is an institution that takes care of people who are idiots and such as that. Oh yes, and people who have fits. I think that this decision should be up to the mother. Especially if the mother is the one who takes care of a child with problems like Ralphie. If she says the child should stay at home, he should stay at home." There was a long pause.

"Where was I? Oh, yes. Despite being on hard-times and taking care of Ralphie, Ruth does a bang-up job feeding and clothing all her children. They're always clean, they do good in school, and are courteous to adults. It isn't as if her children have suffered in any way by having an idiot brother.

"Her husband says he has enough to worry about without 'a little mongrel imbecile runt' of a child to look after and feed. That's what he calls his son, a mongrel runt. This filthy talk is from a man who has never lifted a finger to help care for the boy. He says Ruth has more important things to do. Why, without Ralphie, she could spend more time helping him with farming," Eunice's voice trailed upward and away, mocking the man.

"Bridget, can you imagine being told you would have

to give up your baby? Your very own child?"

Bridget swallowed hard and did her best to keep her composure, blindsided by her long-buried memories and the rage that used to consume her. "No," she said curtly. It was her turn to stare into space, thinking about her lie.

"Men don't know what it is like to have a baby. They're yours, *always* yours, regardless of what happens."

Bridget asked, "How did all this talk about sending Ralphie away get started, anyhow?"

"What happened is that one of Ruth's brothers-in-law went to some meeting here in Grant Grove. It was about a new kind-of-thinking about some of the problems in society. He comes home with this notion that all the idiots and imbeciles and people who aren't right should all be sterilized and/or put into institutions. It also has something to do with genetics and breeding, and feebleminded folks having too many babies. It has some new kind of name, although I don't remember what Ruth called it. Apparently, even famous people believe the same way. These people believe in sending these children to institutions, even if they are no trouble at all. Imagine your child raised by strangers.

"Maybe Ruth loves little Ralphie even more than any of her other children. Maybe he needs more love because he does less for himself. All I know is that she doesn't want to let him go. She is fighting it as best she can. I think instead of giving up the boy, she should give up her husband and his good-for-nothing family. She could move back down here and bring Ralphie and the rest of her children with her. Mom, Dad, and I could help her out some, which would be more than she gets up there from his goddamn family." Eunice turned pink, "Sorry, I'm not normally one to curse."

"Don't worry about it, Eunice."

Eunice stopped for a long break, taking a sip or two of her now lukewarm tea. She sighed deeply as Bridget added hot water to her cup. Bridget let the silence continue because she knew her friend well enough to know she had more to unburden. The silence gave her a moment more to reflect on being unable to keep her baby. A baby she never held before they took it away. *How did these things happen? Eunice was right. Shouldn't the decision about a child staying with its mother be up to the mother and not someone else? Especially if the mother is the only one providing care for the child.*

Before she could delve too far back into her painful past, Bridget commented, "I'm glad you were able to go up there and at least listen to her."

"Yes, I suppose. I mean with times the way they are, what else can we do? It's not like we are rich and can afford nannies to look after our children. All I know is that her heart will break if they take that boy away. The way it sounded, though, I think she's going to have to give in to 'em."

"Did she say anything about why they are trying to do this now?"

"She said her husband and his side of the family were pressuring her on account of this big push to put people who aren't right into institutions. They say they can get a judge to sign some 'commitment' order or something like that, but I don't know if that is a law. Oh, and one more thing, Ruth's husband says it will be one less mouth to feed in these tough times. How cruel is that, to think of your own flesh and blood like they are a dog you can kick out of the house to save a slice of bread?"

"Absolutely," Bridget nodded as she thought of how cruel her father had been. "Cruelty seems to have no limits. When is this supposed to happen?" Bridget asked absentmindedly.

"I don't know. There is this county social worker that came to the house and said that the sooner Ruth agrees, the sooner she can put Ralphie on some waiting list. Apparently, there is a whole lot of people waiting to get into this Helmhurst. I think it's her husband who wants to get this done as soon as possible before Ruth can kick up too much of a fuss."

"Probably... men will sometimes do that. I mean, go ahead and do something before their wives or the rest of the family can react to it. Thank God, my Lars has never done something like that to me."

Bridget continued, "I'm thankful for that. But I've heard a lot of women talk about how they don't have much say in anything. You know, women in my home country, Norway, had the right to vote a long time ago, and yet, here in America, the great symbol of democracy to the world, we women only recently got the vote. It's sad to see women treated like they are lowly kitchen help or breeding stock." Bridget knew she was getting off-topic, but she thought maybe she could distract Eunice a bit, get her mind off little Ralphie, and her sister's heartbreak.

But Eunice wasn't interested in women's rights or suffrage or anything else. "Thank you for listening, Bridget. I would have exploded if I hadn't talked to you." She had a sad, tired look on her face. "I am worn out from worrying about Ruth. I don't know what I can do."

"I think you should do what you have always done. Be

a good mother to your children, and try to see Ruth as often as you can. I can take the children any time you want to go by yourself."

Eunice simply nodded and silently mouthed the words, "Thank you."

She extended her hands across the table and grasped Bridget's hands like she was grabbing onto a lifesaver ring. She held on tight to Bridget and smiled as she looked deep into Bridget's eyes. "Oh, Bridget, I don't know what I'd ever do without you. You make my world so much better by being my friend. I love you!"

"I know you would do the same for me. Maybe someday I'll need to come to you," Bridget said as she squeezed Eunice's hands in return.

"So, what else is new?" Bridget said in a calm and straightforward voice as they released their hands and sat back from each other. Both broke into deep, hearty, laughter and a few tears streamed down their faces as the last of the tension dissipated. The burden on their collective souls had been released, at least for the moment.

When she finally regained her composure and wiped the last tear from her eyes, Eunice said, "Oh, my, look at the time. I must get groceries, run some errands, and be back before the kids get home from school." With that, Eunice almost jumped out of her chair, gave Bridget a hug, and left.

As the screen door slammed shut, Bridget's face turned cloudy, her mind again took her back to her teenage pregnancy and having to give up her baby. *There are no words to describe having your child forcibly taken from you.* The memories of how all that happened were too painful to allow her to recall details. *Probably for the best,* she reasoned. Every time she started to think about her past, it was unpleasant. *Definitely. Best to leave it all alone. But why do those memories keep coming back?*

It was an hour, maybe two before Lars came in, wondering what was for lunch. He looked at Bridget and saw she was upset. "What's wrong?"

"I'm not a bad person, am I? I mean, back then, I didn't know about how to make babies. I was so young then."

"Come here . . . that was a long time ago. Let it go." He held her close and gently stroked her hair. He privately wondered what her baby looked like today. Based on Bridget's age and the few details he knew, her child must be about twenty now. *Where did he or she live? What did they do?* Like Bridget, Lars had questions that would never have answers.

~ ~ ~

"Miss Bridenbaugh?"

"Yes."

"This is Gertrude Bingham, from Helmhurst. We met briefly some time ago and have exchanged letters. I'm calling today to inform you that we have removed Ralph Belkner from our waiting list. We have admitted him to a brand-new unit we call the 'Little Boys.' He will be living with other boys his age and ability level."

"When is this going to take place?"

"His admissions date will be February 20. You can stop calling and writing to us regarding his case. Miss Joan, everyone has an emergency, a story to tell, you know what I mean? Yet when we want to talk to you about a discharge, we can never reach you."

Joan was ready to say "squeaky wheel" when she heard the click.

She looked at the phone in disbelief, *that bitch hung up on me!* Joan seethed about the insult the rest of the day. The joy of her victory of getting Ralph admitted to Helmhurst, lost.

Chapter 8
DR. JOHN PHILLIPS

THERE'S NOTHING MORE DEBILITATING ABOUT A DISABILITY THAN THE WAY PEOPLE TREAT YOU OVER IT.
SOLANGE NICOLE

1930

It was July 12, 1930. Breakfast was wrapping up, the last of the coffee poured, and spoons were clinking against bowls. It didn't take long for Lars to recognize the now-familiar mother-daughter spat.

"Am I going to get to go to Margaret's place or not?" Anna's whiny tone assured any listener she was a teenager.

"Not if you keep up that attitude. Besides, today, we are doing green beans. You know that."

"It never hurts to ask. You know I don't like green beans."

"There are plenty of starving people out there who would eat those beans raw, just to fill their bellies."

Lars was glad that he'd not stepped into the argument. Bridget was more than capable of standing her ground. With the spat ended, he summarized the day ahead. "So . . . you ladies are picking beans, I'm chopping weeds out of the cornfields, and Peter, you, my dear boy, are to finish painting the chicken house."

"Work, work, work, that's all we ever do around here. We never get a break." Anna continued with her attitude.

"Anna, you can stop your sassing right now. I'm not listening to this whining all day." There was a slight hint of crimson emerging in the middle of her cheeks. "Do you understand?" Bridget was close to losing her temper.

"Okay, *okay!*"

"I mean it, keep it up, and you'll be doing beans until midnight."

"I get the message." Anna crossed her arms and leaned back in her chair.

"We'll let's get going then. We want to finish before it gets too hot," Bridget said.

Lars smiled to himself as he picked up his dishes and carried them to the sink. *My children—already so grown up. They help us produce the food we need to stave off hunger and pay the bills.* He gave Bridget a quick peck on the cheek before heading out the door.

The morning dew was finally evaporating off the corn in the fields and the vegetables in the garden. Still, moist air looked faintly like fog as the heat of the day approached. Lars noted the corn was already waist-high, slightly taller than it was a year ago.

In Bridget's garden were peas, carrots, onions, potatoes, squash, and tomatoes, the staples of most Minnesota gardens. Bridget and Anna's goal today was to find and pick the ripe beans hiding in the lush, thick, and dark green plants still coated with dew. Lars raised sweet corn in a separate patch back of the chicken coop. Bridget also liked to plant herbs, which added the tastes her family loved. Anna and Bridget went to the garden, each wearing long-sleeved dresses and large floppy hats to shield them from bugs and the powerful sun rays.

Already, the sun was driving the temperatures up, and

it was barely nine. Lars' mind was wandering as he walked up and down the cornrows, chopping out the tall weeds and pulling the short ones. *I bet it's over eighty.* He thought about John Larson's wife dying, the stock market crash, his boyhood home in Norway, and having sex with Bridget. He stopped at the last thought, recalling how often they made love in hopes of having more children. *The babies never came, but it was fun trying to make them. No, it was more than fun; it was pure ecstasy.*

At that moment, he saw Peter running toward him, waving his arms. He could hear him calling, but the distance muffled his words. Peter kept coming fast, and in that instant, Lars knew something must be wrong. Peter looked frantic as he stopped and made a big windmill like a circle with his arm, waiving him to come. An alarm bell rang inside his head, and fear gripped him.

Peter led him back toward the house. Shortly before Lars caught up with him, he spotted Bridget kneeling over Anna. He arrived on the scene in time to hear Bridget.

"I don't know. I don't know," Bridget moaned, rocking back and forth on her haunches. "One minute she was standing near me, then I heard her make a funny noise. When I looked up, I saw her head roll forward onto her chest, and her body slumped to the ground. By the time she reached the ground, her whole body was shaking and jerking uncontrollably."

Bridget stopped to get her breath and stroke Anna's damp brow. "Thank goodness; she came to rest facing upward." Choking back tears, Bridget continued, "She had this strange, far-away, glassy look in her eyes and her whole body was rigid, her muscles were hard as steel."

"Did you move her?" Lars managed to ask between

deep breaths.

"No, she lay right where she is now."

Bridget didn't continue, so Lars asked, "What happened next?"

"Then, the jerking got stronger and faster. It was as if some demon had control of Anna's body. She had jolts so strong they almost lifted her off the ground." Bridget stopped and allowed her emotions to run free. Tears and sobs made their way up and out of her. Taking Anna's hand, she pressed it to her cheek, her free hand stroking Anna's forehead, wiping away the remaining damp hairs.

Anna's breathing was steady, and her body relaxed. She seemed as if she were in a twilight sleep. *Oh, Lord, what does this mean? What is happening to my beautiful daughter?* Lars could see white foam bubbles that by now seemed to fill his daughter's mouth and was struck with fear. Lars too knelt by his daughter, picking up her other hand.

"Oh, my baby, my baby," Bridget cried softly. "What's happening to you?"

Still panting, Peter offered what he had seen. "When I heard mom screaming and yelling, I came over here and saw Anna on the ground, shaking and jerking and out of her mind, like mom said. Then I came to get you. That's all I know. But it was terrible. She was layin' there foaming at her mouth, writhing and kicking. Mom was trying to talk to her."

Lars took a turn stroking his daughter's face and hair, using his dirty fingers. Left behind were little lines of brown dirt from her brow to her chin. Anna responded to his strokes, turning slightly to him, and making eye contact. Lars took his handkerchief out of his back pocket and wiped away the bubbles and moisture that were pooling under her jaw.

No one spoke for the next minute or two. Lars and Peter finished gaining control of their breathing, while Bridget wept for her daughter. The only other sounds were the crows in a far-away tree and the chirping of nearby sparrows and robins.

Anna began to wake and soon tried to sit up. She coughed and choked a bit; the excess fluid in her mouth was now a problem. As soon as Anna sat up, she tried to stand. But she was weak and unsteady, unable to make it off the ground. A second attempt went better, and Anna made it up to her knees.

Bridget and Lars stood up. After a few more seconds passed, she managed to stand up with Lars on one side and Bridget on the other. The three of them stood there in the beans waiting until Anna was ready to walk to the house. Lars noticed that Bridget was not much steadier than Anna, so he nodded to Peter to take over for Bridget.

"Bridget, go into the house and get some cold water and a clean towel. If we can, Peter and I will help Anna to the steps." He hoped that by giving Bridget something to do, she would begin to gain control of herself. He was right; she immediately ran off toward the house.

Peter and Lars walked Anna toward the back door of the house. They inched along at first, then picked up speed as she gained more strength. Anna was already sitting on the middle step when Bridget came out the door with an enamel pan filled with water and two old dish towels.

Peter sat with Anna in case she needed help staying upright. But she seemed to be regaining her strength and awareness with each passing second. Armed with a damp towel, Bridget faced her daughter and began to wipe her face and neck. Anna seemed to appreciate the coolness. A small smile emerged from her blank face.

"What happened?" Her words were slightly slurred.

"You don't remember?" Bridget asked.

"No," Anna said. "Weren't we just picking beans, or was it peas?"

"It was beans. Then you fell to the ground and started jerking and shaking real bad." Bridget still sounded distraught.

"I did what? I don't remember anything like that."

"It's good you don't remember anything, honey. It was terrible watching you lie there on the ground, doing those strange movements with every part of your body."

Lars broke in with a loud voice. "I think we've gone over enough details. Thank goodness it's all over." Standing at the foot of the stairs, Lars put his fingers to his lips, signaling Bridget to say no more. He felt there was no need to alarm Anna.

The color was returning to Anna's cheeks, and she started to move. She took the damp towel off the back of her neck, where Bridget had let it lay. "It's too wet."

Lars smiled as he went into the house and said, "My daughter's back."

Bridget sat on the other side of Anna and pulled her close, forcing her head to rest on her shoulder. Both were damp with sweat and cold water. Both stared out at the horizon.

Lars emerged from the house in a few minutes with a glass of water for Anna and said, "I called Dr. Phillips. He said to bring her to his office."

He tried to stay calm, but his was heart was pounding,

and rings of moisture under his arms were growing larger. Lars washed his hands and face and put on a clean shirt and better shoes. He came back out of the house with the car keys in one hand. "Let's hurry up and go." His voice was stern as he struggled to keep from showing how worried he was.

"I'll stay home," Peter said. "I have to finish painting before my brush dries out. Besides, I don't think I could take any more sitting around with little miss herky-jerky here." He gave Anna a hard nudge with his elbow and leaned on her, almost forcing her into Bridget's lap.

"Stop it, you creep," Anna replied. Her face contorted as she pretended to be in severe pain.

"Okay, enough! Now is not the time for fooling around. I can't be bothered with you two acting up right now." With that, Bridget stood up and went into the house to wash her hands and face. She returned wearing clean shoes and minus her work apron.

Lars backed the old Model T out of a shed and was waiting for Bridget and Anna to get in. Peter walked Anna and his mom to the car and uncharacteristically hugged Anna. "You'll be as good as new in no time." He suddenly turned toward the chicken coop and started to walk away. He walked fast, and Lars knew why. Here he was, almost eighteen years old, and boys don't get sentimental at that age. His friends would call him a baby if he got all gushy over his sister.

Bridget directed Anna to get into the back seat and slid in beside her. She wanted to be by her side if she started jerking again. On the way into town, she combed Anna's hair, pulling out bits of dirt and leaves.

"Ouch!" Anna tried to push her mother's hand away.

"It hurts."

"Your hair looks like a rats' nest. You've got dirt and broken stems and leaves in it. You don't want to go to town with it looking like this." She soon stopped combing. Licking one finger, she wiped away a speck of dirt she had missed with her towel.

"And stop licking my face," Anna protested.

The rest of the way, both Bridget and Lars sat staring straight ahead, looking tense and worried. Lars assumed Bridget was thinking the same thing he was. Something terrible had happened, and they weren't sure what it was or what it meant. The old car bounced around over the deep dirt ruts, shaking the Olsons and leaving a dusty trail.

~ ~ ~

They sat for about 10 minutes in Dr. Phillip's waiting room as he finished with another patient. Lars bounced his leg up and down, and he hummed an old Norwegian sailor's tune. After a few minutes, Bridget reached over and put a hand on his knee. His mind raced between Anna, Dr. Phillips, and what Anna's seizure might mean for their future. From things he'd heard, Lars understood that he was a good doctor. His family had little contact with him since Anna was born, but they were grateful for Bridget's care during her difficult pregnancy.

"Come on back." He motioned for them to follow him into his office, which also served as one of his two examining rooms. Dr. Phillips patted the edge of the examining table and told Anna to sit there. Bridget sat on the chair facing the table while Lars stood next to her.

Doctor Phillips started with Anna, "Tell me what

happened."

"I don't know," Anna replied. "One minute, I was picking green beans with mom, and the next minute I am on the ground looking up at her. She said I was thrashing about, but I don't remember that."

"How do you feel now?"

"Okay. Mostly I'm tired."

"Bridget. It sounds like you were nearby. Tell me what happened. How long did this last?"

"I don't have any idea; I didn't time it. A few minutes, five, maybe."

Bridget went on to describe what she had seen and how she called for help. She told him about how scared she felt as she watched the movements. As Bridget described it, her body was shaking ever so slightly. She seemed to be reliving it. Seeing how distraught Bridget was, Lars moved closer and put his hand on her shoulder to assure and steady her.

"Has this ever happened before?" Dr. Phillips asked.

"No," Lars replied. By now, Bridget was staring into her lap and crying softly.

Dr. Phillips performed his examination of Anna carefully, focusing on neurological issues such as reactions to stimuli, muscle tension, eye focusing, and pupil dilation. After examining her, he told Anna to return to the waiting room and that her parents would join her in a few minutes. Closing the door behind her, he sat down at his desk. It seemed like it took forever for him to find his pipe, pack it, light it, and turn his attention to them.

"Anna seems to be fine now. She was a bit flushed, and some of her reaction times are still a bit slow, which are typical for a person who has had what people often call a fit. It's more appropriately called a seizure. Sometimes people, especially teenage girls, have one or two of these seizures, and they go away forever. Or, sometimes, they are a severe problem lasting a lifetime. The second possibility is a malady called epilepsy. Other than heredity, we don't know why some people get this disease and others don't.

"Whatever the cause, when the seizure happens, the unfortunate patient is unable to control themselves. Thankfully, they're entirely unaware of what is happening to them. As you saw with Anna, most of the time, when the seizure is over, they are tired and weak. There is a recovery period that can last from a few minutes up to an hour or two. It all depends on the severity of the seizure.

"I don't consider an occasional seizure or two to be serious. However, if the fits become frequent, or stronger, or the family is having difficulty coping with them, the patient may need to go to a place I think is called the Helmhurst School for Epileptics, Idiots, and Feeble-Minded. I may not have all the words in the right order, but I think that's what it's called. Anyhow, it's over near St. Paul. They receive better care there by people who know how to handle such things. But we're getting ahead of ourselves. Anna seems healthy enough. We'll wait to see if this becomes a bigger problem."

He stopped, took another puff on his pipe, and asked, "Do you have any questions?"

Lars didn't hesitate, "We're kinda upset by this. Right now, I can't think of a thing. I'll probably think of a bunch of stuff once we leave. Bridget, you have anything you want to ask?"

Bridget shook her head. Tiny tears were still slowly

making their way down her cheeks.

"If you think of something later, give me a call. For today, make sure Anna rests." Dr. Phillips turned his swivel chair around and grabbed a small towel from a shelf. After handing it to Bridget, he laid his pipe back onto an ashtray and reached over and put his hand on Bridget's shoulder. "Come on, mom, your little girl will be okay. Get ahold of yourself before you go out to face her. It won't do her any good to see you this way."

Lars reached into his pocket and pulled out a small wad of bills and a few coins and asked, "How much do we owe you?"

"One dollar."

Lars paid the fee and put his arm over Bridget's shoulder as they walked silently out of the office. For once, he lost his cheerful demeanor. His clenched jaw made him look as grim as he felt.

Lars and Bridget were quiet on the ride home, and no one spoke until Anna finally asked, "So, what is wrong with me?"

"Nothing," Lars replied. "You had a little something called a seizure, a fit. And it probably won't ever happen again. Dr. Phillips said you should be fine."

"Oh," was all Anna said.

Lars continued, "But I think it would be best if none of us mentioned this to anyone else, not even Margaret or Eunice . . . *nobody*. We don't want people to start making up stories out of one little thing or turning one fit into a big deal. He paused for a response, but when one didn't come, he prompted, "Do you two understand?" His tone was stern, and his question left room for only one answer.

"Yes," they both replied softly.

By the next day, Anna was on her very best behavior. She was cheerful and cooperative as she helped Bridget with canning the green beans they picked before her seizure. However, her cheerfulness had nothing to do with her seizure. It was because she wanted to spend the weekend at Margaret's house. Bridget and Lars worried about her going but decided it was best to let her go. To keep her home would require an explanation they didn't know how to give.

~ ~ ~

Joan Bridenbaugh sat at her desk on the first floor of the Redwood County Courthouse, admiring the tall oak tree out on the lawn. Small wisps of white snow ducked and dove over branches then around the trunk, working their way to the top where they disappeared into the blue sky.

She had just finished reading a letter from Edith Stinson. It was a follow-up to the one she had sent to Joan in 1926 in which she promised that all Redwood County school children would be intelligence tested by the state Department of Public Welfare. What Stinson had neglected to mention back then was that only one psychologist served as the test giver for the entire state.

Joan learned long ago about promises and reality. Each experience with state government fueled her already cynical outlook on life. After all, it was now January 18, 1931, four-and-a-half years after the initial 1926 promise. Joan looked down at the letter from Miss Stinson and re-read the third paragraph.

Dr. A. C. Waters or his assistant will be contacting your

office to arrange for dates to test all the school-age children in your county. I am sending a copy of this letter to your County Superintendent of Schools. He can work with you and Dr. Waters' office to arrange dates for testing. You should also make special efforts to inventory those children who, for some reason or another, are not involved in a school classroom. These children should also be examined by Dr. Waters, who will determine which children he can test. If they can't, he will estimate their mental age.

Joan agreed with Miss Stinson; all the children on her list should undergo testing whether or not they were in school. There were children too crippled to go to school. Plus, those severely impaired idiots and imbeciles who didn't belong in a classroom needed to be classified and dealt with accordingly.

But there were children in the public schools that didn't belong there. They were a menace to those who could learn. It wasn't the child's fault; they were innocent. She blamed the parents. They were the ones producing "feebleminded" children then trying to pass them off as normal. To get all the defective children in Redwood County sterilized and institutionalized, she needed proof to take to the judge. Evidence that would substantiate her request for commitment in the cases where parents didn't cooperate. In many courts, a low enough score on an intelligence test was one form of proof a child was feebleminded, or worse.

She smiled as she reached into her desk and pulled out the notebook she had hidden in the back. Here were the names of people she had identified as being unfit for one reason or another. Sterilized people had a red S by their name. Joan made a big red checkmark by those she had sent away. There was a black checkmark by the names of those discharged from an institution. Her year-end net admissions were growing, but so were the number of people she found still needing to be institutionalized. Undoubtedly, the testing would help increase the number of red checkmarks in her secret book.

Before putting her book away, she scanned through the names. There, in the end, was Ralph Belkner. He had a big red checkmark indicating that as of July 10, 1930, he lived in Helmhurst. She relished that one since she wrested the child from the clutches of his uncooperative mother. Recent scientific studies proved that other members of this family would also be defective. She would watch and wait for the other defective Belkners to emerge, precisely as she was doing with dozens of other families.

Anna Olson's name was in the book because Joan had received a phone call from Dr. Phillips after her first and so-far only seizure. Dr. Phillips privately believed in the eugenics movement and let Joan know when he met people with mental or physical problems that had genetic origins. One seizure wasn't enough to warrant sending Anna to Helmhurst, but it was enough to warrant a spot in her little book. That way, if she had any more seizures, she'd be prepared to push for institutionalization.

Joan knew Anna and her family from Redeemer Lutheran Church. She met Lars and Bridget there within the first month of arriving in Grant Grove. They often greeted each other at church, but other than that, they had few interactions. Living in a small town, however, meant they heard about each other. For example, Joan heard rumors of Bridget's moodiness and Lars' drunken uncle. Now, she would watch them closer, looking for signs the family was a threat to a better society.

CHAPTER 9
MARGARET PETERSEN

THE HIGHER-GRADE FEEBLEMINDED FEMALE IS A GREATER RISK THAN THE MALE.
G.C. HANNA

1931

While most children in the US felt the pain of the worsening economic depression, rural children noticed slight differences in their way of life from what it had been in prior years. They lived in near poverty from birth and harbored little sympathy for others who were now getting a taste of their experiences. Although there was ample food, it tended to be bland. Meats, vegetables, soups, sauces, and fruits were all canned in jars. Summer was an exception when fresh fruits and vegetables made it to the dining room table.

Mended then re-mended clothes made their way down to younger brothers, sisters, or cousins. The patches were sometimes a source of great fun for the children.

"Look!" yelled a ten-year-old boy, "Joey has a patch on his butt!"

"He must have farted so hard it blew a hole in his pants," another boy added.

"I did not. My mom did this before she gave them to me, so knock it off!"

"Fart bomber, fart bomber," the whole group chanted until Joey ran off with tears in his eyes.

"Come on back, Joey. We were just kidding. Come on, don't tell, Joey, we're sorry, okay?"

It was when they started high school and went to Grant Grove for classes that they became embarrassed by their dress. They saw city kids wearing newer clothes on opening day. By comparison, the farm kids looked like hicks. Peter asked his parents for some new clothes right before his freshman year. Bridget and Lars knew he wanted to fit in, so they bought him two new pairs of denim jeans and two new shirts. It was his job to make them last the whole school year.

Clothing wasn't the only thing farm children learned to deal with when money was tight. Without money for movies or expensive toys, children learned the fine art of imaginative play. Peter and Anna were typical children in that their favorite activity was having a friend or group of friends over to their house. Parents set two standard rules for these visits. They took place only after they did all their morning chores and ended before it was time to do the afternoon round.

As Anna and Margaret turned eight, they graduated from playing with ragdolls inside the house to playing outside. "Let's go out and play like we're famous women-explorers, conquering the African jungles—like Tarzan and Jane," Margaret suggested.

"Only this time I get to be Jane," Anna insisted on this condition, with all the courage she could muster. She usually let Margaret assign the roles, and she was tired of always playing the part of a boy.

"Oh, all right. But we need some water and cookies to pretend we are on a long journey."

With a mason jar full of cold well water and a brown

bag holding cookies stolen from the cookie jar, they climbed into the haymow. The rain was dripping down on the roof as they reached the top of the large pile of hay, their footsteps driving tiny bits of dry alfalfa into the air. Anna felt safe and dry inside the dusty confines of the barn. *Let it rain,* she thought. *We're having fun.*

"Careful, so we don't slide down," Margaret warned right before she lost her footing and took a long slide down the hay. After getting her breath back, she hollered up to Anna, "Slide down, you'll be okay. It's fun. Pretend it's a great waterfall, and we survived the plunge!" Anna laughed and squealed in delight as she reached the soft landing below.

"Come on, let's do it again," Anna shouted. She was already on her way back up to the top.

Years passed and climbing around in the hay or trees, and tromping around in the weeds behind the chicken coop began to give way to sitting on the porch looking at magazines and talking about new things.

Anna looked up, "Has your mother talked to you about this 'special time?'"

Margaret blushed. "No, but I know all about it. My older sister's a senior in high school, and she told me everything. I think it's awful."

"I agree, plus you have to go to all that extra work. My mom says it isn't any big deal, and it's normal for women. She also told me I ought to know about having sex, *now that sounds terrible.* Who would want to kiss a boy? Let alone allowing him to put his thing in you. She also said never to do it until you get married. Never, never, never! When you have sex with a man, it makes a baby. Like the bull breeding cows." Anna sat back, satisfied she knew more than Margaret for once.

"Ew! Will you tell me when that 'special time' starts to happen to you? I'll let you know when it happens to me. I'm curious about everything, about what it feels like. My sister gets very moody when it happens to her. Even mean sometimes."

"Sure, I bet it happens to you first, though. You are a little older, plus you're a little more grown up than me."

Soon movies, starlets, and kissing boys were the standard fare for all the girls their age, and they met as often as possible to talk. Talking was the teenage girls' favorite pastime. Their parents would get tired of the noise they would make in the house and shoo them outside. One day when three of Anna's friends were over for an afternoon, they came across Peter smoking behind the chicken coop.

"Oo oo oo, Peter! I'm going to tell mom and papa," Anna gasped.

"You keep your mouth shut, you little twerp, or I'll tell everyone about your little secret."

"Oh, yeah, well, I dare you," Anna said as she stomped off, her girlfriends in tow.

"What secret is that?" Margaret asked.

"Nothing. My stupid brother's talking nonsense." Anna didn't mind telling a little white lie because she recalled her father's strict instructions about not telling anyone about her seizure.

Anna's mood swings and occasional sassiness sometimes tested Bridget's patience. She didn't want to be like her father, punishing every small misdeed she did as a child. So instead of being put off by her small acts of rebellion, Bridget accepted them as a part of being a girl starting puberty.

~ ~ ~

Farm communities were close-knit, often finding relief from the daily drudgery of farm life with picnics or potlucks. For members of Redeemer Lutheran, their Fourth of July all-day picnic was such an event. Held on the Sunday nearest the holiday, it started with a short church service with a brief sermon. Pastor Nygard even canceled Sunday School. Lars and the other men set up tables and chairs. Peter and his friends set up the games, and the women carried food to the tables. The children played tag or simply chased each other around. Each family brought at least one main dish and a dessert. By the time the meal started, the tables had food from edge to edge.

The Country Feed and Supply Store loaned the church a new cattle watering tank. The men's group at Redeemer bought watermelons, and John Dowd provided large twelve-inch square blocks of ice. When they finished putting it all together, melons and chunks of ice floated in ice-cold water. No child could resist putting a hand in the icy water and pushing them around. Older boys had contests to see who could keep their hands in the water the longest.

"Ptew," a seed flew across the grass. "I bet that went twenty feet!"

"No way. Let me show you how to do it." The second boy spat a seed with a long high arc. He was the champion of the day, no one doubted it, but his mother severely scolded him for having watermelon juice spilled all down the front of his white shirt. At thirteen, Anna thought this was all silly and far beneath her. After all, she considered herself more grown-up than these boys.

The afternoon time flew by with sack races, softball games, and conversations under the maple trees. The little ones fell asleep on blankets, and the elders nodded off in their chairs. Soon it was time for families to start picking up their things. Farmers had chores to do before it got dark.

At the Olsons', while Peter milked cows, Anna picked eggs, Lars fed the livestock, and Bridget prepared picnic leftovers. She also cut large slices of white bread and set out both butter and apple butter.

It was dusk by the time everyone gathered around the kitchen table. As usual, the family prayed. "God is great. God is good, and we thank Him for this food. Amen." Everyone was tired, and it was noticeably quiet. The only sound was that of the crickets starting their evening chorus. After the blueberry crisp was gone, Lars read while Peter and Anna helped their mom clean up.

~ ~ ~

Anna was not the only woman in the house with mood swings and an occasional edge in her voice. The stress brought on by Anna's seizure kept boiling in Bridget's mind and often spilled out like hot lava. Lars was the one burned by her sudden eruptions.

One day, Bridget instructed Lars, "I don't want anyone else to know about her seizure, do you understand that?"

"Yes, I do understand. Wasn't it me who said that first?"

"Yes. But sometimes you act like it never happened!"

"What? What do you expect me to do or say? Or not say? I know the labels they put on people. I understand that if you have epilepsy, these eugenics people want to send you to an institution. Better yet, sterilize you." Lars paused for a moment, his face now flushed. "What do you think I should be doing? *Tell me!*"

Lars wasn't quite finished. "What do you do? Sometimes you sit around the house all day with a long sad face. You act like you are a hundred miles away. People are going to think something's wrong for sure if you keep acting like you have melancholy. You don't talk to me, but you always want to know my exact whereabouts. I can't tell you ahead of time every single place I'll be."

Bridget shot back. "I want to know where you're at, so I can find you if it happens again!"

Lars had nothing else to say. He stood up, shook his head, and went out to the barn where he could find some soothing liquid comfort. *Thank God for Ruth and her little side business. At least so far, she isn't shut down, like some of those places in Chicago.* His mind wandered off into other subjects as he sat on an upside-down bucket and stared at the bright stars and brilliant moon.

Lars returned to the house late, expecting to find Bridget asleep. Instead, she was waiting for him in her satin nightgown. As soon as he was in bed, she took it off and snuggled up against his shoulder.

"I'm sorry," she whispered.

"That's okay. I know Anna worries you. She worries me too, although I try not to show it."

"It is hard for both of us, but I shouldn't take it out on you."

She kissed him deeply, with love, and the intent to make him happy. The passion that ensued was genuine, burning as hot as it ever had. They found long ago that sexual intimacy was a release and reminded them of how deeply they loved one another. They went to sleep that night, both feeling complete, gratified, and at peace.

~ ~ ~

Anna sat at her desk by the window, watching dapple-gray clouds roll by. The changing patterns, the swirling curtains of snow, and the howling wind distracted her from her studies. She was somewhere in the land of the mountain kings and gnomes of her mother's old Norway legends. Her mother's favorite piece of music, Edvard Grieg's *Peer Gynt Suite*, filled the sky. She was unaware that two people had entered the warm classroom.

"Anna Olson." Hearing her name, she snapped her out of her daydream. She hesitated. She didn't know where Miss Pratt was.

"Anna Olson, come here this minute. Please don't make me call you again." Anna hated the shrill sound of her teacher, especially when Miss Pratt was talking to her. The voice was coming from behind her.

"Yes, Miss Pratt." Anna raised her hand as she stood.

"Anna, I would like you to meet Miss Bridenbaugh and Dr. Paulis. Dr. Paulis is here to give you a test. I told him we were short of space, so the two of you will work here in the coat closet. Is that clear?"

"Yes, Miss Pratt."

For fourteen-year-old Anna, the entire experience was strange. The man wasn't friendly and acted as if he were in a hurry. Without hesitation or explanation, he began.

"What state are we in?"

"Minnesota."

"What time of the year is it?"

"Winter."

The questions became increasingly more difficult.

"Spell the word *world* backward."

"Dlorw, Dolrw, . . ."

Giving Anna little more time to think it over, he snapped, "Let's move on."

"A man bought three monkeys, and each one costs twenty-five dollars. How much profit would he have if he sold two of them for thirty-two dollars and the third for forty-seven dollars and fifty cents?"

Anna picked up a pencil and tried to do the math quickly. *Two times thirty-two dollars equals sixty-four dollars. Then add the forty-seven dollars and fifty cents.*

"Times up, Anna, let's move on."

During the next hour, there were increasingly tough questions peppered in rapid succession. It might not have been so bad, except for the fact Anna was in a closet with an old man whose breath reeked of cigars. She could hear her classmates going on with their day, and she wondered why she was the only one taking this test.

Chapter 10
NUMBER TWO

THE WORST CRUELTY THAT CAN BE INFLICTED ON A HUMAN BEING IS ISOLATION.
SUKARNO

1931

The bright April sun prevented Lars from knowing who was running toward him. Nor did he understand why. But as the person neared, he could hear him hollering, and he instantly recognized the situation for what it was. His face blushed a tinge of crimson, and his heart sped up.

From a hundred feet away, Lars heard, "Mr. Olson, you gotta come quick. It's Anna."

That was all Lars needed. He quickly unhooked his horses from the plow and turned them toward the barn. "Hup, hup, hup," he called out, slapping their back with the reins, trying to get them to move faster. When the boy reached him, Lars recognized him as one of Paul Hagadorn's children.

"What happened?"

Tom doubled over. Gasping for air, he could barely speak. Out came a brief explanation: "Well sir, Anna, she fell to the floor and started floppin' and jerkin' around, like she was in a devil's spell. That didn't last too long, and then she just laid there all stiff like. Since we don't have no phone at the school. Miss Pratt said I better come git you."

"Okay, Tom, save your breath. Did you tell Mrs. Olson?"

"Yup. She didn't say nothin'. She stood there, kind of swayin' a bit and all white. I figured I needed to get you."

"Good, you go on up to the house and wait by the back steps. I'll get the car."

Lars reached the barn door where he let the horses stand, without taking their harnesses off. He started his 1925 Ford, pulling it up to the house where Tom was sitting on the back step. Seeing no sign of Bridget, he honked the horn, which let out a squawk more like a goose than a modern car.

Bridget finally came dashing out of the house, her old sun hat perched atop her head and an apron stained by fruits and vegetables around her waist. As she reached the car, she realized she had the apron on and quickly undid the knot at the back and slipped it off. The hat she threw in the back seat.

"Tom, hop in, we'll take you back with us."

Once he was in the car, Tom said, "I hope Anna is okay. She was shaking and jerkin' like I never seen before. Is she sick or something?"

"We don't know, Tom, we haven't seen her. I'm sure she'll be alright. She was after the last—I mean we're worried about her, that's for sure."

Their car bumped and jumped down Schoolhouse Road. Lars looked over at Bridget. She was staring straight ahead, her face frozen in a hard gaze. Lars could see she wasn't in a good mental state. She was a mother, Lars rationalized. She had every right to be concerned. It felt to Lars like the two-mile drive to the schoolhouse took an hour, when, in fact, it took less than ten minutes.

They entered the school, not knowing what to expect. What they found was Anna sitting all alone by a wall. Not even Miss Pratt had approached Anna to see if she could help. Anna's face was a fiery red. Her dress wrinkled, her strawberry-blonde hair in complete disarray. A small river of bubbles was slowly flowing down one side of her chin. She was still in the trance that follows a seizure. Anna was having a tough time keeping her head up, and it looked like she was dozing off.

"What happened?" Lars looked around at the mixture of terrified, questioning, and curious students hoping someone would tell him what he needed to know. A little girl he didn't know spoke up.

"Mr. Olson, she was sitting next to me one minute and the next moment, she slumped to the floor. It wasn't like she fell hard. It was more like the air came outta her. Then she started jerking, and her muscles got really tight. You could see them pulling her back and forth. Fast, like I never knew possible. You could hear a soft swoosh of her clothes when she was jerking. Then, the jerking stopped. She lay there real quiet—she seemed to be breathin' all right, so Margaret and I helped her to sit up where she is now. It was awful, Mr. Olson, just awful."

"Miss Pratt, is that what happened?"

"What do you mean?"

"I mean, you are the teacher, and you're staring at Anna like a five-year-old. I thought you would be helping her. Doing something like getting her some water, wiping her forehead, and comforting her. It sounds like it's the students who helped out, not you."

"Mr. Olson, I am not a trained nurse. I am a teacher." Miss Pratt's voice trailed off and away.

Lars turned his head; he didn't want an argument. Bridget knelt beside Anna and took her in her arms. She put her head on her shoulder and rocked her gently back and forth. Anna soon looked up at Bridget and gave her a weak smile.

Finally, another voice spoke.

"You done shakin', Anna?" It was little Jimmy Ellis.

"I don't think she knows anything. She's starin' off into space." The answer came from his friend Russell.

Still another student chimed in, "Yeah . . . that must be what it's like when demons take ahold of you. I heard about that once, demons making your body shake."

Lars knelt, taking his daughter's arm. He could feel that her muscles were still weak. Realizing she needed more time to recover, he didn't talk or move her. After a few minutes, Anna spoke.

"Hi, Papa. I think that thing happened to me again, but I don't feel so good this time."

"Shh. You're going to be okay," Lars replied.

With small tears trickling down her cheeks, Bridget stroked Anna's face and hair with the back of her hand.

"Oh God, not again. Please make it go away." She took a deep breath, followed by a long, slow exhale. "God, let her be normal." Bridget's whispered prayer expressed a mind full of worry.

Anna gradually gained muscle strength and more awareness. She looked at Bridget and said, "I'll be okay Momma, you don't need to treat me like a baby."

Looking at Lars, Anna continued, "Papa, I'm alright. It was one of those, ah, seizures!" She tried to get to her feet, but she was still too weak and disoriented to be able to get up on her own. They heard Miss Pratt clap her hands and announce there was a special recess, and the children should go outside. Some students dashed for the door while others stayed to watch Anna.

Five minutes later, with Lars on one side and Bridget on the other, they managed to get her standing. Once she got up, her balance improved, as did her orientation to where she was. She looked at Margaret and the other girls who were still across the room.

"This happened to me once before, but it's no big problem, I'm the same now as I was before. Don't worry about me."

Meanwhile, Lars went to the coat rack and got her coat.

"Come on, let's go," he said.

"But I am okay now. Why can't I stay and finish the day?"

"No, I think we need to see Dr. Phillips and then get you home. I'm sure you'll be back soon."

Without further explanation or acknowledgment, Lars walked Anna toward the door, with Bridget following close behind. As they were leaving the room, Anna turned around and said, "I'll see ya tomorrow."

~ ~ ~

As they passed their farm, Anna protested, "We aren't going to see that doctor guy, are we? I don't like him. He stinks from smoking that dumb old' pipe." Her objection expressed both disgust and rebellion.

Bridget turned around to face Anna, "We are going regardless of what you say. This is the second time this has happened, and we need to find some answers. We need to find out what to do, so this will never happen again."

After a moment passed, Bridget continued lecturing Anna. "These fits frighten me. Plus, now all the other children have seen you jerking and shaking about on the floor. They will tell their parents, and everyone will say you are an afflicted person. You also told them this wasn't your first seizure. You agreed you understood Papa when he told you not to say anything to anyone."

"What does afflicted mean? Besides, by now, they already know I'm different. Going to see a doctor isn't going to change that. I'm sure they'll forget about it in a few days anyhow. Jeeze." There was a slight hesitation in her speech as if she were searching for the right words. Anna folded her arms and stared out the side window.

Lars glanced at Bridget and noticed her cheeks had turned a darker shade of red. He knew her well and understood her anger and fear. But he also had questions that spun circles through his mind. What was happening with their daughter, and why her? What made Anna this way? He found no answers, so the questions repeated themselves over and over.

The rest of the trip was silent. Lars drove as fast as possible, trying to avoid the deep ruts in the dirt road that caused their old Ford to shimmy and shake. Finally, they reached smooth gravel, and Lars stepped on the gas.

After a brief examination, Dr. Phillips again excused Anna, who was eager to get out of the examining room. "As I said before, this may be her last seizure. Or the beginning of a long, painful affliction. We don't understand what is going on in the brain that causes fits, and there are different kinds of seizure disorders. Epilepsy is one of many, which is why she needs to see a specialist.

They can do the correct types of tests and give you a better idea of what kind of seizure disorder she has. I'll give you the name and phone numbers of two I know and trust. The only thing is you'll need to go to Minneapolis to see them. If you don't have a phone, I can have my wife call and make an appointment for you."

"We have a phone, but if your wife made the call, we would appreciate it. She would know how to explain this and what to say," Lars said.

"I'll have Bonnie see what she can do. It may take her a few days, but she will get back to you."

Bridget stood up. "Just so you know, she's not going to someplace far away to live in an institution. I can tell you that right now." Her voice was tight and hard and cold as steel. Her eyes shot daggers at Dr. Phillips. "We can take care of her at home if it comes to that. There's no way we are going to send her away." She turned to Lars and said, "Let's go. I've heard enough."

Lars let Bridget leave first, and as he followed, he shook Dr. Phillip's hand. "I'm sorry, Doctor. She's emotional right now."

"I'm used to it, Lars. Sometimes it's hard to come to grips with health problems. If I were you, I'd brace yourself for a reaction from the community. People can be cruel sometimes, especially when they don't understand things." As the doctor turned away from Lars, he made a final comment. "Good luck to you people." He said it with a tone of graveness as if this second seizure were a death sentence.

~ ~ ~

Anna was unprepared for the reception she got when she returned to school. The moment the other students saw her, they froze in place and stared. It was a long, awkward moment that was broken by the innocent question from a little six-year-old. "Are you going to fall on the floor again?"

"No, it's only happened twice, and it won't happen again," Anna said with a forced smile on her face. She was anxious about what her classmates were thinking. Her hands were damp, and her muscles tense. She could feel each heartbeat.

"Oh," the little one said casually.

Anna went to her desk, embarrassed by the stares of the other students. She took out her books, noticing that the others were slow getting to their seats, stealing glances at her as often as they could. With the children seated, Miss Pratt said that they needed to concentrate on their studies, not Anna. She began teaching, and the students started their lessons for the day.

Jimmy Parcel continued to stare at Anna.

"What you lookin' at?" Anna snapped.

"Nothin'."

"Then mind your own business."

Miss Pratt's shrill, sharp words rang out, "Anna, be quiet and start your studies. You've already been disruptive enough."

Anna put her head down, angry that she was the focus of attention, *again*.

Margaret helped Anna by silently pointing out the place where they were in their math book. For the rest of the day, Anna concentrated as best she could on her assignments. She tried not to think about the isolation she already felt. Her mind often wandered to a place far, far away, a place without form or substance. She quickly snapped out of her trances each time they occurred and told herself that everything would be all right.

At the first opportunity, Anna leaned over to Margret and whispered, "Did you see the note that Gertrude passed Aksel right before I had my fit? I know that Tomisina had it first. I wonder if Tomisina or someone else wrote it? I know she likes Aksel because she always tries to hang her coat up next to his."

"Uh, huh," was all the reaction Anna received. Margret stared straight ahead, not turning her head to make eye contact. Her lukewarm response was the norm, and it carried over to the day that followed, then the next. No one seemed to want to talk to her, or if they did, their words were short and terse. Anna began to tense up at the thought of going to school since she didn't understand why no one wanted to talk to her. Her frustrations worsened as the days went by. Finally, after six days of getting the silent treatment, her emotions broke loose. She ran outside and cried.

Anna tried to make the big sobs that welled up from within stop. Her emotions needed someone, especially Margaret, to come outside to console her. For the first time in her life, she was utterly alone, and all she could do was cry. Emotionally spent, she wiped her face with the sleeves of her dress. Her eyes and nose were red and swollen. Every few seconds, a tiny sob snuck out. After an hour, she returned to her class.

As the weeks passed, Margaret and a few of the other girls gradually started to talk to her again. Unlike before, however, they didn't share the small secret things that make teenage relationships work. She was more a stranger as opposed to a part of the group. But at least they would give her eye contact now and then and engage in some conversation. As this happened, Anna had hopes that someday soon, things would be back to the way they were. She hoped that everyone would forget what had happened to her.

The boys in her age group wouldn't let her seizure slip easily into the past. Anna heard them laugh at her and call her a freak when she walked by during recess. One or two of them would feign having a seizure to the howls of laughter from the others. Anna looked at her friends and saw them trying not to laugh, but a few of them couldn't contain themselves.

"Ha, ha, ha," Anna said before walking away, trying to separate herself from the group, but a one-room schoolhouse didn't make it easy to hide. The best she could do was to find a place to be by herself. Arms crossed, staring at the floor, she sulked, trying her best to shut out what had happened.

"Come on, Anna," one of the girls would finally say. "They didn't mean anything by it." Reluctantly, Anna would get up and rejoin the group, trying to act as if nothing had happened.

Margret eventually resumed her friendship with Anna. Still, there was a small strain in her voice when she brought up the topic of Anna's seizure. Naturally, she and the other students had questions.

"When did this thing happen to you before? What makes you jerk like that? Do you feel anything when you're jerking? What do you think about when it happens? What makes your mouth foam?" Anna didn't have any answers. Understandably, these were things about which young people, and their parents, for that matter, were curious. To her, the questions and comments were more ways for them to single her out for ridicule.

Occasionally one of the older boys would remember. "Oh, I'm havin' a fit!" he would announce after pretending to fall to the floor, feigning shaking and jerking.

Another would say, "Hi, I'm Anna. I have a jerky disease. It makes me foam at the mouth, and I shake all over!"

Anna had no choice but to accept it. In school, she pretended to laugh. At home, she cried. When school was out for the year, her classmates forgot about what had happened to her.

~ ~ ~

Joan Bridenbaugh and Abigail Pratt were active members of the Southwest Minnesota Eugenics Society. In addition to reading all the literature, they attended every meeting. They met briefly after the May 1931 meeting.

"I don't know if you've heard, but that little Miss Olson had a fit in my class. It was a terrible sight. It's a shame those innocent little ones had to witness such a horrible thing."

Joan Bridenbaugh nodded and smiled. It was a source of great pride, knowing what bad things were happening in her community. She didn't tell Abigail, but she already knew Anna had a second seizure, thanks to Dr. Phillips' secret calls. Privately he believed she had epilepsy even though there was no conclusive diagnosis. Joan agreed with him that from the eugenics point of view, she was a threat to the community.

"I would very much appreciate it if you would tell me all about what happened in your classroom. Tell me everything, and I mean *everything*."

"Well, you wouldn't have believed it even if you had seen it." It took over thirty minutes for Miss Pratt to tell her about Anna's seizure and its aftermath. As Joan requested, she explained every detail and every reaction.

They agreed that it would be proper for Miss Pratt to talk to the superintendent of schools and inform him of the seizure.

The first thing Joan did when she got back to her office was to make sure she had recorded the second seizure in her little book. She went to Anna's name and added March 31, 1931. In tiny print, she wrote, "Seizure two. Sterilize! Remove from school!" Her little book, crowded with entries, would soon need to be with a larger one. *That's okay with me. It means I've been doing my job well—despite what others think.*

While she had her book open, she noticed the name Betty Graham, daughter of the Methodist preacher. Joan got her parents to agree to send her to the Minnesota School for the Deaf. Joan realized she wasn't deaf, but the school also offered intensive speech therapy for stammering. If they couldn't correct the defect, she would argue the girl should remain there simply because she wasn't "right in the head." Page after page had capital s's or checkmarks. She successfully got many defective people sterilized, but most were sent away to one institution or another. Her supervisor told her she had taken sparsely populated Redwood County from nearly last to first in the percentage of its population institutionalized.

She noticed Ralph Belkner's name and smiled. He was a threat to society. If he fathered children, they too would be imbeciles. She averted that disaster, but it wasn't easy. The boy's mother was stubborn. She fought like a wildcat to keep her son home. She felt pity for a woman who would bother to love such a low-grade person. Joan recalled having to work hard on the judge at Ralph's commitment hearing, even though she knew that in the end, she would win. *I'm sure Ralph is happier now with his own kind. I did the right thing.*

But it wasn't only Ralph who was a threat to society. From the Belkner family history, she recorded at her first meeting with Ralph's father, there were siblings, uncles, grandparents, and cousins that she needed to keep an eye on. Many she already documented as heavy drinkers, lazy, and feebleminded. Joan thought about Henry Goddards' book describing the Kallikak family and how many deviants descended from one woman. *These Belkners are just like the Kallikaks, alcoholics, and shiftless no-counts, the whole lot of them. At least they provide me with job security.*

Chapter 11
MINNEAPOLIS

THE QUESTION IS NOT HOW TO GET CURED, BUT HOW TO LIVE.
JOSEPH CONRAD

1931

Lars was pleased with the July 7 appointment with the specialist in Minneapolis. For farmers, July meant a break between planting and harvesting, so the trip didn't cause him to miss any time in the fields. Peter stayed behind to take care of the animals and mow alfalfa.

Lars sensed Anna's excitement. All she talked about was the big city, bright lights, and stores full of beautiful things not available in hick towns like Grant Grove. On the other hand, he felt tension and apprehension oozing from Bridget. She grew silent and seldom smiled.

At night, she talked to Lars about her fears.

"What if they say she's epileptic? What then?"

"Don't get all wound up. We'll wait to see what the doctors say. Besides, Dr. Phillips said Anna might not have any more seizures. Maybe she will outgrow them."

"What if she doesn't have epilepsy, but still has seizures? How are we supposed to deal with that?"

"Same thing. Stop worrying so much, it's making you hard to be around."

"Someone has to care about Anna. You don't seem one-bit upset. She has a serious problem. What if she falls and hurts herself? What if she doesn't wake up after a fit?

I worry about it happening again, and you're not here. I can't handle things as well as you."

Lars put his arms around her, "Shh."

They took the train since Lars didn't like to drive in the big city, and his old car wasn't always reliable. They left the day before the appointment, so they would have time to find the building where it would be. Lars also wanted to be sure they could get a room at the hotel John Dowd recommended. He said it would be clean, inexpensive, and easy to find.

As they stood on the platform in Minneapolis waiting for their suitcase, Ann raised her voice over the background noise, "I like this, Papa. Here we are in this huge place, and nobody knows anyone else. People walk on by you; they don't know you, so they don't judge you. I like that, you know, not being judged as weird, or spastic, or called a witch."

"I kind of like it too, Anna. I like seeing new things and different things. That's what I like about coming here. Plus, seeing the doctor. Maybe he'll—"

"What? You mean maybe he'll tell us what's wrong with me?"

Lars smiled and gave her hand a gentle squeeze.

They made their way through the crowded station and out onto the busy streets. It wasn't the clean, bright, bustling scene Anna envisioned. The Great Depression was deepening. "Closed" signs hung in the window of every fourth store. Where there was a "Help Wanted" sign and long lines of hungry looking men lined up. Some were dirty, and some so tired they could hardly stand. Others had a terrible look of desperation. There were even longer lines where a church was offering free soup and a chunk of white bread. Lars stopped and stared, stunned by the sight of so many people in need.

Three blocks north of the train station, they found their hotel. As John Dowd promised, everything was clean and comfortable. They had a private bath, which Anna and her mother appreciated. Plus, their room had enough space to accommodate a rollaway for Anna.

Lars and Anna enjoyed eating at restaurants and ordering food they would typically not have at home. The pork tenderloin sandwich platter instantly became a favorite. Served with mustard, fried potatoes, and applesauce, it was a meal fit for a king. Both ordered cherry pie and ate with gusto.

Bridget sat opposite Anna and Lars, wearing sadness and fatigue on her face like a mask. "Come on, Bridget. Cheer up! You ought to be happy that you don't have to cook or do dishes. Order something different than what you would have at home. Look, here is a roast beef and mashed potatoes plate, piled high on a thick slice of bread and covered with gravy. That sounds good."

"I don't like eating from a kitchen where I don't know who's cooking or how clean things are. You hear stories about people getting sick."

"Bridget, stop being this way. We are here to enjoy a visit to the city before seeing this doctor."

Bridget said no more. She picked at a piece of pie and took tiny sips of her iced tea, all the while staring out the window at the mixture of strange-looking people walking by. There were rich women with finely tailored dresses, poor women with skirts frayed at the hemlines, and every social class in between.

The next day, their appointment was with a doctor

who worked at the Epileptic and Neurologic Disorders Center. The Olsons were unprepared and disturbed by the odd people in the waiting room.

Anna leaned over, whispering, "Momma, look at that person, moving his arms slowly all around. That is so strange."

"Shh."

A few minutes later, "Momma, that guy keeps falling asleep. One minute he's talking to the person next to him, and the next minute, he's asleep."

"Anna, it isn't polite to stare at people. You don't like it when people stare at you. Now mind your own business."

"I ain't staring. I can see them when I look from one side to the other. These people are creepy, they scare me."

Bridget had to admit some people were hard not to notice, like the person who sat straight and stiff as a board, always staring straight ahead, never moving, never paying attention to anything going on in the room. Bridget and Lars began to wonder if they were in the right waiting room.

A moment later, Anna leaned over to Lars. "Papa, I was thinkin' the kids at school might think I'm scary and weird just like I feel with these people."

Lars whispered back, "Maybe."

Finally, a nurse called Anna's name. They followed her to an examining room where she took Anna's temperature and asked her to step on the scale. They didn't wait long for the doctor. After hearing the description of the two seizures, asking questions, and making notes, he examined Anna. When he finished, he told Anna she could get off the examining table.

"First, I can't be one hundred percent sure we are talking about epilepsy. But that would be my first guess at this point. When a person has two or three seizures like Anna, that's what we call it. However, that's not always the case. We know there are several types of seizures disorders, or fits, as the ordinary person calls them. It doesn't sound like Anna has any of these other seizures, so I'll not go into the details. What we don't understand is why this happens to some people and not others. Some think it's genetically inherited." Looking at Lars and Bridget, he asked them if their parents or grandparents had any kind of fits.

Both Bridget and Lars shook their heads. "No," they each said softly.

"Aunts or uncles?" Again, both said, "No."

"Well, in any case, as of late, more of us think it's more a malfunction of the brain and isn't genetic. With better research, we are finding cases like yours, where no one else in the family had fits. It's easy to blame it all on heredity. But life isn't as simple as that. Do you have any questions?"

Lars and Bridget were quiet until Lars broke the silence. "Will she have more fits?"

"That's hard to tell. Some youngsters have one or two seizures, and that's it."

"Do they hurt her brain?" Bridget asked.

"By hurt, I assume you mean damage inside the brain. We don't think so, but we're not sure."

Bridget then asked, "Why does Anna have foam in her mouth?"

The doctor leaned back and smiled. "That foam isn't anything more than tiny air bubbles. When a person has a seizure, they don't swallow, and typically they exhale through the mouth. This air mixes with the saliva that they would normally swallow, and the resulting bubbles are what looks like foam. It isn't anything to worry about, okay?"

Bridget nodded affirmatively.

"Some people have this affliction their whole life. Like I already said, others have a few seizures but never develop epilepsy. Now, what to do. If Anna has the condition and it gets worse, there may be no choice but to send her to the Helmhurst just outside of St. Paul. They have a special part of their institution which treats people with epilepsy, and they do an excellent job. Sometimes they find ways to get the fits to stop completely. I know their physician personally and consider him quite an expert on neurological abnormalities. They also have a school for the children headed up by top-notch teachers. I believe it's the perfect combination of services."

Lars looked over at Bridget and saw she was about to turn white. He knew what she was thinking. He knew her deepest fears: "Bridget . . . Bridget, take a deep breath."

"Doctor, we don't need no school, no Helmhurst. My wife and I will take good care of our Anna."

"A lot of people say that. All I'm suggesting is that you keep an open mind. But there is good news. There has been some evidence to show a new type of treatment works well for some people. Mrs. Olson, there is a special diet based on the findings of some research done here in Minnesota. It's called a ketogenic diet. This diet, plus a type of medication called bromides are known to completely stop the fits. It doesn't work in every case, nothing does, but it is promising. It's been around long enough to have proven its success.

"On your way out, my nurse will give you some pamphlets on this diet and discuss it with you. Plus, she can put you in touch with a group of people who are using the diet. Meanwhile, I'm going to give you a prescription for some bromides. I strongly urge you to try them."

He patted Bridget's knee. "That's about all I can do for you today. Epilepsy is a tricky problem and hard to understand. But we continue to learn more every year. Why don't you bring Anna back to see me in, say, six months, and we will see how she's doing."

After their appointment, the Olsons headed back to the train station. Once the train got moving, they sat in a trance-like silence all the way to Grant Grove, staring blankly out the window at the farms rolling by. The steady clicking of the wheels, the heat of the afternoon, and the gentle rocking of the train car lulled Lars to sleep.

Lars woke up whenever the train slowed to a stop at small towns he never heard of. He looked over at Anna, who had fallen asleep with her head on her mother's lap. He prayed, *God, please make her healthy again, just like after her measles, and sprained ankle. Is this what you want for her? This curse? I hope you are testing us, and soon, the test will be over.*

Bridget tried the new Ketotonic diet even though she didn't know if it would work. She sent away for more information and received a booklet on why this approach seemed to work for people with epilepsy and a listing of foods Anna could eat. The list was short; the Ketotonic diet wasn't easy to follow since it called for a reduction to near zero of certain common foods.

Anna whined, "I see here where I can't eat things like

bread, pasta, and anything else made with flour. Does that mean cookies are out?

"I think so if that's what it says in that booklet."

"No cream and only milk with the cream skimmed off the top. I can't eat like this! I hate vegetables and fruit. And I don't even know what lean meat is."

"This is for your own good, you know. Your papa and I thought this would be better for you than taking those pills. You don't want to have to be taking some medication, do you?"

"Okay, okay, I'll try it, but it better work. I'm going back to school soon, and I don't want to have another fit."

~ ~ ~

As the weeks passed, Lars worried less about Anna's seizures and more about how they were affecting Bridget. She was becoming more distant. She didn't speak unless spoken to, and her answers to questions were short. He often found her staring off into the distance. Lars knew she was angry that their daughter had these terrible things happen to her. He was worried because he didn't want her behavior to upset Anna and Peter.

There was a warm, gentle breeze moving over their bodies. It was a hot August night, and for Lars, nightgowns or pajamas were optional. He preferred to sleep in his briefs and Bridget her light blue, satin pajamas. He rolled toward her, his head resting on his left hand.

"You asleep?"

"Almost."

"Well, I thought that maybe we could have a little sex tonight."

"That's not a very romantic way to go about it."

"Well, I can make it romantic." He grinned widely as his right hand slipped under her three-quarter length pajamas, moving up past her waistline then onto her breasts. "Is this what you mean by romantic?" he gently stroked her breasts while softly nibbling at her ear.

"No, not that either. It's just sex you want. You men are all the same."

"Sure, men like sex. But if memory serves, you don't find it all that bad yourself."

"Not tonight."

"It's been a while."

"We had sex last week."

"Last week! I think it was last month. At least it seems like a month."

She reached up and gently stroked his face. "Not tonight, dear. Maybe tomorrow night."

Lars complied with her directive. As soon as his hand was out from under her nightgown, she turned away from him.

"Bridget, we need to talk about your melancholy. The only time you act normal is when other people are around. When you are at home with us, you clam up. It's hard when you freeze us out all the time. The kids notice it, you know."

She turned toward him, touched his face, and gently kissed his lips. It was a wet kiss, warm and tender. "I know I am acting differently. I've had a hard time dealing with things. All I can say is I don't mean to hurt anyone. It's just the way I am right now. I'm sure that as soon as school starts and Anna isn't here all the time, things will get back to normal and I'll feel better. I promise."

"What does Anna being at home have to do with it?"

"*Everything*. Every moment I spend with Anna, I think she'll have another seizure. With you out in the fields or doing chores all the time, I'm on my own. I'm scared." Without waiting for his reply, she rolled back on her side, her back to him. Their discussion was over.

With Bridget's growing melancholy and Anna's teenage sassiness, it was more common than not for things to be tense between mother and daughter. Thankfully, the two had several things that drew them together. Sewing, knitting, needlepoint, and mending were as natural for Anna as they had been for Bridget. Of all these, needlepoint was their favorite. Both had won several awards in their respective divisions at the county fair.

At fourteen, Anna was already superior to her mom in several respects. She could think of a scene, a pattern, or a flower and set about to stitch it on cloth. Her choice of thread colors created scenes that were vibrant and often included subtle shades in the transition from one color to the next. Bridget continued teaching techniques like selecting the proper needle size and tying the thread on the back of the cloth.

One evening, Anna and her mother swung back and forth on the porch swing while needlepointing. Lars sat in his rocker, reading a newspaper. The cool, moist air felt refreshing after a sweltering day. Clouds on the western horizon signaled a much-needed rain.

"Do you think the people in town talk about my fits?"

"I suppose they do. People wag their tongues at everything." Lars said without looking up from his paper.

"I think my friends are still afraid of me 'cuz I don't see

them quite so much. I have a feeling they don't invite me to everything they do. That stingy diet you have me on reminds them of my seizures."

"I know, honey, be patient. Everything will work out." It was Bridget's turn to offer some reassurance.

"I sure hope so. I am getting tired of being different."

~ ~ ~

The summer of '31 moved slowly for Anna and Bridget. They needed some relief from their mental and emotional struggles. Bridget found comfort with her friend Eunice. Now, it was Bridget's turn to unload her burdens. Over several visits, Bridget tried to explain her frustration with trying to get Anna to stick with the ketogenic diet. She talked about being angry at the very suggestion that Anna would need to go to Helmhurst. Bridget was disappointed with herself for being unable to shake her melancholy and anxiety. To her, it was both curious and comforting that she could talk to Eunice easier than she could unburden herself to anyone else, even Lars, who had done nothing but love and be kind to her. In the fashion of a close friend, Eunice listened, hugged, and comforted Bridget.

Their time together was essential to their mutual survival. Eunice relied on Bridget to listen as she divulged that financial problems were threatening, and they may lose their farm. Her husband, like many others, had borrowed too much money, and they were gradually sliding into bankruptcy. Both women thought their futures looked bleak.

They often talked about Ralphie, who was now in Helmhurst. Eunice's sister tried to see him as often as she could, but her husband kept telling her she should forget about him. He acted as though in life, you can erase the people you know and love as if they were stick figures on a blackboard.

Eunice updated Bridget on Ralphie's care. "My sister says that Helmhurst is a terrible place. They lock people like Ralphie up in a ward, and they'd leave him and the other poor imbeciles there all day. The ward is very noisy, smells terrible, and some of his fellow inmates go around hitting others for no good reason. The worst part is that no one tries to make things better.

"Otherwise, she says Ralphie is doing okay, except for the fact he tries to hold on to her every time she tries to leave. It makes her cry, having to leave him behind, especially since he wants to come home so bad."

Bridget had heard enough about the boy's treatment to confirm her fears. She was terrified that someday they would treat Anna like they treat Ralph. She'd heard other horror stories about the way people who lived there changed for the worse. *No way is my Anna going to a place like that.*

In mid-August, Eunice and her husband lost their farm. Their eviction notice gave them less than a week to pack and leave. Eunice's goodbye to Bridget was quick and painful, leaving an emotional scar on her heart. Like tens of thousands of bankrupt farmers before them, the Weatherbys drove down dusty country roads to find work in the city.

~ ~ ~

It was August 24, six days before school was to start.

That evening, Joan Bridenbaugh and Abigail Pratt paid a visit to the Olsons. The sun had set behind a high bank of clouds that foretold a thunderstorm. Crickets were noisy, and the air was so close, and thick one could hardly breathe. Bridget heard a car come into their driveway, followed by two doors slamming. Soon, there was a gentle rapping at the front door.

"Good evening, Bridget. I'm wondering if Miss Pratt and I might visit with you and Lars for a short while?" Joan asked.

"About what?" Bridget made no move to let them in.

"Anna and her schooling."

"Just a moment." Joan could hear Bridget spit tense, angry words at Lars. "Here they come, unannounced, leaving me no time to fix my hair or put on a decent dress."

"Better let them in since they're here."

When they were all seated, Joan spoke. "We appreciate your seeing us with no notice. Miss Pratt and I felt it would be best this way."

"Best for you or best for us?" Bridget's tone was on the verge of being angry.

"Everyone. I will get to the point Mr. and Mrs. Olson. We would like to discuss Anna so it might be best if she were someplace where she couldn't hear us."

"She's upstairs in her bedroom."

"And Peter?"

"I would appreciate your getting to the point. Peter's whereabouts should be none of your concern." This time it was Lars who was on edge.

"Good idea, Mr. Olson. Miss Pratt and I have discussed Anna's medical condition with the county superintendent of schools up in Redwood Falls. He has ordered that Anna no longer attend school until you can produce a doctor's statement that Anna is seizure-free. "

The comment drew blank stares and silence. The humid summer air itself seemed to make the tension worse. Abigail Pratt interjected, "You can understand that the students were upset by her seizure in the classroom. They talked about it for the longest time, and quite frankly, it was a serious disruption."

"You're simply banning her from school without talking to us? Is that the right thing to do?" Lars' voice was deep, filling the entire room. "We've been to Minneapolis to see a neurologist, and he gave us a special diet for Anna. It's known to prevent seizures, and so far, it's worked. It would have been nice if you had considered that." His eyes narrowed, and he stopped blinking as he stared Joan down.

"A diet isn't going to change our opinion in the least. An epileptic person will always be an epileptic person. The only thing to do is to place them in Helmhurst. They need to be as far away from the mainstream of society as possible." Joan's voice was cold, showing no emotion in either her tone or on her face.

"We don't appreciate you diagnosing our daughter. You're not qualified to do that. Why even the specialist in Minneapolis said, he wasn't sure she had epilepsy." Bridget glared, her face now flushed.

Joan forced herself to sit as tall as possible, then tilted her chin up, assuming an air of superiority. "I don't appreciate your doubting my qualifications," she snapped. "I am an expert in these matters. I deal with all sorts of problem people, so I know what's best for our society."

Bridget too, was sitting straight, on the edge of her

chair, as she delivered a sharp retort, "Are you saying my daughter is a 'problem' for society?"

"Bridget, no need to get angry." Lars' voice again filled the room. "Joan, it doesn't do any good to go labeling people so quickly." Looking at Miss Pratt, "There must be a way we can work out Anna's attending school."

Miss Pratt explained, "I'll send her assignments home with one of her friends. Plus, I'll grade her work when she turns it in. Perhaps she will still be able to take the eighth-grade exam, although I doubt she has the mental capacity to do that."

Bridget's voice was still sharp, "Homework? Mental capacity?" She stood up and said, "I've heard enough."

"Are you leaving?" Lars studied his wife's red face.

"Yes," she said as she walked out of the room.

"As we were saying, Anna should continue her education here at home. If her fits continue to be a problem, we will send her to the Helmhurst School for Epileptics. I have been there myself seen it with my own eyes and can assure you it's a good place. The children are so happy there. You know, being with their own kind."

"That's out of the question, and I'm glad Bridget didn't hear you. She bristles at the very mention of the word Helmhurst."

"I heard it all right." Bridget came storming back into the room. "You two can leave *now*. There isn't going to be any more discussion tonight. This eugenics of yours isn't worth a shit. I don't care if Alexander Graham Bell and all the big shots in the United States think genes cause everything, my Anna isn't leaving my side. No Helmhurst. Did you get that? No institution for Anna. Now get the hell out of my house."

CHAPTER 12
SECRETS

A WOMAN'S HEART IS A DEEP OCEAN OF SECRETS.
GLORIA STEWART

1931

Ruth Carlson was born and raised in Grant Grove. Yet, in many ways, she did not fit in. In an era when a woman's role was to marry and have children, Ruth did neither. Instead, she ran the small restaurant her mother and father started in 1908. She often quipped, "My business is my baby." Raised to be a faithful Lutheran, she wasn't so committed as an adult. She only went to church on special occasions such as holidays, funerals, and weddings. Finally, underneath her cheerful and extroverted front, lay a stubborn contrarian who didn't mind taking the opposite point of view and sticking with it.

Ruth's Café was the melting pot for the community. It was a place where people like Lars and Bridget mingled and met people. Lutherans mixed with Catholics. Farmers rubbed shoulders with townspeople. Norwegians ate with Germans. Old men used it as a place to play cards and hand out opinions on every subject. The people who believed that the government needed to do more to help the average person met those who felt the government was already too big.

In addition to all the mingling, Ruth became a trusted confidant for men and women alike. She seldom, if ever, passed along secrets or nasty opinions. More often, she was the listener, which endeared her to many. People appreciated a trusted confidant in a town where everybody sought to know everything about each other's lives.

One warm summer afternoon, there were only three people in Ruth's Café. Two were farmers finishing their pie and coffee by the front window. The third was John Dowd sitting in a booth close to the back. The overhead fans gently stirred the warm air as John drank his coffee. Ruth came over to him to see if he needed a refill.

"We could've been good together, you know." John stared deep into the coffee.

Ruth replied, "I know. It was my fault. I didn't want what you wanted. For me, it was all about staying free. Now, look at me, I'm still single. My business is like milking cows. There are no days off. It's funny how the things you wanted so badly when you were young end up being hardships later in life."

"Yeah, you got that right. Still, you had everything I ever wanted in a woman. Sometimes I think about us back then, and what it would be like if we'd married."

"Shame on you, John Dowd. You're a married man. You have a beautiful wife, a big house, and you're doing well financially. All you wanted back then was to have sex. You loved my body, remember?" She turned to face the counter so he wouldn't see her blush. "Besides, you never asked."

"Guilty on both accounts. But you notice how long it took me to find another woman? All those years, I waited for some sign that you'd change your mind."

"I do miss our little rendezvous and the precious few times we spent together. We were a pair, but not a pair.

You know?"

"It was something like that. I better get going."

Before he could get up, Ruth sat down across from him. "I'm lonely sometimes, especially at night, reading the paper by myself. There's no one in bed to keep me warm. Are you unhappy, John? You sound unhappy."

"No, I just felt like talkin' to you, Ruth." John reached into his pocket for money. "There is something I'm curious to know. Why did you get into the booze business? And when was that, by the way?"

"1922."

Ruth leaned closer to him. "This here restaurant is hardly making it. I'd have lost it by now if I hadn't gotten the extra income. Not all of us are rich, you know. I don't have a husband or a farm or another way of support. I've got no way to save for the future."

"Times are hard, Ruth, no one has any money right now. That'll change one day."

"A *few* people got money. *You* got money, and *your* businesses go on no matter what. But most of us don't have what you have. So, when this guy came around lookin' for a place to distribute his goods, and when I saw how quickly his stuff sold, I offered to partner up with him. Besides, it ain't nothing more than giving people what they want."

"Yeah, which just happens to be illegal."

"Sure. *Who cares?* These big, rich tycoons use poor people up and spit them out, and no one does a thing to help the little guy. People are out there starving, and all the politicians worry about is some hard-working guy who wants a shot of rye or schnapps now and then. To hell with it. At least that's the way I see it." She paused. "Screw 'em.

All I do is give people a chance to have a little fun." She stood up and headed back to the counter.

John spoke before she had taken a second step toward the counter, his words barely audible. "To answer your question, me and Erica. Were doin' good."

~ ~ ~

Joan had always sat in the same place in the same pew since she was a little girl. Her seat was next to the aisle in the third row from the front. Anyone who didn't know better and took that seat, got an angry stare down from Joan until they moved. Regulars knew it was her seat. Like many, Joan was often guilty of coming to church and going through the motions. Singing familiar hymns, saying the responses during the liturgy, and letting the sermon float gently in one ear and out the other.

For Joan, today was not one of those days. Pastor Nygard delivered his sermon like a father speaking to his children. "In the King James Bible, turn to first Corinthians the thirteenth chapter and thirteenth verse, 'And now abideth faith, hope, love, these three: but the greatest of these is love.'" Pastor Nygard paused for a moment. "Here, I believe God means charity springing forth from love. For without love, nothing is possible, no faith, no hope. Love first from God to man and then from man to God. From this loving relationship comes many things, including love for others, which gives rise to charity. Charity, how many of us display love for our fellow man by being charitable?"

Pastor Nygard's comments struck her like a thunderbolt. It was as if God were speaking to her directly. *"Joan, this message is for you. Wake up. You need to be charitable.*

You need to give with love in your heart." She thought of her life and how she always seemed to be fighting with people. *Yes, God is right. I need to give more than what I put in the collection plate every Sunday.*

It was true, she was a regular giver, second behind John Dowd in supporting the church. But she didn't give as much as she could. *I have the money. I have a job, plus I have my farm income. I don't spend much on myself, so I should be able to give more.*

Pastor Nygard stood at the top of the steps to the church and shook the hands of everyone attending that morning. Babies, toddlers, and teenagers could not escape from a genuinely warm embrace from their spiritual shepherd. Joan leaned in close to his ear, "Might I come by to see you later this week? I need some guidance regarding a church matter."

"Certainly. I'm here most mornings. In the afternoon, I see the sick and shut ins. We have a phone now, you know. You can check on my whereabouts with Mrs. Nygard before you come."

Later in the week, Joan came to his small, cramped office. Cigar smoke filled the room with a stench that reminded her of her father's pipe.

"Pastor Nygard, I come to church every Sunday. I pray, and I give every month. But last Sunday, listening to that verse about faith, hope, and charity, I felt like God was speaking to me. It was strange, but I saw a bolt of light which moved my mind, and I guess, my soul."

"Sounds like you had a Paul moment."

"Paul moment?"

"Yes, you know Paul on the road to Damascus. God

spoke to him, and he fell to the ground. He became a Christian at that moment."

"Oh, yes, yes! It was something like that. In any case, I had this feeling I needed to love more — to be more charitable. So, that's what I wanted to know. How do I do that?"

"Joan, do you recall the story of the poor woman with the alms? How God pointed her out as giving more than the rich people?" Joan nodded. "What was really going on in that story is that she was making a great sacrifice. She was a pauper, yet she gave of what little she had. We could easily excuse her for not giving anything. As a pauper, she sacrificed the things she needed so that she could give to others.

"The rich people were giving, but they weren't making a sacrifice. God calls on each of us to make a sacrifice to give something up to help others. Does this make sense?"

Joan thought for a moment, then smiled and nodded her head. "Yes, it does. Thank you, Pastor." After a pause, Joan continued, "Do the Lutherans still have those missionaries in Africa?"

"Yes, as far as I know. Although a lot of missionaries have had to come back to the US because they simply can't raise the money they need to continue their work."

Joan said, "What about building a school or a church in Africa? They have no idea about Jesus and how He can save their souls. That would be exciting. To be able to build a missionary church. How much would something like that cost?"

"I don't know," Pastor Nygard replied. But I'll check with some people I know."

Two months later, Pastor Nygard found a missionary who was looking for money to build a church in Africa.

After Joan corresponded with him, she gave him enough money to build a church. As the years went by, Joan continued to support that missionary, and eventually, she paid for a small medical clinic and school.

She did, however, have one strict condition for all her gifts— that she remain anonymous. So, Joan Bridenbaugh, the very personification of the eugenics movement, including its racism, and its goal for a genetically pure society, became a significant giver to an African missionary. In her mind, she was proving to God that she was making a First Corinthians type of sacrifice. Secretly, she believed her charity was her way of redeeming herself for her sins.

CHAPTER 13
PASTOR NYGARD

DRUNKENNESS IS VOLUNTARY MADNESS
SENECA

1932

Lars Olson stepped into the sunlight from the relative darkness of the Grant Grove Sales Barn. The late winter sun temporarily blinded him. Its rays became more intense as they bounced off the snow. Or, it might be that the sunshine seemed brighter because it replaced the dark gray winter days that are common in southern Minnesota.

He stood there for a minute or two, letting his eyes adjust to the light. His right hand formed a visor over his brow. For the moment, the troubles and worries of his life seem to recede in the same way the winter snow slowly melts. Time stopped, and his world felt magnificent and warm.

Lars focused on the world around him and began to live in the moment. He looked first at the field west of the sales barn, where he saw some black patches of earth and brown grass. *Soon,* he thought, *they will thaw and be muddy, then later in the spring, ready for plowing and planting.* Everything would soon be mud, especially the roads and the barnyards. If sunshine brightens the spirit, mud dampens it. As he walked across the parking lot towards his horse and wagon, there was already a bit of it sucking at his shoes, slowing his stride.

When Lars reached his destination, he jumped into the wagon. He pulled an empty pail and a feedbag out of a wooden box just behind the seat. He draped the feedbag over the horse's head so it could eat the oats inside while he went to the back of the sales barn to fill the pail with water. Upon returning, he took off the feedbag, placing the water bucket on the ground in front of the horse and returned the bag to the wooden box.

Lars was in no hurry to get home because life was often tense there. Besides, he needed a quick nap since he had been up since four a.m. He was still smiling as he situated himself on top of the wooden box, resting against the back of the driver's seat. He dozed off while thinking about sailing into the horizon with his childhood friends from Norway.

Twenty minutes later, he awoke with a jolt. *Time to get busy!* There were a few things he needed to do before heading home. He hopped down from the wagon and emptied the water pail. He quickly took off his coat and bib overalls, replacing them with a thick, red and black checkered flannel shirt and a pair of gray wool pants.

As he switched his pocket watch and the money from the sale of his hogs to his clean pants, Lars stopped to count. It was the most he had ever gotten per pound for his pigs in at least ten years. Plus, each was heavier than he'd thought. His five hogs collectively weighted two thousand one hundred and thirty-five pounds. At five cents a pound, they netted him a whopping one hundred six dollars and seventy-five cents. He would use the money for seeds for the spring planting, groceries, and farm supplies. To be sure, it would pay for a few small extras—things like spools of thread for Bridget and Anna and magazines for both Anna and Peter. For himself, he'd get a newspaper and a bottle of schnapps—or whatever Ruth had on hand.

Lars made a mental list of all the things to do as he drove his horse, Ginger, into town. On that list, he included a bit of personal time. Lars used to call on Olaf and Gorine Carlson because of all the help they gave him and Bridget when they first came to Grant Grove. After they passed away, Lars liked to spend time drinking coffee with his farmer friends at Ruth's Café, where he heard about new farming tips, seeds, and the latest news and gossip. Today, he was interested in a more personal conversation.

He drove six more blocks then turned into the alley behind the Country Feed and Supply store. After securing Ginger to a fencepost, he walked a few more blocks to Pastor Andrew Nygard's home. Lars reflected on the bond the two shared. He was one of the several people, like the Dowds and the Carlsons, who helped Bridget and him settle into Grant Grove. Today, Pastor Nygard would be in his livery stable turned workshop. After retiring from the pulpit, his new job was minor repairs to broken things or woodworking for friends and neighbors. He always welcomed visitors to help him pass the time.

The moment Lars stepped into the garage and closed the door, heat engulfed him. Two small oak logs cracked and spat out embers in the belly of a stove. Sparks bounced up and down before settling against the wood, adding tiny bits of mass to the glowing embers. Lars loosened his thick shirt.

Familiar smells, such as oil mixed with sawdust and fresh-cut wood, told him he was in a comfortable place.

Hardwoods like oak, cherry, and mahogany were all neatly sorted, stacked, and waiting for just the right use. Finally, there was the ever-present cigar smoke that had soaked into every piece of fabric the old pastor wore. Those familiar with Pastor Nygard knew cigars were part of who he was. "It's my only vice," he would explain to a newcomer.

"Ah, my good friend," Nygard's lovely rich baritone voice filled the room.

"Good morning, Pastor."

Turning away from a bicycle he was tinkering with, the old man reached for his short fat cigar, smoldering in a coffee can cut down to be an ashtray.

"How are you holding up these days?"

"I am doing pretty well, thank you. I got a reasonable price for some hogs this morning, but not much else is selling for a whole lot. It is hard, you know, but at least we eat three solid meals a day. There plenty of people who don't, so we aren't as bad off as them."

"I know what you mean, Lars. We are always looking for the bright side, hoping and working for something better. Which is why I'm sure our country will work itself out of this depression. When, I don't know."

Usually, the two of them would be chatting along like schoolgirls, but today, Lars was quiet, hesitant. He suddenly realized that he'd lost the "good feeling" of earlier in the day.

Lars finally broke the silence. "Things are harder for Bridget and Anna, you know since they barred Anna from going to school last fall. The thing is, there isn't anything I can do about it. Poor, brokenhearted Anna misses seeing her friends every day. The fact is they have both been feeling low."

Lars took a deep breath, exhaled, then continued. "At least Peter and I get out some and come to town now and then. We have our routines, and our lives go on. But Anna and her mom, well, they spend a lot of time together now. Bridget insists Anna does her school lessons just the same, and she's got her normal chores. Sometimes they get to fussing at each other, and when they do, I might as well be a fly on the wall. If I say anything, regardless of what it is, it's wrong. The only thing that pleases them or that takes their mind off things is needlepointing. They spend so much time doing that and sewing. It is a good distraction, I guess."

"I can imagine," Andrew offered. "How is Bridget holding up? You know, with the sadness."

"Well, between you and me—"

"Always," Andrew replied.

"Bridget goes through the motions each day, but I can tell she isn't quite right. There is something about her spirit that seems to be gone. She's withdrawn and sometimes just stares off into space. She talks about waiting for the next fit and terrified by the mere fact that it could happen again."

Lars continued, "Anna is a teenager. She skulks around the house. She gets her feathers all ruffled up at any little thing. Sometimes I don't blame her. I hate to say this, but it would be better if she had a common disease. Then everyone would know what was wrong with her. *We* would know what was wrong with her. Honestly, Andrew, I prefer being outside or here in town to being in my own house. There's too much tension hanging in the air."

Lars realized he had gone on, pouring out his soul. He

stopped and turned his gaze toward the garage's only window leaving Pastor Nygard with a moment to reflect.

"This all sounds perfectly normal to me, given the circumstances. Experiencing the shame of suspension from school plus having to stay at home with your parents would bother any modern teenager. Used to be in the old days, girls were at home with their mothers all the time, many of them never got a formal education. But today, things are different.

"I can imagine that dealing with this epilepsy is hard, though, never knowing when the next seizure will happen or if it ever will happen. But you're good, solid people and you will figure out a way to get through this. I predict that eventually, everyone will be fine."

"I hope so. But what makes me mad is the way people treat us now, like we have leprosy. Not so much me, but they stay away from Anna and Bridget when they go downtown or to church. Sometimes, it's even hard for me to get them to come to church since they feel like everyone is staring at them. They complain about being home all the time, but they don't want to go out."

"I'm sure this will pass with time," Andrew replied. "People are uncomfortable with things they don't understand. Yes, and sometimes they keep their distance." The old pastor sat down on a pail. He put his well-smoked cigar in his mouth, and the ashes started to glow.

"That is one way to account for this popular thinking, you know . . . this eugenics thing. It's an awful way of thinking, in my opinion. They want to put people who don't fit into a neat round hole called 'normal' into an institution. In the old days, no one paid much attention to the feebleminded and epileptics and the like. If they were worse off, they stayed at home or lived with a sister or brother. Otherwise, they just tagged along with their mother or father. A lot of people had an old uncle who wasn't quite right and who would sit in a rocker on the porch all day."

Lars took in what Andrew said with considerable interest. That's why he came here today, to unburden himself and to listen to Andrew's wisdom. Perhaps there was something that would ease his troubled spirit.

"Pastor Nygard, the way kids, and parents, have been treating Anna is shameful. Where is their so-called Christianity? Aren't we supposed to offer comfort and aid to those who are sick, poor, and afflicted?"

"I don't know, Lars. People are what they are; they're flawed in some way. We're all flawed. Keep in mind that it's hard to judge the whole person based on the way they treat Anna. I try to see the whole picture even though it's difficult sometimes. I think this will get resolved if you stay patient like I know you always are."

Lars didn't respond. He wanted some biblical answers to his problems. He wanted a miracle, and so far, none was forthcoming.

Andrew continued, "Did you know that way back in the Middle Ages they used to burn people at the stake for having seizures? They thought the devil possessed them. In the not-too-far past, they beat people of lesser intelligence, or those who were odd. They also put them in prison or sold them off at auction to folks who would use them for menial labor. Horrible things, so in a lot of ways, we are making progress as a society. You see, there's a lot of history of people doing bad things to people they don't understand. I know you can't tell all of this to Bridget and

Anna, but perhaps it will give you some understanding."

"Yes, you're right. I'm sorry for carrying on about others acting like Christians. Here I am doing the same thing they are doing, being judgmental."

"No, no, that is quite all right. We all have our questions and doubts about the role of religion in daily life. We wouldn't be human if we didn't. Even you, my eternally optimistic and happy friend, you have a right to have your doubts, your sadness, and your anger.

"Meanwhile, take the family to a movie in Mankato or take a trip out west this summer. I'm sure you can shake the cookie jar and come up with some funds to do that. When your crops are on their own and before harvesting, see the Black Hills if you can afford it. How about the Iowa Great Lakes and Arnolds Park? These places aren't very far away. Always try to keep something special planned for them, something fun and positive they can look forward to. That will help them get through their feeling so bad."

He looked deep into Lars' eyes like searching for a response. All he got was an ever so small nod. He turned back to the bicycle.

"As for me, I have to figure out why this chain keeps coming off. I promised my grandson Mathew I'd have it ready for him this spring, and spring is almost here. What do you think?"

Lars bent over the bicycle and offered an opinion, and the two chatted away over a few other projects Pastor Nygard had started. Soon Lars realized it was past lunchtime, and he was hungry. Plus, he had his list of things to pick up before heading home.

"Thanks, Andrew. You've been a good pastor and friend."

On his walk back to the Country Feed and Supply store, he thought about how his farewell comment seemed so final. He concluded it was an accidental choice of words. He also noticed there were gusts of wind, and it was getting colder.

~ ~ ~

As soon as Lars entered the back door of the store, familiar sounds and smells greeted him. There was the squeak of the door, the creaking of the floorboards, the scent of seeds, lumber, and axle grease. Here was where he bought his farm supplies and picked up little tips about farming. He recalled looking through the front window the first days he and Bridget came to Grant Grove. *Ah, those were pleasant days. We were scared as rabbits and so ignorant of American things, but we didn't care. We were glad to be here.* Lars knew and liked old Mr. Tobias, who originally owned the store. He gave Lars honest advice on what was needed to run his farm. Later, he grew to be friends with Tobias's son Bartholomew or Bart as everyone called him.

"Hey, Lars, you old Norski, how you doin'?" came the same warm greeting he always received from Bart.

Bart was somewhere on the other side of the room. Lars finally found him over by the fencing supplies, pricing, and stocking new inventory.

"So, how you doin'?" Bart asked for the second time.

"Okay. Some things better, some the same, and some things worse. Same as always." He continued with a coy smile. "I came in to look at seed corn and find out how much you are going to gouge us this year."

"How much money you got? That's what we'll charge."

Lars laughed. "I also need a pound of number eight nails, some axle grease, and . . . oyster shells. My hens keep clucking for it." Lars chuckled at his farmer humor.

"Well, you should talk to the seed corn guy, but he's out calling on some farmers out east. Won't be back till maybe three. They got three kinds of seeds this year. He'll have to explain what each one does. How much grease did you say you need?"

"Give me a full bucket and one bag of oyster shells. I'll pass for now, on the seeds, and check back with you next time I'm in town."

"Okay, I'll get all your things set out by the back door; I assume you parked that old nag in the alley as usual. By the way, when are you going to get with modern times and buy a truck like everyone else?"

"When you stop charging three arms and a leg for supplies," Lars replied with a light and almost festive flair. He didn't feel up to light banter and wished he had his good mood from earlier in the day.

"I'm going on over to Ruth's. I'll settle up with you on my way out of town."

The minute he strode through the restaurant door, came another loud and familiar greeting, "Hey, Norski, long time no see. Come on over here and let me feed you!" This time it was Ruth greeting him in her usual, bombastic manner. She also liked Lars and felt like his sponsor of sorts since she and her parents had taken the Olsons under their wing in the early days. The Norski part of the greeting was Lars' nickname that everyone used as a term of endearment.

He had barely gotten himself seated at the lunch

counter when Ruth had two warm dinner rolls and a cup of coffee at his reach. Still holding the coffee pot, she leaned over to whisper to him.

"Today is your lucky day. I've got some top of the line, finely distilled moonshine, white lightning—the kind you hear about them making in Kentucky. Only this stuff comes from someplace up north. I guess some German guys make it in the back of their barn.

"You don't need a whole lot of it to feel good. I tested a bit of it myself, and it made me smile right quick. Whew, it looks innocent enough, but man does it carry a kick. Go on back to the kitchen, and Joe will give you a sample while he gets your pork chops ready." She no longer bothered with a menu since he ordered the same thing every time.

"Ohhhh," Lars pronounced as he returned to an upright position on the stool, "Yes, I will try that." He winked and smiled at Ruth. He stood up and went to the back of the restaurant. Instead of taking a left to the restroom, he walked straight ahead, into the kitchen.

The cook gave Lars a fleeting glance. He was furiously trying to get all the orders filled, but he knew Lars and why he was there. He nodded to a shelf and said, "Behind the flour."

That was all the instruction Lars needed as he'd been through this routine many times before. Lars moved the flour over to one side and saw a pint bottle and a small glass. It held a clear, odorless liquid that looked like water. He poured a little into the glass and braced himself as he put it to his lips, tilted his head back, and let the liquid flow over his tongue. At first, it felt warm and soothing, but as it went down, his mouth and throat exploded with the hot, sharp sensation only distilled liquor can deliver. Its fire burned all the way down to his stomach. The heat lingered for longer than usual, causing Lars to cough a bit. He squinted as he shook his head and took a deep breath.

"Damn," Lars whispered to himself.

After a few seconds, he looked over at Joe, who was still busy and decided to cheat. He took a second drink, this time about half the size of the first. Once again, the small sip of liquor soothed, then burned his mouth. He liked this stuff.

He was halfway through his meal when Ruth stopped by to give him a refill on coffee,

"Well, what do you think?"

"Wow," he whispered. "I think I feel a little warm already. Put me down for either a pint or a half-pint, whatever it comes in."

"I've only got pints, and they cost $2.50 each. I know it's expensive, but it is the clearest and best I have ever had. Think of it as doubling the effect of each drink, you know, so you don't have to buy so much to have a good time."

Lars thought for a moment. He knew he shouldn't spend money on this selfish indulgence, but he had made a good profit on the hogs. He also rationalized it was his only vice.

He grinned as he said, "Why, yes, that would be fine, put me down for one. And the chocolate cake would be good as well." He felt like he had to cover up their conversation, to make it look like they had been talking about something else other than liquor. He needn't have bothered since everyone else in the café knew Ruth was a bootlegger. Most were also her liquor customers and didn't care one way or the other.

"You can pay me along with your check, just like we always do. You know where I put things out back."

Lars finished eating, paid for both the lunch and the liquor, and greeted familiar people on his way out the door. As his hand reached the old creaking front door, Ruth called out, "Lars—you drive in today?"

"Nope, Ginger and I brought in a load of hogs."

"Well you better get scooting on home or plan to stay here, a big storm is comin'. It's on the radio."

"Thanks for the warning. We'll be fine." He gave her a wink and a nod, and he was out the door. The chill hit him. He had to admit it was a lot colder than when he went in.

At the back of the shed was a pile of empty old wooden crates covering the booze. As Lars unstacked them, he had some thoughts of regret. *I should have used that money for something pretty for Bridget, maybe a silk scarf or hairpin. Too late now.* He took his pint and returned the empty crates to the pile. He looked the bottle over, as if inspecting it for some quality or another, then unscrewed the cap, put the bottle to his lips, and took another small drink. Like his first taste, it was smooth but soon burned his mouth. He understood why most people mixed it with something else.

"Whooo yeah." He shuddered as he put the bottle in his pants pocket.

As he neared the wagon, he suddenly began to feel the full effects of the first drink of Ruth's liquor. He felt terrific— calm, warm, and relaxed. This sensation was the reason people drank. "Ah, yes," he whispered to himself, "It will be a warm ride home." He felt his mood lift as well.

He transferred his bottle to the heavy coat he left in the wagon. As soon as he turned around, he looked at his watch and saw it was 1:30 p.m. Bridget would be furious by now, and he still had to pick up the main things on his list. "Shit. She's going to be mad, alright. I shouldn't have talked to Andrew for so long." Lars knew she would be very agitated and worried until he got back. That was always the case.

With cheeks flushed, a smiling Lars struggled a bit with finding the right bills and coins to pay Bart for his purchases. He didn't know if it were the sudden anxiety over being late or the alcohol, but he was having trouble focusing.

"You know you need to stay here in town. There is a big ol' spring storm coming, and you don't want to get caught in it." Bart noticed Lars was slightly drunk. "You alright, Lars?"

"Yeah, sure. I'm fine, right as rain. You know good old Ginger knows the way. Hell, we can get home through anything. I'll be ready to go soon, I just have a few errands to run," Lars said as he headed out the front door to Main Street.

"Okay, but it's better to be on the safe side."

As soon as he got outside, Lars grumped, "Oof da." The weather had gone from perfect to terrible and he knew he would get cold on the way home. Then came a comforting realization, "Ah . . . but I have some liquid heat."

He went down to the general store and bought yeast, a can of coffee, a package of Bridget's favorite dried fruit, and a ten-pound bag of flour. Breaking with his conservative tradition, he even bought some pre-packaged cereal and two cans of tuna. Lars slurred the phrase, "Gotta treat 'em right."

Taking his cardboard box of food, he went to the drug

store and bought some liniment for when his feet got sore, a small mirror for Bridget to have in her purse, a mystery magazine for Peter, and another about movie stars for Anna. He also bought Anna a paperback romance novel for her upcoming birthday. The owner of the shop was busy in the back, so Lars simply plopped down a dollar and fifty cents on the counter, assuming it was enough.

Finally, he went to the dry goods store and bought several spools of fine thread, a spool of red yarn, and some blue dye so Bridget could spruce up some old jeans. He always did this when he came to town, and Bridget and Anna were happy to have extra thread, regardless of the color. Not really knowing what to do, and not caring, Lars simply grabbed the spools and headed to the counter. He hoped he had gotten all the right things. *Jesus, that is some powerful stuff,* a hint of a smile returning to his face.

He took a tarp from the wooden storage box and covered his purchases. Reaching into his heavy coat pocket, he pulled out the bottle. He made sure no one was watching before he took another sip, a larger one. *I can handle it.* Lars seldom drank during the day, and he had no explanation for why he did today. The buzz felt good, and it helped him forget about Anna's seizures and Bridget's melancholy.

He believed that the three drinks he had taken of the high powered alcohol were small sips. But they had been shot size, enough to cloud his thinking. Lars knew he was drunk, but was sure he could pull himself together. He was also sure he would be sober enough to finish the chores Peter hadn't completed when he got home. He didn't pay attention to the fact it was now snowing heavier, and the temperature had dropped to twenty-eight degrees.

Bart came out the back door with a handful of old crates to stack on his small loading dock. "Lars, you still here? You better wait here in town! I heard warnings on the Mankato radio station; it's turning out to be a huge blizzard. People are callin' in to report whiteout conditions all over the place."

Lars wasn't sure he heard everything Bart said, but he waved back just the same. "Okay, thanks."

He looked at his watch, and it was 2:15 p.m. *Shit, she's gonna be mad as hell.* He slapped the reins gently on Ginger's wet back, the leather causing the sleet and snow to spring up into the already heavy air.

By the time he reached the west edge of town, the road already had a coating of snow that had not yet gotten mushed into the gravel by car wheels. He noted he seemed to be the only one on the road. *Good. The fewer cars, the better—fewer ruts."* The one car he met blinked its lights at him, and the driver's arm hung out the window, moving up and down (the universal signal to stop). Lars simply waived and kept going. He took note of the fact that it was difficult to see the auction barn off to his right, "God damn!" Lars shouted to Ginger. "This is a real snowstorm."

CHAPTER 14
SNOW

THE SNOW DOESN'T GIVE A SOFT WHITE DAMN WHOM IT TOUCHES.
E.E. CUMMINGS

1932

It was mid-March. March 14, to be exact, and in his mind's eye, Lars believed it would soon stop snowing. Early spring snows were often fierce but brief. It wasn't obvious which was opaquer, the snowstorm, or his rational mind. The cumulative effect of the several drinks he had numbed his senses and made it hard for him to concentrate. He struggled to stay seated upright as his head bobbed back and forth and up and down.

Lars was in a pure grain alcohol world, ninety-nine proof and deadly as poison. But even if he were sober, the whiteout would have erased his ability to use any of his senses. On he went. As they left town, Lars and Ginger became immersed in a cloud of soft white light, void of all colors. Further out in the country, the wind picked up until it roared and howled songs of danger and death.

"What time is it?" Lars asked himself. "I don't know." He answered his question as if he were two people. He fumbled for his watch. No luck. He tried to think about time, but he couldn't comprehend it.

During one lucid moment, he thought about the fact that either the alcohol or the driving snow deprived him of visual and auditory senses, *I'm driving blind here but no worry, Ginger will make her way home, she has been on this road a hundred times.* He continued with a one-way conversation with his horse. "Besides, you haven't been drinkin', have you? No, no, no. You know the way by instinct, no need for me to see."

On they went, and Lars said, "Oh, look, I'm floating in a cloud." Lars faded in and out of self-awareness. Time and distance passed, unknown amounts of snow fell, as Ginger took them further out in the country. When Lars once again emerged from his stupor, he realized he wasn't even sure if he was moving. He came up with a drunken man's plan to find out. Lars had the presence of mind to get down on the floorboard carefully. Then, while he was on his hands and knees, he felt for the wagon wheel. Sure enough, it was slowly moving. *Good.*

On they went, without the benefit of knowing where they were. Suddenly Lars jerked to attention. "God damn it, my hands got a bit of a tingle." The tingling indicated his hands were numb, but he had no idea what to do about it. A fleeting thought, like a brilliant spark of colored light, shot through his mind. It disappeared in an instant. *Too bad,* he reasoned. *I hope I won't need it later.* Ginger plodded on.

God damn, I'm drunk. Lars created an apology. "I'm sorry, God, normally I don't talk like that." The whiteout raged on as Bart predicted. *Hopefully, it will stop soon.*

He thought he could see further ahead, at least he could see Ginger's haunches. *It's letting up.* He believed it was a sign the fierce storm was about to stop. It must be time to turn on to County Road 15 and soon after that, onto Schoolhouse Road, the road leading to his farm and safety. He tried to focus on finding the turn. By now, he could even see the snow-covered road below him. *If the snow and wind would let up for even a moment, I could see where I am. I can make myself get sober enough to do that, Yes I can.* Blinking and nodding and moving about, he tried to concentrate. Then, he saw a clue. Ahead was a small boulder left in the ground due to its size that told Lars County Road 15 would be to his right fifteen feet ahead. "Gee, gee, gee," he shouted as he pulled hard on the right rein. Slowly, Ginger and the wagon swung to the right.

He settled back and waited. Once again, he closed his eyes, and his mind went blank. His body swayed gently with the slow movement of the wagon. At times he felt as if he might topple off the seat. Somehow, he managed to stay upright. He leaned sharply to his left, causing him to wake with a start. Ginger plodded on at a slow, steady pace, and soon he was sure he was at the correct place to turn. Now, he could see the bare outline of a road on his left. *School House road! We're just about home!* With a pull of the rein from Lars, Ginger swung left.

Lars slipped back into a dream. *He was young and sailing in the North Sea, the Norway coast within eyesight. A friend yelled, "Here comes a swell." Lars pulled back hard on the rudder to face the wave head-on. As the small boat descended from the crest of the wave, he felt himself lurch forward.* His dream interrupted, Lars rejoined the real world, struggling to orient himself. He realized the wagon had suddenly stopped. With his eyes now open, he took note that the soft white light of the sky was turning gray as daylight slipped toward dusk.

"We're home. Ha! Ol' Bart was wrong. I was right. Ginger did know the way." Again, he crouched down on the floorboards and felt for the wagon wheel. This time it wasn't moving. Doing this made him aware of how frozen his hands were. His fingers were numb and hard to move. Spears of pain made their way up to his brain, breaking through the alcohol stupor. "Oh, shit. I should have put on my gloves. And my coat! Damn. I should have put on my coat," he hollered into the storm.

By some miracle, he remembered where his gloves and coat were. He reached back into the wagon and fumbled around until he found them. With significant effort, he managed to get his jacket over his thick wool shirt and his gloves over his stinging hands.

Staying low, he struggled to get down, backing off the wagon, trying not to fall. Something was wrong. His feet stuck deep in thick mud, and it wasn't this deep in his yard. *Where am I? I can't be at home.* Moving about sobered him up enough for him to realize the mistake he made. He turned too soon. He was on the old Indian path, dead-ended at the bog. He bent over for a closer look and found the snow piling up, at least as high as his knees.

Leaving his position by the muddy wagon wheel, he willed himself to move forward, toward Ginger. He tried to pull one foot then the other out of the mud, but it pulled back, making every step a battle. He was inching forward now, along Ginger's left flank, his hands knocking the snow off her back, leaving a trail of water as it slid down her midsection. He would have to pull on her to get her to go forward. He was now sober enough to believe that he could get her moving again.

He felt his way over her shoulder then his gloved hand worked its way up her neck. The going was slow, the mud thickening as he went. With each step, he grew more aware of his surroundings and the problems he had created for himself. Still, he was sure nothing was going to stop him, neither mud nor blizzard, nothing. He roared into the howling storm, "I'm a damn immigrant! Nothin' gonna stop me!"

Finally, he stood in front of Ginger and stopped for a moment to rest. *I got to keep moving, or I'm going to die.* He wondered to himself, *Why is it still snowing so much? It's supposed to let up because spring storms don't last this long.* It was almost dark now. The swirling snow and dusk left Lars with very little light.

He reached up around her nose to grab both sides of the bridle. Moving his frozen hands onto each side of the bit, he leaned back and tried to pull her forward. She didn't move. Lars stopped, tilting his head forward until it rested on Ginger's forehead. He rested for a moment before he pleaded. "We have to move, you damn horse."

After trying two more times, Lars stopped to get his breath. He pleaded. "Come on, Ginger, come on. We gotta go home." Lars had an insight. *If I pull a little harder, I could convince her to lift her feet out of the mud.* He crouched a bit, then quickly stood upright, all the while pulling her forward. He lost his sense of balance and fell backward, jerking down hard on the bit. Startled by the pain in her mouth, Ginger finally freed her front feet from the mud. When her right hoof came down, it landed squarely on Lar's lower left leg, snapping it in two. Lars let go of the bit and fell backward into the mud as the sudden intense pain seared its way into his brain.

Lars had endured all kinds of pain. He stabbed himself with a pitchfork, put a finger into a pulley, and nearly crushed himself while repairing machinery. Lars had experienced all these and more. Yet, as he lay there with his heels stuck in the mud, his shattered leg in two pieces, he felt the worst pain of his life. Not even the alcohol was enough to dull the thousands of daggers that instantly and violently shot their way up his leg where they would torture and overwhelm his senses.

"*Oh God, oh God, oh God!*" he screamed as he went into shock. The two parts of his broken leg were at a 20-degree angle. The pain was shooting and tearing through him as if the devil's own pitchfork was stabbing him repeatedly. For a long while, there was nothing else in Lars' world, nothing but mind-numbing pain.

Finally, he became aware that he had to free his broken foot from the mud so it could lay level with the rest of his body. He struggled mightily to sit up because even a tiny move threw new arrows of pain to his brain. Slowly, he moved his left hand down to the top of his left foot. With his eyes closed and his teeth clenched, he pulled on the toes of his left foot until it was free of the mud. Now at least, his broken leg rested horizontally. The pain eased some as he fell backward into the cold black muck. His nervous system drove flaming arrows up his leg while it automatically shut down blood flow to the rest of his body in order to send it to the wound. Lars lost consciousness for several minutes.

When he came to, he realized that he was lying only one foot in front of Ginger. What if she decided to move forward? To avoid Ginger accidentally stepping on him again, he knew he needed to pull away from the horse. Slowly wriggling back and forth, pushing against the mud with his elbows, he pulled away, inches at a time. Each tiny move intensified the pain, but finally, he was out from under Gingers' front feet.

As the alcohol slowly released its grip on his senses, Lars remained in a dreamlike world of pain and shock. He was still living a nightmare. *For sure, this is a dream. That booze is playing tricks on me. I'm in a hell of my own making. My God, what have I done?* He closed his eyes. The roar of the storm completely blanketed him as the snow began to cover his body.

Laying there in the cold mud, he realized he couldn't move anywhere. Any attempt to do so would bring more unbearable pain. *I need help. I need someone to fetch Dr. Phillips.* As he grew more rational, he knew no one would come because it was too dark, and the storm was still raging. No one in their right mind would go out in a storm that swirled and spun around like a child's toy top.

Eventually, he was sober enough to know that he was at the end of his life. *So soon?* "I am still young," he screamed out in anguish. The wind instantly muffled his words. He lay there, tormented by pain and terror, once again realizing that he had been careless and foolish. He had brought all this on himself. His breaths shortened, his heart raced, and he felt the sensation of blood rushing to his face.

In his panic, he screamed, "Peter, come get me. I'm so close to you, not more than a half a mile away! I'm down in the bog." The panic subsided. He closed his eyes and drifted off into a mindless, sleepy place. The darkness had now settled in on the bog. How long had he lain this way? He had no way to know, and his frozen hands were too muddy to find, let alone pull out his pocket watch. It occurred to him that he hadn't known anything for sure since he left Grant Grove. It was all a blur.

Another drink, yeah, another drink. It'll keep the pain

down and warm me up. What does it matter now, you know, if I'm drunk? He struggled mightily to sit partway up and to get the bottle out of his coat pocket, trying to avoid the sharp pain. He finally reached a forty-five-degree angle and managed to get the bottle out. He looked forward to the added relief and warmth the liquor would bring.

This drink will be a big one, he reasoned. *I'm not sure I'll have the energy to do it again.* Success, he managed to make his numb fingers get the cap off. Sure enough, the mouthful of searing heat felt good as it spread its fire down into his stomach. He took two large gulps and gently laid himself back down.

Lars tried one more time to see if he could think of any way out of his plight. Could he get to the wagon to get his overalls? *No.* Could he get to the road? *No.* Could he start a fire? *No.* He had no matches nor kindling nor wood. He was going to freeze to death unless someone came to help.

It was odd, he thought. Reaching the end of all hope now brought him to a state of peacefulness and tranquility. There would be no more panic nor fear. Laying there in the dark, the storm raging above him, he thought that death was not going to be so bad. *Let it come. I am ready.* He realized that alcohol and pain would cause him to be unaware of his death. He would die a shameful death, stuck in a bog.

In a moment of lucid thought, he remembered it was Anna's birthday. His last words were, "Happy birthday, Anna. Happy birthday."

He recalled that earlier in the day, he was in the soft white light of the blizzard. Now he was moving into another white light. This light was brighter, luminescent, piercing the darkness and snow. As he neared it, his pain gradually went away, and his frozen hands began to thaw. He was sure he could hear his beloved grandfather's voice calling him from somewhere out in the roaring blizzard.

~ ~ ~

It was March 15, one day after Lars died less than a mile away from his home. Anna woke to the sound of the wind still howling. Snowflakes blew against the side of the house, then upwards against the eave and finally over the top as if they were in a hurry to get to a snowbank far away. One time she stood close to a train track as a train roared past at sixty miles per hour, sucking her clothes away from her body. The overwhelming sound waves shook her. She thought the storm and its roaring wind sounded the same way. If she were outside, it would sweep her into the clouds.

"It's my birthday," she whispered to herself.

She lay under the warm layers of quilts, wondering if her papa had come home during the night. Someone had stoked the furnace below because she felt the warm air rising through the floor register, slowly driving the chill from her room. Sounds were coming from the kitchen, and that was a good sign because he was always the first one up in the morning. Papa was the one who put coal in the furnace to get the house warm before everyone else got up. She braved the remaining chill in her room to dress.

Downstairs, there was no sign of her father. She found her mother still sitting by the kitchen table near the door, waiting for Lars. Anna noticed her mother had not changed clothes. *Had she been there all night?* Peter was at the stove, making coffee and boiling water for oatmeal. There was heat radiating from the woodstove, and it was comforting, an oasis of warmth in the still chilly house.

"Did Papa come home last night?" she asked.

"No, he didn't," Peter snapped back. "He stayed in town because of the storm. Don't you understand anything?"

"I was just asking," Anna said, hanging her head a bit. "You don't have to get so sore about it."

Peter ignored her retort, and Bridget sat still, looking off into the distance. She hadn't spoken since the storm began. Anna and Peter ate their oatmeal in silence while their mother pushed hers away the moment Peter sat it down in front of her, still not saying a word. Peter, who had just recently declared himself old enough to drink coffee, sipped at the steaming brew and winced. For a while, silence hung uncomfortably over the table.

"Coffee too strong for you?" Anna mocked.

"Shut up," Peter snapped.

"Aren't you supposed to be out doing the chores?" Anna asked.

"Not in this weather. I ain't goin' out there and getting stuck in the snow and freeze my hands off. Besides, those animals can wait a while. This here snow can't go on much longer."

"You think it'll be over soon, and Papa will come home?" Anna continued.

"Yup, as soon as the storm is over. Like he always does, isn't that right, Momma? The county will clear the roads; then, he'll be here."

She turned to him and very slowly nodded. She

seemed determined to continue her silence. Anna didn't understand. Neither she nor Peter did anything wrong to deserve the silent treatment. They had seen short spells of silence, but they usually lasted no more than a few hours. Both hoped this wouldn't be any different.

"Are you okay?" Peter asked, looking directly at his mother. His question met with silence.

"Momma, I know you are worried, but don't be. You can't sit there all the time. He'll be home like I said. He had to wait in town because of the storm. Why don't you go to bed for a while? When you get up, the storm will be over."

Bridget nodded but didn't move. Anna got up, scraped her uneaten oatmeal back into the pot, and walked into the dining room and then the living room, looking out each window to see how high the snow had piled up. It was deep, deeper than she had ever seen. Finally, her curiosity satisfied. Anna sat down and picked up her needlepoint. She listened as the grandfather clock measured the time with steady ticks. Eventually, after two hours, she tired of the sewing and got up to stretch and use the bathroom. She noticed that the storm was starting to let up, and the sun was peeking through the steel-gray canopy. At least her mother had gone to bed since Peter was alone at the kitchen table, a copy of Life magazine, and a half-empty cup of coffee in front of him.

"She finally went to bed," Peter said. "Got tired enough to sleep. I know she gets nervous when Papa isn't around, but she's worried sick this time. I figure it isn't any use to fret about it. There isn't a thing we can do anyhow."

Peering out the back door, Anna commented on the storm, "The snow sure looks deep out there. I'll bet it's a good ten feet high in places."

"Oh, don't be silly. There ain't no ten-foot-high drifts. Nine feet eleven inches, maybe, but not ten."

Anna went over and tried to smack him on the head, but he grabbed her arm and smiled. After a few seconds, he continued with his thoughts. "I'm going out pretty soon since the storm is letting up. You clean off the table, wash the dishes, and try to make yourself useful. I have a feeling you'll have to fill in for Mom until Papa gets home. Start making something for lunch. In another hour or so, I'll be damn hungry."

"Okay," Anna said, "but I don't know what to do. She usually tells me."

"Figure something out. Look around, if the floors need dusting, do that. If the ironing needs doing, do that. Decide something for yourself for once. Hell, you're almost fifteen. Surely you can do something other than sitting around doing that damn sewing all day and night."

"I *am* fifteen, you dumb pumpkin. My birthday was yesterday, and I doubt you even thought about getting me a present. By the way, Momma made me a cake yesterday. She said it was okay to break this stupid ketogenic diet since it was my special day. Maybe we'll have cake for lunch."

"Well happy birthday, you little runt. But no, we ain't eatin' no cake till Papa gets home. He'd be furious if we did that."

Anna replied, "I was just kidding, by the way. You're as dumb as a cow, not a pumpkin." She quickly received a blow to her arm, a reward for her insult. "That didn't hurt a bit." She darted to the kitchen doorway to avoid another blow.

"Just so you know, I don't do needlework all day and

night. Besides, if I did, it isn't any of your business. You aren't the boss of me. Plus, Momma and Papa would be mad if they heard you swear like that. They would give you a good scolding."

"Grow up and stop whining. All I'm saying is help out around here until Momma gets up, and Papa gets home." He looked at his sister with a smile on his face.

She hated him sometimes. He could get her angry with just a look or a few words. *He must think tormenting me is his job. He always seems to get some evil pleasure out of doing it.* "Grow up yourself, you lousy excuse for a brother."

After finishing their morning chores, Anna and Peter went up to their mother's room. Peter was the only one who spoke. "Mom, it's time to get up and get something to eat." He was firm, "You *have* to eat something." She finally obeyed.

Later that day, Anna's supper of boiled potatoes, canned corn, and roast beef was cooling on the table. Anna's head was down, and she was near tears. Her cooking wasn't satisfactory. The roast was barely warm in the middle, and the potatoes were undercooked. Peter still ate the food with gusto. His appetite was huge after laboring all day against the large snowdrifts. On the other hand, Bridget just picked at her food. She did drink a cup of tea Anna prepared for her.

Her silence continued. Anna thought that somehow, she seemed sadder and more remote with a hint of harshness in her stare. *Please, Momma, act normal, like you used to.*

Chapter 15
SHERIFF JOSEPH SMITH

EVEN THOUGH I WALK THROUGH THE VALLEY OF THE SHADOW OF DEATH, I WILL FEAR NO EVIL, FOR YOU ARE WITH ME; YOUR ROD AND YOUR STAFF, THEY COMFORT ME.
PSALM 23 KING DAVID

1932

On March 22, Joan Bridenbaugh took the 7:06 a.m. train to Minneapolis. Bright sunshine dancing off a blanket of snow nearly blinded her. She closed her eyes and put her head back, letting the gentle rocking of the train lull her into a meditative-like state. Her mind wandered through issues and problems in no particular order. Some were routine, daily things like who to call to fix her heating boiler. Others were disconcerting, like the 1931 food riot in Minneapolis. It shocked everyone to find out there were so many hungry people.

The meeting between Minnesota's county social workers and Mildred Stinson took place in an auditorium at the University of Minnesota. Arriving early, Joan hung up her coat and got a front-row seat. Her peers soon started trickling in with their briefcases and purses.

"I have been trying to warn everyone that these so-called poor trashy people are a menace. Who would listen? Not a soul that's who," Joan offered to the lady sitting next to her.

"What are you talking about, Miss Joan?"

"The food riots here in Minneapolis. Why those criminals destroyed a man's business."

"I see it as a failure to provide enough food for people. The food was there, in warehouses, but without money, the hungry couldn't benefit from it. The government needs to do something. People are starving."

"They sure do. These criminals need to be put in institutions or sterilized. Whatever it takes to keep them from breeding more criminals. I suppose you would simply give them the food."

"Why, yes," replied the stranger.

"Before we go on, let me introduce myself. I'm Joan Bridenbaugh. It sounds like you already know my first name. I am curious as to how since we've never met."

"Everyone knows you, Miss Bridenbaugh. You're the eugenics lady."

The woman stood up and moved to another seat. Joan sat alone, her back perfectly straight, eyes forward and face emotionless.

The social workers listened to speakers who covered problems they were all facing. Number one was a lack of money to build new residential buildings at all the mental institutions. Problem number two was the growing waiting lists, a result of problem number one. Better coordination between the institutions and the communities was three. Especially interesting to her was the speech by Dr. Murdoch, Helmhurst's new superintendent. His speech was on the growing menace of the feebleminded, and it fit her mindset to a tee.

~ ~ ~

The storm came to be known as the "Blizzard of 1932." It left behind downed telephone lines, closed country roads, felled trees, and damaged roofs. It took three days to clear the main roads. Remote side roads, like Schoolhouse Road, stayed closed for two more days. The storm cut a wide swath through Minnesota as well as northern Iowa and Illinois before heading out over Lake Michigan. There it gathered more moisture before hitting Ohio and Pennsylvania.

At first, Anna believed that her Papa got trapped in Grant Grove. No one could travel without passible roads. But as traffic began flowing on County Road 15, fear and anxiety set in. As the days passed, Anna spent more time with Bridget, staring out windows, looking for the first glimpse that would free their souls from the terrible tension growing tighter and tighter by the hour. Peter worked from dawn till dusk clearing snow, feeding and watering the animals, and milking their two Jersey cows.

On March 20, Peter made his way into town to see if he could learn anything about his Papa's whereabouts. He came home late that afternoon, and dejectedly recounted his day to his mother and sister. Peter told Anna and his mother about driving through the mud that was starting to emerge on Schoolhouse Road and the slush on County Road 15. He said several shop owners had seen Lars on March 14, but they hadn't seen him since. He found John Dowd at his grain exchange, told him about his father, and asked if John had seen him. "No, but I'll find him."

Everyone expressed concern, but no one had anything more to offer. Peter sat slumped in the kitchen chair with a warmed-up cup of coffee, and for the first time in his life, smoked a cigarette in the kitchen. For a long time, he sat quietly, sipping his coffee and blowing clouds of smoke that hung in the air.

Two days later, Lars had still not appeared. The sullen group ate lunch in silence. Finally, Anna spoke.

"Why isn't Papa home?"

"How would I know?" Peter replied.

"You said he would come home when the roads were clear!"

A tired and overworked Peter finally broke, "*Okay, okay, okay*, I don't know what happened to him. Maybe he's sick or hurt somewhere. Maybe . . . all I need to do is check all the homes on his way home. Could be someone took him in and is caring for him."

"Yeah, probably another of your hair-brained ideas."

"Why can't you say something positive for a change instead of criticizing and doubting me! You keep sniping at me, and all mom does is stare out of that goddamn window."

"All I did was wonder why you keep saying Papa will be home soon," Anna screamed back.

"You two stop it." Bridget finally spoke after days of silence. "We are all worried. Do your best to carry on, and Peter, you can stop your profanity and smoking in this house right now." Without another word, she slipped back into her melancholy, her slate-blue eyes gazing off into some other world. Anna noticed that tiny tears were making their way down her cheeks. She had no way to know what her mother was thinking, but Anna believed Bridget feared the worst. All she could do is encourage her to eat, sleep, and get up in the morning.

Later that day, Anna and Bridget heard the old Ford pull into the garage. They could tell from Peter's posture as he walked to the house that he had more bad news.

"Nothing. No one knew a damn thing. Sorry, Mom." His face tightened, his eyes narrowed, and his mouth pulled together like he had eaten a sour berry. Peter was ready to cry. "What are we going to do now? That's what I want to know. What do we do next?"

There was silence, and no one had an answer. Peter eventually got up and put on his overalls. It was time to feed the animals and milk the cows. "Anna, don't forget to pick the eggs and come get the milk."

She nodded. Anna was nearly as depressed as her mother, but she snapped out of her daze and prepared to do her chores. On her way out, she put another lump of coal in the stove. She would soon need extra heat to fry the pork chops she was planning to serve for supper.

In the barn, Anna listened as Peter spoke. "I knew something was wrong with Mom from the get-go. She's acting like a widow." Peter said as he squirted milk into the pail.

"How would you know what a widow acts like?"

"I know. Trust me, I can tell."

"Like you knew Papa would be home right after the storm? Then when you went to town and knocked on all the doors of people along the way. So far, you have been wrong about everything."

"Shut up. I was trying to talk to you like an adult. If that's a crime, then arrest me!"

"I'm sorry, Peter. I'm afraid. What'll we do if Papa doesn't come home?"

"He'll be home soon. Keep on hoping, and he'll be here." Peter got up and took his sister in his arms and gave her a strong hug—something he had never done before.

"Now go get those eggs picked, and don't forget to make sure the water in the chicken house isn't frozen."

During their dinner of pork chops, canned green beans, and boiled potatoes, Anna hung her head and picked at her food. It seemed impossible that her papa still wasn't at the table. After a few nibbles, she spoke for everyone when she simply said, "I wish Papa were here."

On March 25, late in the afternoon, a car pulled into their driveway, and Anna ran to the window to be the first to see who it was. "It's John and Erica Dowd," she announced. "Maybe they've come to give us some good news about Papa."

They didn't have any news about Lars, but they were a welcome relief. Erica brought a box, brimming with food, a cornucopia of good things to eat. In the center, was half a smoked ham covered with a brown sugar glaze. Stuffed around it were two loaves of freshly baked bread, cookies, one jar of canned peaches, a smaller jar of raspberry jam, and a bag of hard candy. A cherry pie lay precariously perched on the top. John brought a stack of magazines. For a few minutes, they seemed to forget about Lars as Erica cut the pie, and Anna set out clean plates.

They talked about all the stops Peter made to see if Lars had stopped at a farm along the way. Then John gave them his report. "I don't want to alarm you, but I've been investigating what happened to Lars. Like you, Peter, I didn't turn up anything. For sure, he headed out of town that day, around two-thirty. Then, it's as if he disappeared into thin air. So I talked to Sheriff Smith and asked if he had heard of anything. He hadn't, which, in a way, is good news. But he is going to keep his eyes and ears open."

Bridget stared at John. To everyone's surprise, she

said, "Thank you."

~ ~ ~

Sheriff Joseph P. Smith opened his desk drawer and took out a clean sheet of paper. On the top, he wrote LARS OLSON, April 1, 1932, followed by 'Disappeared on the afternoon of March 14.' He started his official investigation by visiting the Olsons.

At first, he interviewed the family as a group. He listened to Peter explain how his father had loaded pigs into the old farm wagon and headed to Grant Grove early on the fourteenth. That's all Peter knew for sure. Bridget listened intently as the Sheriff asked questions, giving one-word answers or shaking her head. He noted that the family appeared somber and tearful. They were clearly in shock over Lars' disappearance. He wrote several things about Mrs. Olson in addition to her answers, pale complexion, how little she spoke, and that she sat by herself.

He also interviewed them individually, changing the questions based on the person. Were there problems between Lars and Bridget? Did Lars owe money to someone? Was there a fight or a problem with any neighbors, friends? Did he gamble or drink alcohol? Was he taking up with another woman? Was he a good father? Each burning question was an arrow to their hearts. Red faces and anger built with each incriminating suggestion until Peter finally exploded.

"My father's not a two-timing drinker like you think." Peter nearly flew out of his chair.

"Whoa, hold on, son. I'm only doing my job. I'm sorry

if some of my questions upset you, but they are routine in this type of disappearance."

The next day Sheriff Smith went to Grant Grove to talk with John Dowd, who told him what he knew of Lars' activities the day he disappeared. From there, it was easy to piece together Lars' day. Starting with the sales barn, he interviewed the men who worked on March 14. He noted a time gap between his leaving the sales barn until he showed up at the Country Feed and Supply store. He interviewed Ruth Carlson, who turned pale white and had trouble describing how Lars behaved that day. Finally, he went up and down the street, interviewing the business people where he learned of Lars' purchases.

At the general store, the owner said: "Yes, he was here. For sure."

"Did you notice anything unusual about him?"

"Well, when it came time to pay, he seemed a bit tipsy."

At this point, all he knew was that Lars, a usually levelheaded and sensible farmer, disappeared into a white blanket of snow against the repeated warnings of both Ruth and Bart. *Strange*, Smith thought. Lars lived in Minnesota for twenty-one years, and he had to know about early spring storms.

Sheriff Smith returned to his office, pondering two things: Where was Lars from approximately ten a.m. until noon? Second, why did Ruth Carlson turn pale and get flustered during her interview? He knew for sure there was more to her story. Ruth Carlson must have sold Lars liquor. Everyone knew she was a local supplier, providing something people wanted.

He finished his day by calling his counterparts in

Mankato and several of the surrounding towns. Lars had not shown up in their jails as sometimes happened when a local man went on a bender.

Eventually, Sheriff Smith found out about Lars' friendship with Pastor Nygard. He noted how their long chat filled in the missing two hours. Next to the good pastor's name, Smith wrote, "Discussed family problems."

He went back to interview Ruth Carlson. After bearing down on her hard, she finally admitted that she had sold him some hard liquor. His face turned red, and his knuckles white as he simply turned and walked out the door.

Given what he had learned about Lars, he was somewhere nearby. It was only a matter of time before he found out where. Finally, he went public by giving the story to the local radio station in Redwood Falls. Everyone in the county would now know that Lars was missing.

It didn't take long. On April 6, a farmer who lived two miles north of Lars' farm called him to report he had seen something unusual.

"Mr. Sheriff Smith?"

"Yes, this is Joe Smith."

"Maybe I have somethin' useful for you about that Olson guy. I stopped there on County Road 15, just south of Schoolhouse Road, where that old Injun path leads to the bog. I had to fix a flat tire on account of the potholes in the road. In any case, I noticed what looked like a farm wagon down towards the bog. My curiosity got to me, so I went on down there to git a better look."

"Now hold on a minute. First things first, what's your name?"

"Marvin Habash. I live up the road a bit from the Olson

farm."

"Hi Marvin, I recall who you are. Now, go on."

"Well, sir, as I said, I was fixin' a flat tire on account of all those darn potholes in County Road 15. In any case, I walked down that old trail, and the closer I got to that wagon, the more I could see a horse that looked to me like it was dead. I didn't feel too good about going closer, but I thought it might be that was where that Olson fella disappeared."

"It could be Marvin. I'll check it out. I sure thank you for calling, and be sure to greet your Mrs. for me."

Sheriff Smith put down his pen, stood up, and went to the large county map on his wall. The lane Marvin referred to appeared as a thin line running off County Road 15 and parallel to Schoolhouse Road. The thin line was little more than a path that didn't go very far before it disappeared into the bog. He knew the history of the little road. Long ago, it was a Sioux Indian trail leading out to the western part of the county and into South Dakota. As he picked up his hat and coat, he considered the fact that if the wagon was where Marvin said it was, it was no more than a mile, as the crow flies, from the Olson farmhouse. He stopped at the door and returned to his desk to make a call.

"Betty Jean, I might be a bit late tonight, you and the kids go ahead and eat without me."

"Something serious?"

"Yup. I just got a clue about that missing Olson guy."

When Sheriff Smith saw the wagon, he noted it was invisible to anyone passing by on Schoolhouse Road or County Road 15. Six to eight-foot-tall reeds surrounded the path down near the bog. That and the weathered old brown wooden wagon blended into the brown grasses surrounding the area. The shallow mud was turning to a sticky, gooey, paste that grabbed at his boots. He stopped when he got to the right rear wheel, the wagon. It was impossible to go further. At least from there, he could see the horse on the ground and beyond it a body. His heart skipped a beat. It had to be Lars Olson.

No matter the number of times he witnessed a death scene, he felt a little queasy. He closed his eyes for a moment, leaned against the wagon, and took a deep breath. Each death he handled was unique. Every dead person stuck in his mind, and his memory of them surfaced from time to time, often when he least expected it.

When he opened his eyes, he realized the mud was too deep. He would need some way to get to the body, then retrieve it. He returned to his office and called Herbert Bracken, a retired railroad detective, and asked him to help. Bracken worked part-time as a deputy for Redwood County. He knew law enforcement and knew how to keep official business to himself. His help was invaluable in solving cases as well as in routine matters like serving summons' and taking prisoners to court.

After talking with Herbert, the Sheriff stopped at the Lloyd and Larson lumber yard. He asked Harold Larson if he could borrow their old Chevrolet delivery truck. Sheriff Smith also bought twelve eight-foot-long rough-cut pine boards.

At the bog, he and Herbert placed the boards on the mud making a walkway to the body. Leaning over, he saw it was Lars Olson. Sherrif Smith didn't know Lars personally, but from the description Peter gave him, this body was the missing father and husband. The first thing he noticed was that both the tibia and fibula bones were protruding from a large tear in his left pant leg. He winced and stopped for a moment.

The horse had collapsed within inches of Lar's body. Its head rested near the broken leg, making it clear Lars was trying to get the horse out of the bog. Then, the bottle caught his eye. Smeared with mud and laying near Lar's right hand, it was a half-empty pint of clear liquid. He quickly noted the cap was missing. Sheriff Smith picked up the mud-covered bottle and took a whiff of the contents. It had no odor. He took a small sip to confirm his suspicion. It was high-quality moonshine, something he had never seen bootleggers in this area sell up to this point. He was sure this was close to pure alcohol. *It wouldn't take much of this to make a person drunk, and the bottle is nearly half empty. Where in the hell did he get this? Would Ruth have this kind of booze? It had to be, that was the only place he went that bootlegged.*

He poked around the mud for the cap, and after finding it, put it back on the bottle. He wrapped the bottle in his handkerchief and put it in the inside pocket of his jacket. Looking at Bracken, he silently shook his head from side to side, signaling him not to discuss this with anyone. There was no use in divulging that this otherwise upstanding, well-loved person was very drunk when he drove his horse into the bog during a howling blizzard.

Working together, they rolled the still frozen Lars over on his side. After placing a large canvas tarp next to him, they gently lifted him onto the grayish-white square. They wrapped the tarp tightly around Lars's body with a long piece of rope. It was hard physical work moving the body, made heavier by his saturated clothing. They pulled him over the mud: every inch a struggle to stay on their wooden walkway. At the truck, they had a tough time getting a good grip on the now mud-caked body, but they were finally able to lift it onto the truck bed. As soon as they closed the back gate, the old truck temporarily became a hearse.

"They're all hard." Sheriff Smith said as he turned to pick up the boards.

"Indeed, they are," Bracken replied.

Sheriff Smith's first call after returning the truck was to John and Erica Dowd. He shared the grave news and asked them to go with him when he met with the Olsons. It was dark by the time they reached the Olson farm. Smith explained why it had taken so long to find Lars to a stunned and silent family. Their worst fears confirmed, there were deep breaths, sobs, and tears. He also told them he had temporarily left the body at the county coroner's office.

"Miss Olson, do you want me to contact the Randal Jones Funeral Home here in Grant Grove?"

Bridget nodded.

He also asked Bridget if it was okay for him to have Pastor Albertson come out to see her about making further arrangements, and to guide them through their time of sorrow. Again, she nodded. Erica held a now sobbing Anna close to her while a somber John Dowd stood beside Bridget, his hand on her shoulder.

Sheriff Smith stood to leave. "Mrs. Olson, my sympathies to you and your family."

~ ~ ~

Lars' body returned home a day later. Bridget, Peter, and Anna accepted callers for a day and a half. Erica Dowd and the Redeemer Church women took over the Olson home, cleaning, arranging food, and finally, helping Anna and her mother get ready for receiving callers. Anna spent most of her time holding her mother's hand or with her arm wrapped around Bridget's shoulder. Their job was to come to grips with the reality that Lars was gone forever.

The funeral took place at eleven a.m. at Redeemer Lutheran Church on April 10, 1932. There were no seats left by the time Sheriff Smith arrived, so he stood along the back wall, hat in hand. He always tried to pay his respects by attending the funeral of someone whose death he had investigated. By being there, he knew he could learn more about the deceased, their family, and other people who might be involved with the death. It was often the trivial things that helped him the most, a look, a stare, someone anxiously pacing. Tiny details often led him to the bigger story or helped him write a better, more accurate final report. He noticed Joan Bridenbaugh was in attendance. He immediately found himself thinking. *I hope she isn't intending on stirring up trouble for this family and bothering that girl with the fits.*

Pastor Nygard agreed to come out of retirement to conduct the service since he knew Lars and his family so well. Peter, Anna, and Bridget sat in the front row with their close friends John and Erica Dowd. Anna leaned over to Erica, "I hate it. They're all staring at us like we're freaks." Erica took Anna's hand and put it on her lap, in a gesture of kindness and comfort.

Pastor Nygard's sermon was a short, touching remembrance of a man the old pastor loved:

"Many people talk about Christian life. Lars Olson lived it. He lived the Golden Rule, and as best as he could, he followed what Jesus instructed.

"I'll never forget that day when he and Bridget came to my house looking for help, not speaking more than a few dozen words of English. From there, he became a friend to all of us and helped many people in many ways. He and Bridget went through the immigrant life— Lars working two jobs, doing the things most of us no longer wanted to do, and Bridget worked caring for Petra Dowd. They bought their farm and went on to become a successful and welcome part of our community.

"As a part of our church community, Lars helped with painting or reading the Bible lesson of the day. He served on committees and helped comfort those who were suffering and in need. Most of you know these things about Lars. But there are some things you may not know.

"You may not know that Lars and I became good friends. After I retired, he often called on me in my workshop, where we would discuss the events of the world. I loved those visits, especially the one we had on the day he died."

Looking directly at Bridget, Anna, and Peter, he continued. "He told me of his love and concern for you as you journey through trying times. You should find comfort in knowing that he wanted your life to be happy and for you to enjoy a return to good health.

"You may not know that Lars gave extra to help poor people. Even when he and Bridget were in tight financial times, he found a way to help someone who was worse off than himself. You may not know that Lars loved to follow baseball and that he was an avid reader."

Pastor Nygard used the Twenty-Third Psalm to turn his sermon toward the promise of eternal life. But Anna's mind was straying into a vast unknown place where her grief disappeared. In that space, she found peace and tranquility. She liked it because it offered her relief from her aching loneliness and sadness.

Soon, she found herself standing for the benediction.

~ ~ ~

By early 1932, it was customary practice for law enforcement agencies in America to look the other way when there were Prohibition violations. Still, the first thing Sheriff Smith did the day after Lars' funeral was to call the new Federal Bureau of Investigation to find out how to get Ruth Carlson's illegal alcohol business shut down. To his way of thinking, she killed Lars Olson. Yes, he was the one who drank the booze, but she was the one who sold it to him. Sheriff Smith believed it was like giving a loaded gun to a child.

It took only a few days for four FBI agents to show up at Ruth's Café. Two went into the front door with Sheriff Smith, and two covered the back door. Smith strode up to where Ruth was standing and pulled the half-empty and still dirty bottle of liquor out of a sack he was carrying and set it on the counter.

"Ruth, if I could, I'd charge you with manslaughter in Lars Olson's death. Since I don't have enough direct evidence for that, I did the next best thing. I found some new friends here who are going to stop you from hurting anyone else."

Ruth stared at the bottle, and soon tears started to flow

down her cheeks. Between sobs, Ruth said, "I welcomed Lars and Bridget to Grant Grove. My folks and I helped them settle in. I served their family meals all these years. Now, you're treating me like a common criminal. I had no idea that things would end up like this."

The FBI men started to tear her restaurant apart, finding a bottle here and a bottle there. But it was in the back that they found several cases of high-quality whiskey, some homemade wine, and various other types of liquor. The FBI closed Ruth's Café, and she was one of the last people in Minnesota prosecuted on bootlegging charges.

Things are seldom private in a small town. Exactly a week after closing Ruth's Café, Sheriff Smith had a visitor to his office. Joan Bridenbaugh stood in his doorway.

"Mr. Smith, I would like to see your file on the Olson family. Some people think Lars was drunk the day he died. From the rumors going around, it sounds like you sicked the federals on Ruth because she sold booze to Mr. Olson the day he died. Is that true?"

"What's in my file is none of your concern, Joan."

"Oh, I'm afraid it is. I already had my eye on that family ever since I found out that epileptic girl Anna had her first fit. Now, I wonder about the severe melancholy her mother has. So far, her son Peter seems to be okay, but he may end up being a drunk like his father. And if memory serves, Lars had an uncle that was a drunken waste of a man. I see a trend here, don't you? It's obvious: these Olsons are descendants from someone in Norway who shouldn't have been allowed to have children. The grandmother, whoever she is, should have been sterilized."

"Joan, you're entitled to your opinions, but I'm going

to stick with mine. These are good folks. And unless some judge somewhere tells me to give you what I have, you can go straight back to your office and stay there. I got nothing in that file you need to know about."

"Listen here, Mr. Smith. We are both county employees, so you have to give me that file." Joan was bright red, wagging her finger at the sheriff as if he were a child in a schoolroom.

"I'm not givin' you squat. But here are two orders: Number one, leave that Olson family alone. They are good folks who've simply had a hard time. They don't need you pokin' around. Number two, go straight to hell and take that eugenics shit with you. People ain't breeding stock like pigs, despite what you say. You and your self-righteous talk about bad genes and a pure race, it doesn't mean a thing in the real world." By the time he finished, he was on his feet and glaring straight into her eyes.

CHAPTER 16
BRIDGET OLSON

*... WHAT WE DO TO PEOPLE WHO ARE THE MOST VULNERABLE ...
WE 'SHOOT THE WOUNDED.' AS IF THEY HAVEN'T SUFFERED
ENOUGH, WE ADD TO IT BY GOSSIPING AND TREATING HURT PEOPLE
LIKE OUTCASTS.*
LYNN DOVE

1932

The best way to describe the Olson household was somber. There was a sadness that sunk deep into everything they did. Darkness engulfed their souls, and one could see it in their eyes. Anna watched Peter struggle with the farm chores. Her mother's melancholy continued. Anna tried to help her as best she could. It was all too much for a young fifteen-year-old.

She was understandably angry. It sometimes spilled over into fits of rage where she would take chicken eggs and throw them at the wall of the chicken coop. If her mother or Peter ever caught her throwing eggs, she would be in big trouble. Selling them brought desperately needed cash. Deliberately breaking eggs simply wasn't done.

She went to the grove of trees and broke branches. She raged against God. "Ahh, You shouldn't have taken my papa. Why did You take my papa?"

An unfortunate doll would sail across the room. "If You love people so much, why do You let them die?" her screams filled the air.

Time helped only a little. Although Anna was demonstrative in her grief, and Peter simply carried on with life, their mother suffered her pain in silence. But her silence only made things worse for Anna and Peter. It was hard for them to understand how their mother could ignore them every day for such a long time.

Old Pastor Nygard made regular trips out to the farm to see the family. He was especially concerned about Bridget's near-catatonic condition. The pastor held her hand and prayed for understanding. He counseled Bridget. "Lars may have passed away, but he's with God. Someday you will join him in heaven. But for now, you have to try to get better for your children's sake."

He tried to explain to Anna that Bridget was sick and that "time will help, be patient with your mother, and trust God."

How was that going to help? Anna asked herself, looking down at the floor. The old pastor read the Bible and prayed more, but the sorrow lingered.

Elizabeth and other friends came more frequently. They brought Anna her schoolwork assignments, which she burned in the woodstove. The magazines they brought would often sail across the room after her friends left. Still, she had to admit she enjoyed having them come to her house. Sometimes they would pick her up and take her to a movie in Mankato. Getting out of the house was a welcome relief from living with Bridget. Anna laughed with them as best she could. She tried to act normal. They helped her feel good, if only for a little while. Then, after they left, the anger often returned.

She talked to her favorite baby doll comparing her life to her friends': "For one thing, I can't go to school like them. For another thing, I don't have a papa, and they do. Plus, I have these stupid fits, and they don't. Because I have fits, I have to eat this stupid diet. It's all stupid, stupid, stupid! Now here I am talking to a doll like I was a five-year-old."

Peter got out of the house as often as possible. "Being around you two sad sacks isn't what I call enjoyable." Anna couldn't blame him for his evening escapes, but she resented the fact his leaving left her in charge of their mother.

"Why don't you try staying home more and watching Mom in the evenings," Anna blurted out one day at lunch.

"For one thing, I do all the farm work, like care for the animals twice a day every day. That's hard work even though it's not in the house. Besides, I have friends. I don't want to lose my friends. They depend on me to liven up the party," Peter calmly replied with a grin.

"You know Papa wouldn't let you get by with this if he were here."

"But he's not. Is he? And Momma's crazy. She ain't here either." Anna tried to slap him, but he caught her wrist.

Both sat back in silence at Peter's revelation. They were orphans even though their mother was alive.

One day, there was a knock on the back door. It was Eunice. "I heard that Lars died, and I came as soon as I could." She held Bridget in her arms, put her head on her shoulder, and rocked her back and forth. They didn't say much, but at least Bridget said a few words.

Holding Eunice's hand, Bridget said, "I hurt so bad, Eunice, terribly bad. What can I do?"

"It takes time, honey. Time will heal you. You'll feel

better soon. Anna will take good care of you." She looked at Anna with a weak smile and a slight nod.

There was one thing left between the Olson women: needlepoint. Anna could get her mother to smile a bit when she would suggest they work on their projects. There wasn't a lot of conversation, but there was a rapport. Anna enjoyed listening to her favorite shows on the radio as they stitched. Radio brought Anna different things to think about and enhanced her understanding of the world. Most of all, it brought her relief. She would laugh at the jokes that George Burns and Gracie Allen told on the Guy Lombardo radio show. She would swing with Duke Ellington and sing with Perry Como.

The days drug on for Peter and Anna. It seemed odd that a teen was caring for her mother, doing her best to get through each day without crying.

~ ~ ~

Joan was an active member of the Redeemer Lutheran Church, Dorcas Circle. This small group of women performed a combination of social, religious, and charitable functions. On May 18, it held its quarterly meeting at Susan Johnson's home. There were cakes, pies, and cookies of all types arranged on the kitchen table for what most ladies felt was the best part of the meeting — coffee, tea, and desserts.

The meetings always opened with a short prayer and a Bible study led by someone who had volunteered to lead the discussion. A business meeting was an endless discussion on how to make and disburse money for charity. Everyone had opinions and expressed them, except Joan. She felt that such petty matters were below her level of importance.

Joan joined the circle in 1912, and during that time, she had done her share of raising money. She even led a few Bible studies, although she admitted she wasn't a Bible scholar. Today, Joan hoped to hear what the ladies thought was going on in the church and the gossip about the Olson family.

"Why that Bridget, she hasn't been right since Lars died. She was a little bit different before, you know, on the melancholy side, but now, she's much worse. A time for grieving in silence is one thing, but she has two children to think of."

Another woman added, "All I can say is that I was over there twice, once right after Lars died, and the second time when my Henry went to help with the crops. In any case, both times, all she did was stare out into space. The poor thing seemed frozen to her chair. Pitiful, in my opinion."

A third woman chimed in, "That's no way to be when you have children who miss their father. A woman must be strong, you know. That poor girl, she looks after her mother, *plus* she has those fits. It ain't right. It's been two whole months since he passed!"

"I hate to bring up rumors, but has anyone heard anything more about Lars being tipsy before he drove into that terrible storm? No one in their right mind would do that, you know, go out into a whiteout blizzard unless they were drunk."

Finally, someone looked at Joan and asked, "What do you think?"

"Ladies, I frequently see melancholy and excessive drinking. It started to pick up right after the crash of '29. I know everyone gets tired of my preaching, but these are the precise behaviors that we hope to avoid in the future. It's sad. I genuinely feel bad for the Olson children. Their parents have these flaws, and their little girl, Anna, has those seizures. I can't say any more, of course, because I'm reviewing the situation professionally."

~ ~ ~

Bridget Olson sat alone, lost in a sea of problems. Some were real, and others made up of bits and pieces of anxiety. The greatest of her problems, in fact, the largest, was her inability to make her melancholy go away. Her rational thoughts were in a prison her mind had constructed, and she believed the jailor had thrown away the key. Evil thoughts kept racing through her mind, one after the other. Before she could think about one problem for too long, another crowded its way to the front of her mind, demanding her attention.

I can't believe I had a baby stolen from me. Why? My crazy father, that's why. I hate him. Then my Lars got himself killed by that snowstorm. I hear them talking about his being drunk. I know he would never do that. Would he?

Then there's my Anna and her fits and me not able to help her one bit. I'm a terrible mother. My girl deserves better. For a moment, her thoughts were interrupted by the sight of a stray cat running across the yard. In an instant, her mind went back to her problems. *My poor Anna can't even go to school. How can she learn if she can't go to school? I can't teach her. I'm nothing but a dried-up flower.*

Why me? Why am I stuck with this curse? I've gone

mad. Here I am, day after day, every waking moment spent trapped inside my skin. Oh, how I'd like to break out, but this curse has me pinned to the floor. It's like a giant invisible hand is holding me down. Then there's Peter, with his smoking and carousing. He misses his loving father. Lars treated us all so well. Even in tough times, he never took it out on his family. But Peter, when he needs a father figure to set him straight, he has no one.

It was needlepoint that broke through the veil of sadness but only for short periods. As Anna progressed with her skills, her mother would smile. Bridget was able to answer questions and demonstrate a challenging knot or how to create an intricate pattern. These were the only times Bridget felt safe, free from the weight on her soul.

Anna's growing up angry. I'm afraid she'll be like me, bothered by dark thoughts and terrible fears. It hurts me to see my beautiful American family under this kind of pressure. This is the only family I have. Father made sure I didn't have any Norwegian family because he drove everyone away with his tirades and belittling. This bitch Joan reminds me of him. Both are relentless fanatics. Father with his religion and Joan with her eugenics, neither giving a damn about how they affect others.

Where is my Jesus? I need Him. He'll take me to heaven one day, and I'll be with Lars. I know Lars is there because he was righteous, kind, and a true believer. Jesus, will you please come show me how to break my chains? No, I'm probably not worthy of Thy salvation. Here I sit, glued to this chair, and with so much work to do. Tomorrow I'll be better. I'll get back to being a mother who cares for her children. I'll cook and clean. Why do I have this darkness? I'm so sad it hurts. I'm so terribly sorry. My poor Anna and her terrible fits, she doesn't deserve them.

Such was Bridget's life, hour after hour, day after day.

~ ~ ~

It was June 2, 1932, and Joan was on her way to make a surprise visit to the Olsons. As she drove through the country, south to Grant Grove, then west to the Olson farm, she noticed the beautiful late spring flowers. Today, the high temperature would be somewhere in the mid-to-upper-seventies, but the evenings were still chilly. Residents would often say, "This is why I put up with the Minnesota winters."

As she pulled into the Olson's driveway, she could see Peter off in the distance, weeding the ankle-high corn. Laundry was on the clothesline, and a garden was well underway. Leafy vegetables poked high above the green beans. Onions were ready for harvesting, as were the early planting of carrots. *At least she can still grow a garden, for all the good that will do her.*

Anna looked like she was hard at work, her hair tied back, a scarf covering and protecting it as she answered a knock on the back door. "Yes?"

"Is your mother home?" Joan tried to sound cheery, casual, and upbeat. The moment she spoke, she knew it didn't come off that way.

Anna simply stood at the screen door, the only thing protecting her and her mother from this woman. "Yes, but she's busy."

"I've come to pay a little visit. Perhaps she can take a moment to say 'hello.' I'm sure you know who I am. We go to the same church!"

Anna stood staring, unsure of what to do. "Well, okay, for just a minute."

As soon as she was in the kitchen, Joan went to work in a polished, professional manner. "Perhaps we could put some tea on while we wait for your mother to join us?"

Anna didn't make a move or say a word.

"Here, I can put some water on to boil. Where do you keep the tea? You do have tea, don't you?"

"I can do it. I don't need you coming into our kitchen doin' things for me." After throwing another piece of coal in the stove and putting water on to boil, she turned back to Joan. "I know who you are. You and Miss Pratt told my parents I couldn't come to school."

"Now, Anna, that tone isn't very respectful, is it?"

"No, Miss Bridenbaugh, it isn't, and I'm sorry. It's just that my life has been awful miserable since I've been stuck here all day every day with my mother."

Joan made a mental note of her comment and sat down at the table where some of the trappings of breakfast remained — a half-eaten slice of buttered bread, a slice of brick cheese, and a bowl of half-eaten oatmeal sat drying out in the morning sun. These items bothered Joan as did the crumbs still strewn across the tabletop. *Messy, this looks like a pigpen.*

As Anna cleared the remnants away, she apologized. "I'm sorry for the mess. I kind of got distracted before I finished cleaning up."

"Do you usually have to do all the kitchen work?"

"Pretty much. Sometimes I can get Momma to help me. But that's alright. I'm learning. At least Peter isn't complaining quite so much."

"You pitiful thing. I'm sure you must be so frustrated.

By the way, how is your mother doing?"

Anna didn't answer the question and went about getting the tea ready. She placed the box of tea on the table and took three china cups out of the cupboard, but she was so nervous she forgot the saucers. After sitting a cup and spoon in front of Miss Bridenbaugh, she got out their best cream and sugar set. There was sugar, but no cream since Anna hadn't bothered to skim any off the top of the milk. She hadn't expected company. Anna stood by the stove, giving Joan one-word answers to questions. She jumped when the water kettle finally blew it's shrill, piercing whistle. She carefully poured the hot water into the cup and returned the pot to the stove.

"Do you have a tea strainer, honey?"

"Oh, sorry." Anna quickly put the tea strainer in front of Joan and promptly left the room.

Joan sat alone in silence. Anna had not yet come back into the kitchen. *Poor child, she doesn't even know how to serve tea properly.* She looked at the kitchen windows, still in need of a spring cleaning. Kerosene lamp soot and dust still lay thick on the windowsill. No respectable woman would let a house get this dirty. After a moment, she was sure she could hear loud whispers coming from the parlor. Sure enough, Anna was pleading with her mother. Joan got up, put her teacup into the sink, and followed the sound.

Bridget was sitting on the couch, Anna leaning over her; "Come on, Momma. Please, wake up and help me. That scary lady is here, and she wants to . . ."

"She wants to what, Anna? I'm standing right here. Tell me, what do I want to do?"

"Talk to Momma."

"That's right. I came out here to see you and your mother. To see how you are getting along now that your father's no longer with us. Don't worry about making her move. I'm here now."

Anna sat down close to her mother and pulled a blanket over Bridget's knees. Meanwhile, Joan brought up a dining room chair and placed it directly in front of the Olson women. "So, Anna, how have you been getting on? Have you been having more of those terrible fits?"

"No. Not a one."

"Well, that's a good thing, but from what I know, it's merely a matter of time before you have more. Once the fits start, they are hard, if not impossible, to stop, which is why I would like to talk to you about going away to school. Helmhurst has a nice school where all the other students have epileptic fits. You would be around other girls who are just like you, not stuck in this old house, cooking and cleaning and looking after your mother."

Joan noticed that Bridget was glaring at her, so she stopped and waited. She didn't have to wait long.

"She isn't going to any school, Joan. You know full well I'll forbid it." The strength and forcefulness of her voice took both Joan and Anna by surprise. Her pronouncement came like a thunderclap, cracking and loud.

"Oh . . . Miss Bridget speaks! I heard you've been in a catatonic state ever since that Lars of yours went running off into the snowstorm. Too bad really, he was told not to, but some say he wasn't quite in his right mind. But I won't go there."

"What do you mean?" Bridget's tone now softened a bit.

"Oh, nothing, I said the wrong thing. I'm a bit nervous, you know, coming out here, not knowing what I'd find. Surely you know I'm here out of Christian love and concern." Joan leaned back. She sat so straight, her entire spine pressed against the wicker backing of the chair.

There was a long uncomfortable pause.

Joan leveled her gaze at the women before she continued. "Here are the facts as I see them: First, Bridget, you suffer from an extreme case of melancholy. Second, you need help to cure this condition, and a hospital is an appropriate place to get that help. Of course, your hospitalization will leave poor little Anna home alone with her brother, which isn't in her best interest. I believe we need to send her to Helmhurst, and that is what we are going to do."

Bridget started to remove the blanket from over her knees. "I want you to leave right now. Stop this silly talk about Helmhurst." Bridget was gradually, slowly emerging from her dark mood.

"Bridget, it isn't silly talk. We need to help Anna and protect her from the advances of young men who may want to take advantage of her weakened mental condition."

"You think my Anna would have sex with any man who asks? Do you think she's a whore? What weakened mental condition are you talking about?" Bridget was getting louder with every sentence.

"It's obvious. Look at Anna . . . she's feebleminded. She scored low on the standard mental age test, and a few minutes ago, she didn't even know how to serve tea properly. A girl her age should know to bring a saucer, tea strainer, and creamer when serving tea, and she did none of these. I'll talk to the judge about both of you. I can force you to go if you don't cooperate."

Bridget suddenly stood up. She leaned over Joan. "Over my dead body. I will fight you every step of the way. Now get out of my house!"

"Sit down, Bridget, we're not done yet. I decide when I leave, you no longer have control of your life. I do. I have a clear mind, and I know what is best for both of you. I see you for what you are, a family with inferior genes. *So, sit down.*" Joan glared at Bridget as she pointed to the couch.

Anna watched her mother's temper flare, her face was bright red, she was shaking. "I have rights, you know. *We* have rights. You can't just throw us into some institution. We'll take care of our own problems. I will get better soon, and Anna and I will be fine. *Now leave.*"

Bridget walked over to the front door and, her face still red and repeated, "Joan, get out of my house!"

By now, Joan was standing fully erect. She was at least four inches taller than Bridget, and her tight-fitting dress made her look lean, almost muscular. "You're making things much worse than they need to be. Now stop this foolishness. It isn't good for your daughter or you. Your behavior is the kind that proves you need to go to Springhill Hospital. You're mentally unstable."

Bridget looked the opposite of Joan. Everything about her was askew. Her bathrobe and nightgown fit loosely around her body. Her hair was unkempt, sticking out in every direction.

Anna watched her mother in disbelief as she repeated her demand: "Get out. *Please, please, please, go!* You should hear what people say about you. 'Old maid,' 'snobbish,' and my favorite, 'bitch.' Oh, yes, they say all of that and more."

"Settle down, Bridget. You're out of control. If you don't cooperate, I'll send Sheriff Smith out here and have you forcibly taken to the mental ward. We'll see how you like it there." As she spoke, Joan made a move for Bridget. Her self-control was gone. She grabbed Bridget's arm and tried to pull her back from the door. It didn't work, Bridget wouldn't budge. In turn, she grabbed Joan's right arm and tried to pull her out of the house. The two were at a stalemate.

"Stop it!" Anna screamed at Joan. "Leave us alone! Momma and I don't want to go anywhere, except I want to go back to my old school."

"I'm only doing my job!" Joan shot back.

"Leave!" Bridget screamed again at the top of her lungs, tears now flowing down her face. She let loose giving Joan a free hand to grab her hair. She started pulling Bridget back toward the couch. Anna sprung off the couch and tried to get between the two women.

"That'll be enough, Joan!" The tone of the voice was clear and assertive. The four words were not a request.

The two women froze, their attention drawn to the voice. It was Erica Dowd, standing about six feet away. Erica came close to the two women and firmly grasped Joan's hand, moving it away from Bridget.

"Joan, I don't think you can accomplish anything more today. You need to leave. We can talk about what we need to do to help Anna and Bridget when everyone is calm."

Joan stared directly into Erica's eyes and saw in them the calmness and assuredness she wished she had. She was jealous of Erica's demeanor, and she realized she'd let her emotions gain control. Her typically cold, self-assured composure was gone. "Alright, I'll go, but this isn't over."

"We all understand that," Erica responded. "John and I should have done more sooner. We'll step in and make sure Anna and her mom are safe and get whatever help they need."

~ ~ ~

From the minute she confronted Joan Bridenbaugh, Erica knew what she and John had to do. They would have to take all the right steps for them to keep Bridget and Anna out of institutions. Plus, they would need the cooperation of both Joan and the Olsons. It was a challenge under the best of circumstances.

Erica put her arms around Bridget and Anna. She had no idea what emotions she should be feeling at this instant. Anger at Joan? Remorse for not being at the Olson house more frequently? Should she be sad for the wretched condition of the Olson women? The one thing she did know, things were going to change—immediately.

"Come on, let's go sit down in the kitchen. We'll have tea."

"Anna, are you okay? Did she try to grab you?"

Between deep breaths, hiccups, and tears came a quiet "N-n-no."

On their way to the kitchen, Erica held onto her friend, trying to untangle her hair and tighten her bathrobe. She served tea as emotions began to calm. The three women sat in silence. Erica tried to come to grips with what she and John could do. She thought they had an evil enemy, one who would tear this grieving family apart at the seams. *It's ironic*, Erica thought, *Joan is a member of their church.*

She turned to Anna, "Can you tell me what happened?"

"Well, it started with her inviting herself into the house. I didn't know…"

Bridget interrupted her daughter, "I'll tell you. My poor daughter has had enough and seen enough." She went on to describe in detail what had happened, how the atmosphere deteriorated, and how she defended herself and her daughter. For the moment, her melancholy lifted, and she sounded as clear-headed and sane as she once was.

"It's all on me and my melancholy. I watch Anna try to cope with her brother and me. What a strong and wonderful girl she is. God, how I hate what I've become. I'm sorry, Anna." She reached across the table and held Anna's hand, a few tears still running down her fair skin.

Erica stood up and said, "Come on, Bridget; let's get you a bath." As she washed her hair, her back, and her face, she saw her friend slip back into her dark world. She tried to engage Bridget in more conversation, but it didn't work. Her only response was to grab Erica's hand, squeeze it hard and smile. Then she disappeared totally and completely, absorbed by her madness. Erica tried to get her to come downstairs to sit on the porch swing and do needlepoint, but Bridget shook her head. Instead, she went to her bedroom and laid on top of the covers and closed her eyes.

Downstairs, Erica found Anna sitting on the porch swing, needlepointing.

"Are you going to be okay?"

"I think so. But that mean Joan lady is going to send Momma and me to institutions, isn't she?"

"Not if John and I have anything to say about it. We're going to take better care of your family. I'm so sorry I haven't spent more time with you two. But that will change. I promise you things will be better." She sat down by Anna and took her in her arms, making the soft, comforting sounds of a mother consoling a hurting child.

Over their evening meal, Erica filled John in on what she encountered at the Olson home. She told about the anger, the aggression, the fear, the horror of it all. Two people who did nothing to hurt anyone were being preyed upon by a single-minded eugenicist, hell-bent on creating a perfect human race.

As he listened, John's face turned red, and he fixed his eyes on a place far away, as if he were in deep thought. Erica thought about how he was a stoic man. Outwardly, he looked as cold and hard as the winter soil on which he often stood. Yet as they were lowering Lars into the ground, she saw how he held back his tears. The tears would come later in their bedroom, with her holding him close. She had never seen him cry, not even when his mother passed.

"We'll do what is necessary," is all he had to say, which was precisely what Erica wanted to hear.

Chapter 17
ERICA DOWD

HAPPINESS WAS BUT THE OCCASIONAL EPISODE IN A GENERAL DRAMA OF PAIN.
THOMAS HARDY

1932

Erica was still grieving, although it wasn't for Lars. She gradually realized she was now grieving for the loss of her friend. No, Bridget wasn't dead, but she might as well be. *It's like Bridget was being blown away bit by bit by the prairie winds as if she were dry dandelion seeds. Perhaps Lars took her soul with his, leaving a shell of a person behind.* Bridget was Erica's anchor when she first came to Grant Grove. A new language, a new job, new customs, new everything, and it was Bridget who smoothed her way. They grew close, as did the rest of their families. Unable to have children of their own, she and John treated Peter and Anna as their nephew and niece. The Olsons and the Dowds were also alike because neither couple had family nearby. Erica did have a sister in Minneapolis, but their relationship turned out to be cordial, not close.

"John, what do we do?"

"Do?"

Erica was frustrated *as if he doesn't know what I mean.* Her response was curt, "The Olsons. What do we do about the Olsons?"

"I don't know. What are you thinking?"

"For one thing, I think Bridget needs medical help. I've heard some new medications could help her."

"I agree. Go ahead and make an appointment with Dr. Phillips and take her in. We'll pay the bill." John turned away and picked up his magazine, his face a hard block of ice, frozen somewhere between angry and sad.

He soon turned back to Erica, "I still can't comprehend how my closest friend, a guy who was always sensible, would get drunk in the middle of the day and drive out into a blizzard. I'm trying to think of any time I ever saw Lars drunk. Probably never." His fist came down on the table, rattling the china, "Bullshit!" His eyes were moist as Erica reached for his hand. It was then that Erica realized John was still grieving for Lars.

After a moment of silence, Erica spoke for them both. "It's like we've inherited the family we never had. Don't you think?"

"Yup." John looked up to heaven and whispered, "Don't worry, Lars. Erica, and I will take care of them. They're kin to us now."

Erica wisely put off discussing Anna. She knew it would be best to discuss her options later that evening.

~ ~ ~

On June 30, Dr. Phillips examined Bridget with Erica standing along the wall of his small examining room. "Does she ever come out of this state?"

"Very rarely."

"And how long since Lars died?"

"Almost four months."

"That's a long time to be so seized up with the melancholy. Have you considered admission to a sanitarium or mental hospital for treatment?"

"Yes, we know it may come to that."

"Maybe you and John should talk this over again and see what Joan Bridenbaugh can do to get her admitted to Springhill."

"We know what Bridget would want, and she would be distraught at that idea. We would like to see if there isn't anything else to try before we go that route."

"Sure, I understand. Listen, we can try Pentothal. It's new, and some doctors say it can help. I've never prescribed it, but it's worth a try."

Erica nodded her approval.

Erica and Bridget were leaving when Dr. Phillips asked Erica. "She's lost a lot of weight. Has she been eating okay?"

"We try to get her to eat, but it's hard. She doesn't seem to have an appetite."

~ ~ ~

Erica and John decided that it wasn't a good idea to let the Olson women remain on the farm. Bridget needed more care than Anna could provide, nor would it be wise to leave Anna behind with Peter.

That evening they talked with Anna. "Erica and I believe it would be better for you and your mother if you come to live with us until she feels better. Then you can go back to your own home."

Anna replied, "I like that idea. Maybe I can hang around with my friends again, and I won't have to do so much of the work by myself."

"Right," Erica smiled and reached for Anna's hand.

On July 12, 1932, Erica and Anna packed the Olson women's clothes, along with their sewing and needlepoint supplies, and moved into the Dowd home.

When September arrived, and school started, Erica and Anna drove down the bumpy, dusty Schoolhouse Road to her school. On the way, she explained her reason for making the trip. "Anna, I want to talk to Miss Pratt face to face to let her know how we will handle your homework, and I thought it would be nice if you came as well."

Erica told Miss Pratt about how Anna was going to be doing a better job on her homework. "I'm going to check it over before she sends it in. I hope you find her work satisfactory. She's a bright girl, you know."

All she got back from Abigail Pratt was a curt, "We'll see."

As the ladies were talking, Anna and her friends were chatting away as if nothing had happened. One of the little girls came up to Anna, "Are you coming back to school?"

"No, they still won't let me." Anna suddenly felt sad, being forced to face the reality of her isolation.

Erica watched the little group for a moment and had an idea. On the way home, she shared it with Anna. "What would you say if one Saturday, you invite three or four of your friends to go to Mankato with us? We'll take in a movie and go to the soda fountain. I think it would be fun."

Anna's eyes became as wide as saucers. "Oh Erica, that would be *so* great!"

Anna and Erica picked a date, and Anna contacted her friends. As promised, after the movie, they went to the soda fountain. The noise level grew as the girls laughed and teased each other until Erica eventually had to remind them to be quiet. Anna hadn't smiled this much since before her father died. She was glad for Anna and knew the extra effort she and John spent on caring for the Olsons was paying off.

John and Peter spent more time together. John occasionally took a few hours off from his businesses, to come out to the farm to help Peter plan and prioritize his work. Peter knew the farm routine well, but he was young and, on occasion, made the wrong decisions.

John related to Bridget that he didn't think Peter would end up being a farmer. "His heart isn't in it. But he's young and still affected by the loss of his dad. Maybe he'll grow up to be a great farmer."

~ ~ ~

In July, Erica listened as John made phone call after phone call.

"Gerald? I need one more man to help put up the Olson hay this Saturday. Can you help?"

In mid-October, there was a different need. "Max, listen, I think we have a date set for taking in the Olson corn. Can you bring your wagon and tractor over next Thursday morning? We have two pickers, but we need one more wagon and one more tractor. That should be plenty to get it all picked in one day. Yes, I'm sure your missus can bring some fried chicken but why don't I have Erica call her? She is handling all the food."

John Dowd and the Olson neighbors were carrying out a standing rural tradition. Whenever a farmer died, they would volunteer to plant, then harvest all the crops for one year. This help would ensure that the family would have income and feed for the livestock. After that, it would be up to the family to decide if they should keep, rent out the fields, or sell the farm.

Along the way, John talked to Peter about what to do with the farm.

"John, I mean Mr. Dowd, I think I'd like to try working the farm. A couple of the neighbor guys said they would give me advice from time to time. You know, until I learn things for myself. Heck, I ain't got anything else to do. Besides, I know some things from workin with my dad."

"Peter, I think you can do it. But one thing you're going to have to do is spend less time running around having a good time. It'll be a full-time job and then some. You won't have time to do a lot of the party stuff with your friends."

"Aw, I'm just a young guy blowing off some steam. I'll get the work done, don't you worry."

By the end of October, Erica and John agreed the Pentothal wasn't working. Bridget's melancholy continued. "I think the time has come, John."

"Time for what, putting her in an asylum?"

"Yes. I hear there is a good one on the other side of Mankato. They've got a section where they do all the newest treatments. It's a private place. Some say it's a lot nicer than Springhill, where Miss Joan wants to put her. What do you think?"

John shrugged his shoulders. "That's probably the best thing to do. Still, I hate to send her away and leave Peter and Anna without a parent."

"John, you know as well as I, they have no parents other than us."

"Yup. You're right. Let's see if they have an opening."

~ ~ ~

Once a week, Anna would go out to the farm to help Peter by cleaning the house. Often, tensions would spring up.

Anna chided Peter, "How come you can't keep the kitchen table clean? It's always got crumbs and stuff on it."

Peter replied with a question of his own. "Why don't you get out here more than once a week?"

"I'm so sorry, your majesty. I have a lot of work to do. I clean house here and when I'm with the Dowds. Then, I still help take care of our insane mother. Plus, Erica makes me do homework. What do you think I do, sleep all day? Sit on the porch and needlepoint?"

"I didn't say that. Jesus, you are getting to be a cranky little bitch." Peter was angry, no longer a taunting big brother.

"Cranky bitch? You call your sister a bitch? Well, you're a goddamn tomcat, that's what you are. I know you come home drunk most of the time. I'm gonna tell the Dowds."

"Oh, sure, and what are they gonna do? They're not in charge of me. I'm almost twenty, and I can do what I damn well please."

~ ~ ~

Erica's Thanksgiving table was a cornucopia of dishes. She prided herself on her cooking skills and made a wide variety of American and Norwegian foods. John, Erica, Peter, and Anna stood and held hands while John gave a short prayer of thanks. Bridget sat silently, staring at the food.

"Well, then, let's dig in, shall we?"

It took Anna and Erica an hour to clear the table, store the leftovers, and wash the dishes. Meanwhile, Erica glanced towards the parlor where she saw John and Peter smoking cigars.

"You're not teaching him to smoke those filthy cigars, are you?"

"Erica, this young man is soon to have his twentieth birthday. We're merely having an early birthday celebration."

Erica glanced down at Peter's hands and saw a brandy glass. She just shook her head and went back to the kitchen. *I suppose a young man needs a little something special. Especially one who has shouldered as much responsibility as Peter.* Begrudgingly, she tabled her opposition to both drinking and smoking.

While Bridget rested in her first-floor bedroom, Erica called John and Peter back to the dining room table. "Dessert's served!" When everyone had their choice of pie or cake, Erica nodded to John.

"Anna and Peter, Erica and I think your mother isn't much better. Do you agree?"

They nodded.

John continued. "Perhaps it's time we take more dramatic action. We think your mother should go to a private sanitarium for a while. To get treatment."

"What's a sanitory?" Peter asked.

"Sanitarium. It's a place like a hospital; some call them asylums. They know how to heal those with problems like your mother. It's also a place where the sick can rest while they get back to their natural selves. Perhaps they can cure her of her melancholy."

Anna stared at Erica, a blank expression on her face. After a moment, she said, "I knew this was coming. Momma died when Papa died, and I miss her. I mean, I miss the old way she was before everything got so bad. Now she isn't going to be here at all!" Anna put down her fork, started to cry and bolted. Erica quickly got up and followed her upstairs to her room, where she held her close.

"Shh. I'll take care of you. We can't be your parents, but we can help. We very much want to help. You know John and I love you and Peter."

"When is she going?" Anna asked.

"We don't know for sure. We have your mother on a waiting list. They think they'll have a room for her sometime in the middle of December."

"What about that witch? Will she be involved?"

Erica smiled. "You mean Joan? No, I don't think she needs to be involved. Although I suppose we should tell her what we are doing." Erica stopped for a moment, then continued, "John and I would also like to become your legal guardians, so we have the right to make decisions for you. It would only be temporary until your mother gets back to normal. Do you think that would be okay?"

Anna nodded, then whispered, "I suppose."

The next morning, Erica found Anna, fully clothed, lying next to Bridget. Anna's head rested on her mother's shoulder as she gently stroked her hair. Erica could tell from the redness around Anna's eyes she had been crying.

Later that morning, Anna told Erica about her sleepless night. She talked about being afraid of separation from her silent and listless mother. Anna said it was as if her life flashed before her eyes. She saw her mother in the garden, kitchen, and on the porch, all like a silent movie playing at twice their average speed. Anna remembered her needlepointing, cooking, her mother's reaction to her seizures, and her mother kissing her papa passionately when they thought they were alone. The garden, and church, and each image took its turn in rapid succession. Anna slumped back in her chair, put her head back, and closed her eyes.

Anna was not the only one to worry about Joan Bridenbaugh getting involved. Erica was anxious about their plans for Bridget, but she resolved to herself that Joan was not going to work on her mind. Christmas was coming, and she had two young people who needed love and care.

Two weeks later, John came home from work early complaining he didn't feel well. For the next five days, he battled the influenza virus before finally turning the corner. He appeared at the breakfast table with a broad smile on his face and a joke for Anna, who rolled her eyes.

Erica put a damper on the light-hearted mood when she announced, "Bridget won't be joining us this morning. She's picked up John's influenza and has a fever. Plus, she's starting to vomit."

Bridget worsened as the days went by. Her breathing became more labored, and her fever stayed high. Anna spent all her free time with her mother. She held her hand, put a damp, cold, washcloth on her forehead and petroleum jelly on her chapped and cracked lips. Dr. Phillips called on Bridget daily until he finally announced, "I think it's time we move her to the Methodist hospital over in Mankato."

Erica walked Dr. Phillips to the front door. Once there,

she stopped. There was a tone of sadness in her voice, "Dr. Phillips, John and I have talked about this, we think she should stay here. She's not likely to get better, is she?"

"No. Bridget was in a worn-down condition before this came along. I would give her a few days to a week at the most."

"If you can give her something to keep her comfortable, her children will be here when she dies."

Dr. Phillips nodded in agreement.

Chapter 18
JOAN BRIDENBAUGH

1933

Bridget Olson lingered on longer than Dr. Phillips predicted. All the while, she had a rattling sound like something deep inside her lungs was broken. Peter drove into town every evening after chores. Meanwhile, Anna spent every free minute holding her mother's hand and secretly wishing she would die so she could finally rest in peace. Ladies from Redeemer Lutheran stopped by often with food and well-wishes. Finally, the death vigil was over. Bridget died in her sleep sometime during the early morning hours of January 19, 1933.

Two days later, Redeemer Lutheran Church was three-quarters full for Bridget Olson's funeral. Joan Bridenbaugh sat in her usual spot and listened to Mrs. Johnson plod away at the organ pedals and keys, trying to play simple versions of traditional church hymns. Joan loved the hymns but winced every time Mrs. Johnson played them. *Silence would be better, but maybe I'm too picky.*

Joan's mind continued to wander. *Now is my chance to get Anna sent to Helmhurst. She's an orphan in addition to everything else. The best of all worlds would be to have her sterilized and sent to Helmhurst.*

Two men from the funeral home rolled the casket down the aisle. It was draped with a white linen shroud with a small red cross at each end. The men left it at the foot of the altar and walked to the back. Soon, Joan saw the Dowds usher Peter and Anna to the front pew.

Anna and Erica looked devastated, and the whole church could hear their quiet sobs. Peter looked somber faced, but not distraught. *He is strong.* Joan admired that. *Strength, endurance, carry the load with grace,* she could hear her father as clear as it was yesterday. The service began, and Joan followed the liturgy, bowed her head for the prayers, and pretended to listen to the eulogy. Joan looked down at the small bulletin summarizing Bridget's life. There wasn't much there.

> Born in Bergan, Norway, on April 4, 1890, and died January 19, 1933. Daughter of Timothy and Dagmar (nee Johnson) Androder. Preceded in death by her husband, Lars Olson, and survived by daughter Anna and son Peter. Mrs. Olson was an active member of the Redeemer Lutheran Church.

What did she leave behind? Not much. A defective daughter and a son who may or may not turn out okay. She should have been in a mental hospital long ago. Her melancholy had been evident for years. Still, when she wasn't in one of her melancholy states, she showed some desirable qualities. She provided for her family, was a good Lutheran, and tried her best through good times and bad.

Joan stood outside the church with a small group of women, mostly old widows, and watched as the hearse pulled away, followed by four cars. Only a few people were willing to brave the weather and go to the cemetery, especially for a person who had lived here so long and whose husband everyone loved. As Joan turned to leave, there was a slight spring in her step, a sense of purpose. She had to get back to the office. There was work to do. She needed to get a date for Anna's commitment hearing.

~ ~ ~

Her quick steps echoed off the oak floors onto the marble walls. The click-clack of her leather shoes tapped out the sound of an angry woman on a mission. She was disgusted with Judge Thorton's bailiff and mad at John Dowd. The bailiff wouldn't schedule Anna's commitment hearing until the second week of February because the judge agreed to fill in for an ailing jurist the next county over. She also learned that the previous week, John Dowd's attorney filed a petition for John to become Anna's guardian. If granted, that could derail her chance to get Anna committed.

She had been planning on a late January hearing, which would give her the ability to put Anna on the Helmhurst waiting list. When Joan wanted something done, she wanted it done *immediately*. Now, she had no choice but to wait. Whenever it did take place, she knew this hearing would be a hard-fought battle between her and John Dowd. One which Joan was determined to win.

~ ~ ~

Dinner in the Dowd home was quiet. Everyone was grieving, thinking over all the ill fortune, emptiness, and sorrow that comes with death. The soft clink of knives cutting roast beef or forks laid back to rest on a plate were the only sounds in the room.

"Are you guys going to be my new parents?"

"Anna, we will try our very hardest to keep you with us. Don't you worry about that right now." John looked Anna straight in the eyes, his voice soft and reassuring. "You and Peter are family to Erica and me, and we love you. Like Erica told you at Thanksgiving, we've instructed our attorney to draw up the papers, and hopefully, the judge will approve your living with us and make me your guardian. But we'll have to wait for the Judge to approve our request."

"Yeah, but that ol' witch what's-her-name probably still wants me to go to that Helmhurst place." Anna was slouching over her plate and picking at her mashed potatoes.

"Anna, let's not start calling people names." It was all she could do to keep from laughing at Anna's candid observation.

"Well, Peter and me got a big problem."

"I think it's Peter and I. And yes, honey, you do have a big big problem. Then again. you have us."

"That's about the only good thing."

~ ~ ~

On February 25, Judge John Thorton held a hearing to determine who would become Anna's guardian — John Dowd or the Minnesota Department of Welfare. He already adjudicated Bridget Olson's will. Thanks to their family attorney, Bridget had a will that stipulated half of everything going to Peter and half to Anna. Since Anna was a minor, she would need a separate guardian whose only job was to handle her share of the money until she became an adult.

Although the judge preferred to hold commitment and custody hearings in his office, there were too many people present to make that workable, so he moved it to the courtroom. That morning, the courtroom was still chilly as the group entered. The chill seemed to make the sounds of shoe leather and chairs sliding on the oak floor even crisper, louder.

Peter, the Dowds, and their attorney, Mr. Harold Granderson, sat at one large table. At the other table were Joan Bridenbaugh, Miss Abigail Pratt, and Arlys Shoemaker, current president of the Southwest Chapter of the Minnesota Eugenics Society.

Harold Granderson and John Dowd wore suits. Peter had on a worn pair of slacks and a white shirt with a dirty collar. Joan Bridenbaugh dressed in a black full-length skirt that stopped just below her knees. She wore a cream-colored silk button blouse closed at her neck, and a light brown waist-length jacket accented with a red rose pin. A white silk scarf gave her an almost stylish look. Joan sat in the middle of her chair, her back straight and her head unmoving.

Joan often viewed John Dowd as a threat because he was everything she was not. He graduated from Augustana College in Minneapolis with a four-year degree in English and Business. She had but a two-year Social Work degree from Mankato State. He was intelligent, rich by rural Minnesota standards, and highly respected. Throughout the years, he challenged many statements she made, tweaking her inner sense of vulnerability, and causing her to avoid him.

There was a palpable, electric kind of tension in the

air. A cough startled Joan and broke the almost perfect silence. Everyone seemed frozen in place as they waited for Judge Thorton. He broke the pressure when he walked briskly into the room, followed by a court recorder. He wore a crisp, dark blue, double-breasted suit, a white shirt, and a red tie. As soon as he sat down, he surveyed the room, then a sharp rap of his gavel echoed off the walls.

"This hearing is now in session. Let me remind you that this is a hearing, not a trial. I expect courtesy and proper professional demeanor. However, since this is a legal proceeding, everyone who is speaking to this matter must first state their name and swear an oath they are telling the truth. I will take everything presented this morning into consideration. Then, I will make my decision regarding Miss Olson's future. It will derive from the appropriate sections of the Minnesota Revised Code, which are collectively known as the Children's Code of 1917.

"Mr. Granderson, I believe you will speak for Miss Olson and Mr. Dowd. Miss Bridenbaugh, you are here on behalf of Redwood County. Is that correct?"

Both nodded yes.

"Good. I have before me two petitions for the custody of the orphan Miss Anna Olson. One from Mr. Granderson and the other from Miss Bridenbaugh. This hearing will address both. Please keep in mind that what is at stake here is what is best for this child. That is the only thing that matters."

Joan nodded but thought. *Not in my mind, What's best for society, that's what's at stake. No feebleminded child matters one way or the other.*

"Mr. Granderson, you first. Oh, Mr. Granderson, do

you swear to tell the truth, the whole truth, and nothing but the truth, so help you, God?"

"I do." Mr. Granderson continued, "Thank you, your honor."

"John Dowd met Mr. and Mrs. Olson three days after they stepped off the train in Grant Grove in 1911. Within the first month they immigrated from Norway, Lars Olson began working for Mr. Dowd and Bridget Olson for his mother, Petra Dowd.

"When the Olsons were ready to buy their farm, Mr. Dowd loaned them the money they needed. Since Mrs. Olson would no longer be able to work for the Dowds, she and Lars recruited Erica Tomlinson from Norway to be her replacement in the Dowd household. Eventually, Erica and John wed but were unable to have children of their own.

"The Olson family and Mr. and Mrs. Dowd became lifelong friends. The families exchanged holiday gifts, shared meals, and enjoyed the benefits of a close relationship. Mr. and Mrs. Dowd grew to view the Olson children like a niece and nephew.

"There are many reasons they are qualified to serve as Anna Olson's guardian. Mr. Dowd is a college-educated and successful businessman. He has more than adequate financial resources to support Miss Olson. Both the Dowds are church-going people with good moral character. They are known for their honesty and compassion for those less fortunate.

"Mrs. Dowd is an intelligent and cheerful woman who will teach Anna all the things a young lady needs to know to have her own home someday. Erica and John Dowd will be sure she grows up with good manners and will obey the laws of God and man.

"Your honor, Miss Olson isn't allowed to attend school due to her having just two spells of epileptic-like shaking and jerking. I would like to point out that the two documents Miss Bridenbaugh submitted do not say she has epilepsy. They only *think* she might have this malady."

"Mr. Granderson, what does this have to do with Miss Olson's custody?"

"Your honor, if the attendance exclusion stands, Mrs. Dowd will supervise her education in their home. The Dowds will hire a tutor if Mrs. Dowd isn't able to teach the subject matter. They'll be able to provide her medical care if and when it's needed. Living in Grant Grove, they are but a few blocks away from Dr. Phillips.

"Finally, the Dowds have grown very fond of Anna. They love her as their own daughter and will treat her as such. Therefore, we believe they are well suited to serve as Anna's guardians should you grant Mr. Dowd's request."

"Thank you, Mr. Granderson." Before continuing, he administered the oath to John Dowd. "Mr. Dowd, did he leave anything out?"

"No, your honor, I believe he covered our qualifications and interest very well," John spoke with confidence, his voice calm and smooth. "I do want to add that we are very fond of Anna. She has lived in our home since before her mother died so we can testify to the fact she is a wonderful young lady."

"Thank you, Mr. Dowd."

Looking at Peter, Judge Thorton continued, "Mr. Olson, I have some questions for you. First, do you swear to tell the truth, the whole truth, and nothing but the truth, so help you, God?"

"Ah . . . yes."

"Do you think everything Mr. Granderson said is true?"

"Uh, yes sir, your honor. I can say for certain my folks were good friends with the Dowds, and we were over to their place all the time."

"Did they treat you and your sister well?"

"Yes . . . yes, Mr. and Mrs. Dowd did. I mean, they still do."

"Do you think you can look after your sister?"

"No, sir. I am too young. I don't know how to look after her, especially if she is home all the time and me bein' out doing the farming things. Besides, we seem to be fighting all the time. I know that ain't the best for Anna."

"Thank you, Peter." Judge Thorton made a couple of quick notes then proceeded.

"Miss Bridenbaugh, it's your turn. Before you begin, do you swear to tell the truth, the whole truth, and nothing but the truth, so help you, God?"

"Yes, of course," she said, brushing the oath off like lint from a dress. Joan stood straight, her shoulders pulled back, her chin high. She hesitated for a moment, looking down at the table to find her notes. "On behalf of the State of Minnesota, I wish to extend my heartfelt sympathies to the Olson children. My heart and prayers go out to them both. Their parents were good people and so unjustly taken in the prime of their lives.

"I believe that it's in Anna Olson's best interest for the State of Minnesota to serve as her guardian. I have two reasons: First, she has a diagnosis of epilepsy. I've submitted to you written statements from Dr. Phillips as well as a second opinion from a neurological clinic in Minneapolis. Both say that it is highly likely Miss Olson has epilepsy. She has only had two seizures—that we know about, at least. But being an epileptic, she may have more fits at any time. A person in her condition, therefore, requires the correct medical care and education that is currently only available at the Helmhurst School for Epileptics.

"Point number two, Your Honor: the superintendent of the Grant Grove School stated that Anna would not be allowed back at school until a doctor states in writing she will be free from fits."

Without waiting for the judge's approval, Harold Granderson blurted out,

"That is like banning a child from school for life!" His voice was loud, his fists clenched, and he was visibly tense.

"Harold, stop. You, of all people, know better."

"Sorry, Your Honor."

"Miss Bridenbaugh, you may continue."

"When Anna had a fit at school, it was traumatic for her fellow students to see her twitching and jerking around on the floor. It was all very disruptive. We must protect the students from the sight of her having another one of her terrible fits." Joan paused for a dramatic effect. "After that episode, the other students were unable to concentrate on their studies when she was in the classroom. A fit is heart-wrenching to watch, even for an adult.

"I feel it is important for Miss Olson to finish her schooling with children who have similar problems. That way, when she has more seizures, no one will think a thing of it. Again, your honor, the only place that provides for that is Helmhurst."

Joan began to pick up the pace of her delivery.

"Proper medical care for epilepsy will make her less susceptible to injury from falls. Plus, as I said, she will be happier being with people of her own kind." She paused for effect, to let the comment sink in. *Who could be against making a child safe and happy?*

"Now then, there is also this issue of Anna being feebleminded. How do we know this? In a moment, I will let her teacher describe her behavior in the classroom. I will only point out that when she took an intelligence test administered by a Doctor of Psychology from the state, she scored in the low normal range. Her low-test score, plus her backward behavior at school, adds up to this diagnosis of feeblemindedness."

John Dowd exploded from his seat. "Your Honor, if I may!"

"No, you may not, Mr. Dowd. I will give you another chance to speak, but for now, it's Miss Bridenbaugh's turn." Nodding in Joan's direction, he said, "Please continue."

John Dowd slumped onto his chair like a large sack of potatoes thrown on the floor. Harold Granderson patted his knee and whispered something to him.

"I was saying before I was so rudely interrupted, young Miss Olson is feebleminded. It is a well-documented fact that these types of people are incapable of benefiting from formal education. Only the professionals working at Helmhurst can provide the care and training Anna needs. Now, Your Honor, I would like Miss Pratt, Anna's teacher, to speak for a moment or two. She can tell you about the problems Anna had at school."

Judge Thorton nodded it was okay for her to speak and gave her the oath. She blinked several times rapidly, hinting at a sense of insecurity.

"I am kind of nervous being here this morning, so excuse me if I don't speak so well in public. I've had Anna in my classroom for eight years, the whole time she has been in school."

"And this is a public school?"

"Yes, sir."

"What's the name?"

"The school name or my name?"

"The school, please. Give me the name of the school you teach at and where Anna attended."

"Sorry, sir. Well, it's the Schoolhouse Road County School number three. But of course, she doesn't go there anymore."

"When did she stop attending school?"

Miss Pratt blocked on an answer staring blankly in the judge's direction.

"Come come, Miss Pratt, I don't have all day. It's a simple question."

By this time, Joan whispered to her, "September 1931."

"Miss Bridenbaugh, are you the teacher here? If I wanted you to answer the question, I would have asked you." Judge Thorton had a hint of a scowl on his face. He looked back at Abigail Pratt.

"Surely you must know this . . ."

"September 1931, sir. She had a seizure in my class in the prior school year, so Miss Bridenbaugh and I went to the parents and told them Anna wouldn't be allowed to return to school. Do you want me to continue with my comments, sir?"

Judge Thorton nodded.

"Well, she never volunteered to answer questions; she

held back every time. She often didn't know the answers to questions. I would say she was mentally slower than the other students. It wasn't until they came around from the state and did those tests that I realized she was feebleminded."

"Help me get this clear: Are you saying the whole time Anna was in school, she never volunteered, and she never knew the answer to even one question?"

"No, sir, she usually knew the answers. She knew the material. The thing is, I had to pry every answer out of her."

"But she knew the answers?"

"Well, yes. Pretty much."

"Would you say she knew the material most of the time?"

"Yes, she usually knew the answers. But it was difficult getting them out of her." Miss Pratt repeated.

"I don't get this. You are telling me you had a girl in your class for seven, excuse me, eight years. First, you tell me she doesn't know the material you ask her to learn. Then you say she knew most, if not all, of the information in her studies. *Now* you are calling her feebleminded?"

"Yes, sir, that is what the doctor from the state called her."

Judge Thorton shook his head as if he didn't believe what he just heard. "Miss Pratt, please finish your comments as quickly as possible."

As Abigail Pratt was about to speak, Joan could see the scowl on John's face. She smiled at him, taunting him. She enjoyed seeing him uncomfortable. Even though Miss Pratt wasn't doing so well, his precious little Anna Olson would soon belong to the State of Minnesota. He was in her territory now. Commitment hearings were her specialty. She put feebleminded people in Helmhurst as often as possible.

Miss Pratt continued, "It's hard to get my students to concentrate on their studies when they have to worry constantly if she'll have another fit. Since we removed her from school, my class has returned to normal."

"Miss Pratt, one more thing. Have you ever been to Helmhurst, have you seen one of their classrooms?"

"No, sir, I ain't. I mean, haven't done that."

Judge Thorton looked back at Joan Bridenbaugh. "Is there anything else you wish to add? I see you have one more person sitting over there at your table."

"Yes, Your Honor. One more thing, and it may be the most important of all. Miss Arlys Shoemaker is here to tell you about a new research finding."

Judge Thorton interrupted her. "Miss Bridenbaugh, I am a busy man. Is this research going to be relevant to young Miss Olson's guardianship?"

"It is important because I want Miss Olson to go to Helmhurst. It will be best for her and best for society. This new research demonstrates that point."

"Okay, but please let's keep this brief. Miss Shoemaker, do you swear to tell the truth, the whole truth, and nothing but the truth, so help you, God?"

"I do, Your Honor." After receiving a nod from the judge, Arlys Shoemaker weighed in, "Your Honor, as you may know, I'm the President of the Southwest Chapter of the Minnesota Eugenics Society. We're one of the oldest and most important chapters in the nation I might add, thanks to Dr. Dight's leadership.

"Your Honor, I have received a follow-up study to that

done by a Dr. Goddard back around 1917 or thereabouts. I'm sure you know about his famous study of the Kallikaks. This new study brings eugenics close to home. It illustrates the considerable number of degenerate descendants of one woman now in prison up in Duluth. They found a total of twenty-three of her children and grandchildren have ended up in jail for robbery or making mischief. Or, they ended up in places like Helmhurst because they were feebleminded. That all of these problems arose from one person is shocking, Your Honor, and it frightens many of us.

Unless she is sterilized, or put in Helmhurst, Anna Olson could have countless descendants who would also be genetically inferior. They would have these fits and suffer from melancholy like her mother. The good, hard-working taxpayers of Minnesota could end up paying for their care and treatment."

"Okay, that's enough, Miss Shoemaker. I'm way behind schedule, and I have heard and read all about eugenics. But these matters don't pertain to the custody of Miss Olson. Thank you for coming just the same." He noted both John Dowd and Harold Granderson were now on their feet and gave them a hand gesture to stay quiet and sit down.

Arlys Shoemaker remained standing and continued speaking, not understanding that Judge Thorton ordered her to stop.

"Then there is this here copy of a letter written to none other than our own Dr. Dight, by the Chancellor of Germany, Mr. Adolf Hitler.

"'Dr. Dight, thank you for sending me the newspaper article praising our work toward creating a better future *by eliminating people with genetic flaws.'* You see, Dr. Dight had written this article for the Minneapolis Journal that praised Germany . . .

"Miss Shoemaker! Stop. Nobody here gives a damn about this Hitler fellow, nor Dr. Dight for that matter. Please sit down and be quiet."

"Your Honor, sir, let me state the letter is relevant. It recognizes the importance of race science the way they do it in Germany. They have set out a roadmap for the future of a better world."

"*Stop.* One more word from you and I'll put you in jail for contempt."

"Sorry, sir, I'll stop, but you should be smart enough to see how all of this is very relevant to that defective girl, Anna Olson."

"Joan, get her out of here right now, and if she doesn't leave, I'll call Sheriff Smith up here to take her to jail. Do you understand!" His face was red; his eyes narrowed as he glared at Joan.

"Yes, Your Honor."

Rebuffed by the judge, Joan lost her composure. She leaned over Arlys Shoemaker, plucked her purse up off the floor, grabbed her by the arm, and briskly led her to the door. Calling over her shoulder, Arlys Shoemaker left a final comment. "History will show I'm right. *Send her to Helmhurst!*"

With the door shut and Joan back at her seat, Judge Thorton tried to get the hearing back on track.

"Now, are you finished?"

Trying to get her breath and composure back, Joan replied, "Not quite, Your Honor. Miss Schoemaker mentioned sterilization. Should you grant custody to the

Dowds, I will file a separate petition to the Director of the Minnesota Department of Public Welfare, asking for the sterilization of Miss Olson. At the very least, we must be sure she doesn't bear any children."

"Miss Bridenbaugh, stop it. Don't you ever do this again. First of all, I don't need these housewives who've gone to a meeting or two marauding as experts peddling their brand of elitism into my hearings. I have half a notion to slap you with contempt.

"Secondly, don't come in here and threaten a young lady with something as serious as forced sterilization as a way to sway my opinion. I won't have any of that. I'm just about ready to grant custody of this young lady to John Dowd right now."

Harold Granderson suddenly stood. "We think you're right, sir. There is no real science behind this whole eugenics or genetic movement. Many of the things they espouse simply aren't true."

"Harold be quiet. I didn't invite your opinion." Taking a deep breath, Judge Thorton continued, "I've had enough. Let's try to stick to the facts at hand and only speak when I ask for your input. Just maybe we can get through this."

By the time the last word was out, Joan Bridenbaugh was standing. "Your Honor, I'm not quite finished. I do have one more item that's hard to discuss in an open hearing. I prefer discussing it with you privately."

"You know the rules, Joan. You have been through this process more times than anyone. This is an open hearing. Everyone who has a legitimate interest in Anna's welfare gets a chance to hear what I hear. Everyone gets to clarify things for the record. Do you have something to add, or not?"

"Yes, Your Honor, I would like to draw your attention to the moral character of John Dowd. Sir, he may not be the best man to direct the future of an impressionable young lady."

John forgot he was in a formal hearing, forgot that it was the judge who ran it. He rose to his feet and turned to face Joan. "What? What are you implying? You better be careful what you throw around, Joan."

Judge Thorton rapped his gavel and shouted over Dowd's voice, "*Sit down, Mr. Dowd. Sit down and be quiet!* Next outburst and I'll throw you out as well. Miss Bridenbaugh, this better be good, or I will dismiss you from any future guardianship hearings."

"Well, Your Honor, I think it's relevant enough because it has to do with Anna's over-all well-being." She stole a glance at John Dowd, the hint of a smile still on her face. "In Grant Grove, it used to be common knowledge that Mr. Dowd frequently and secretly called on Miss Ruth Carlson, the lady who ran the café there. Everyone knew they were having a liaison of the carnal sort, the kind of relationship not endorsed by the Bible."

Harold Granderson rose. "Your Honor, I object. These allegations are neither factual nor relevant to the matters you are considering today. Her comments are very inappropriate and nothing more than old rumors."

Without waiting for Judge Thorton to get his breath, Joan continued, adding her last comment in one quick blast of words. "Plus, he had the same kind of affair with his current wife before they were married." Pointing at John, she added, "This was back when she lived in *his* house caring for *his* mother. Everyone knew it." Then she promptly sat down.

Erica Dowd rose, her face flushed with anger. "You filthy, filthy woman. Judge Thorton, what she is saying is a lie." The gavel came down hard again.

"*Mrs. Dowd*, now it's your turn to sit down and be quiet. That's enough, every one of you. I'm sorry I even bothered with this hearing. I should have talked to Anna and made my decision on how she answered my questions. Joan, you are done, and I'm not considering any of the things this Arlys lady brought in, nor any of your innuendos regarding Mr. Dowd. I've known John for most of my life, and I know the quality of his character. You just wasted everyone's time and put the quality of *your* character on display."

"Now, Mr. Granderson, do you have anything to add on behalf of Mr. Dowd?"

"Yes, Mr. and Mrs. Dowd feel that Anna can get a better education with private tutors in their home than in some faraway school. Perhaps we could work out a plan with the superintendent of schools that would allow Miss Olson to start high school there in Grant Grove. It seems to me some accommodations must be possible. Plus, she has been faithful at following a special diet known to reduce or even eliminate the fits. It could be she will never have one again. We feel she at least deserves another chance.

"Plus, the Dowds feel that sending her away now would be adding more shock and trauma to what she's already suffered." Harold Granderson was smooth, confident, his self-control evident.

"Your Honor, we have all seen young people go to Helmhurst and never return. The reason they go there is that it's supposedly a place where proper education and training can be delivered. Yet, we all know it is simply a place to dump the people Miss Bridenbaugh doesn't want in our community. How sad to see her ruin home after happy home with her eugenics crusade."

"*I object, your honor!*" It was Miss Bridenbaugh's turn to stand up and shout.

"Sit down, Joan, and be quiet until I ask you to speak. Mr. Granderson, are you about done?"

"Almost, Your Honor. I think anyone in the Grant Grove community would agree that Mr. and Mrs. Dowd are upstanding, good people. They worship the Lord every Sunday, and they participate and support all the charity events. One could not find nicer people to raise a teenager. Thank you."

"Now, it is my turn." Judge Thorton sat forward, his elbows on the bench, hunched over Anna's file, quickly looking at his notes and the material there. He looked up at John Dowd. "Mr. Dowd, how old are you?"

"Sixty-six."

Looking at Erica Dowd, he repeated his question.

"Fifty-two, Your Honor."

"Mrs. Dowd, do you have anything to add?"

"Yes, sir. Anna must stay with us. She has had enough loss for a lifetime. Please let her stay with us. We will take loving care of her and finish raising her properly." Tears welled up in her eyes and she put her face in her handkerchief.

"Thank you, Mrs. Dowd."

Then, without warning, the gavel came down hard. "This hearing is now over."

Chapter 19
ANNA OLSON

YOU NEVER QUITE KNOW WHEN YOU MAY HOPE TO REPAIR THE DAMAGE DONE BY GOING AWAY.
ELIZABETH BOWEN

1933

Judge Thorton reached a decision and summoned John Dowd, Harold Granderson, and Joan Bridenbaugh to his office on March 14, 1933.

"The issue is what is best for Anna Olson. In these matters, I always try to turn to family first, but sometimes that doesn't work out. Peter Olson admits he is too young to serve as her guardian. Mr. Dowd, although you and your wife seem to be a logical choice, you are too old. But that isn't all, perhaps even more important is this issue of her seizures. I'm going to think of Anna here: where can she best get both an education and treatment? From what I've learned, Helmhurst is that place. So I'm committing her to the Department of Public Welfare for placement in that facility.

"This was a hard decision for two reasons. John, your wife was correct. A move to a faraway institution may add more shock and misery for Miss Olson to handle. I'm betting, however, that she is a resilient young person who will adapt well to her new environment. I know you and Erica are good and decent people. Your charity and character were never in doubt. In this case, however, your age works against you. You're getting to be an old man. I heard the other day that we men, on the average, only live to age sixty-two. If something happens to you, we are right back here again.

"Anna needs a longer-term solution. She needs to be in a place better suited to continue her education." He paused to take a drink of water. "Minnesota law provides courts the authority to commit people based on their mental or physical condition. Two physicians feel that Anna probably has epilepsy. I realize the word 'probably' doesn't equal the word 'has,' but in Miss Olson's case, I think she'll have more seizures.

"We have this doctorate-level psychologist from the State of Minnesota, who evaluated Miss Olson and said she was borderline feebleminded. There is no corroborating evidence, no second opinion other than this teacher, and she contradicted herself at every turn. Therefore, I am instructing Miss Bridenbaugh to drop the classification as feebleminded when she makes her placement request to Helmhurst.

"I'm also ordering the State of Minnesota to ensure that Mr. and Mrs. Dowd serve as foster parents for Miss Olson until I rule otherwise. She is to remain in their home until a bed is available in Helmhurst."

Judge Thorton found eye contact with Miss Bridenbaugh, "Do I have your word and assurance that the Dowds will be Anna Olson's foster parents indefinitely? Do you understand that?"

"Yes, Your Honor."

Later that day, Joan opened her desk drawer, took out her little book, and turned to Anna's name. With her red pencil in hand, she placed a large checkmark on it. She was especially happy. *I just won another victory that makes our future more promising. Plus, I bet you are suffering, John Dowd, you almighty, self-righteous do-gooder.*

~ ~ ~

On July 16, 1933, the morning clouds hung low, trailers from a pre-dawn thunderstorm. Erica and Anna were at the farm to get a suitcase and sort through the few items that remained there to see if Anna needed to take any of them to Helmhurst. The first thing Anna did was to get the small wood locker her father and mother brought with them from Norway stored under one of the pantry shelves. She put the box on the kitchen table and joined Erica in her room.

They didn't find much in Anna's room. One dress and a blouse Anna used to wear when she went to church were all they decided to take. The rest of Anna's clothes were already at the Dowd home, where they would finish packing.

Erica shook her head and said, "This is so unfair . . ." Her eyes were welling up. She couldn't say more.

"I know." Anna turned and kicked an old doll under her bed.

Erica wiped the corner of her eyes and took a deep breath. "Well, we must do what the judge says, so we might as well get this finished. Anna, why do you want that old wooden locker? We can get you another suitcase."

"I just like it. Plus, it was my papa's. His dad made it, and my papa brought it all the way from Norway. It's kinda like a piece of my family history."

"Okay, it's just unusual for a girl to want to take a

wooden locker. Anyhow, it doesn't look like we're going to get much here. We'll finish packing at our house."

"Fine." The word came out cross, as if spoken by a teenager about to lose connection to the only home she had ever known.

Erica paid no attention to Anna's attitude. "After you leave, I'm going to pack up the rest of these clothes and move them to our house." Erica stopped for a moment realizing this detail may be too much for Anna to handle. "I'll get to that sometime later, though."

"What about Momma and Papa's things?"

"I don't know, Anna. John and I haven't talked about that yet. I guess we'll probably try to donate the clothes to the poor. We'll have to see what Peter says too. Everything belongs to the two of you, fifty-fifty."

"Erica, do you mind if I spend a few minutes looking at Momma and Papa's things? We're not in a big hurry, are we?

"Take your time, honey. I'll wait downstairs."

Anna went into her parents' room, and on a bookshelf, she found a stack of her mothers' completed but unframed needlepoint projects. She selected a few of her favorites and placed them in a sewing bag already filled with a variety of threads and needles.

She then moved to her parents' dresser, where she opened what she knew to be her papa's drawer and reached under a pile of socks where she found a small knife he had gotten from his grandfather in Norway. She turned the knife over in her hand, stroking it gently, and with a quick, impulsive move, tucked it into the sewing bag.

As she turned away from the dresser, her mother's

diamond ring caught her eye. Bridget wore the ring on special occasions only. The last time Anna remembered her wearing it was the day they buried her papa.

Without thinking, she scooped up the ring and placed it in the bag. She felt like she was stealing since her mother hadn't given it to her. On the other hand, her mother was no longer here. *Besides, if things had worked out differently, she might have given it to my fiancé before he proposed to me. Anyway, it's better that I have it than Peter.*

Anna knew the story of this ring. Lars got it as a gift from a rich, older man when he found out he was planning to marry Bridget Androder. Her eyes shone brightly each time she told the story of Lars proposing to her by the side of a little lake in Kleppe, Norway. Bridget recounted his blushing, how his hands shook when he took her hand, and how softly he spoke as he proposed. Bridget also talked about how the diamond was somehow related to the Norwegian royal family, but she didn't exactly understand how. At this moment, its importance was that it belonged to her mother.

There was one more thing Anna wanted. Downstairs, on the top of the dining room bureau, there was an exquisite round lace doily made by her maternal grandmother. Anna marveled at the intricate design and how perfectly the knots held the design in place. After a quick dash downstairs to retrieve the lace, the sewing bag was complete, as was her packing.

Anna plopped down close to Erica, who was resting on the sofa in the parlor. She leaned her head on her shoulder and let a few tears make their way down her pretty but sad face. Erica started humming an old Norwegian folk melody, the same one her mother used to sing. *I'm breaking into a thousand pieces,* Anna thought. What seemed like hundreds of memories came flooding in and out of her mind, quick scenes, so short she could barely recognize them.

"Come on, Anna, let's go. We need to get home for lunch."

"Home? But your home isn't really my home." The word 'home' stuck with Anna. *How can it be that the only home I've ever known isn't going to be my home any longer?*

~ ~ ~

Erica looked at the calendar on the wall. It was July 18, and she knew that this would be one of the worst days of her life. Joan Bridenbaugh was taking Anna to Helmhurst. Today was the day they would lose Anna. She tried to understand how this was yet another "worst day" of Anna's young life.

John was waiting at the dining room table, his breakfast getting cold. He was silent, sullen-looking, and only occasionally taking a sip of coffee. So far, Anna hadn't appeared at the table.

"When's she gonna get up?"

"I called her fifteen minutes ago because I knew you two would want to say goodbye to each other."

"I gotta get to work." With that, John stood up, placed his napkin on his still clean plate, and went upstairs to her room. "Anna, I have to get to work."

A faint "goodbye" came from the other side of the door.

John knocked then opened the door. A fully dressed

Anna was sitting on her bed, head down, and crying.

He walked over to her, and as he did, she stood up, hugged him, then immediately sat back down on the bed. He sat down next to her and put his arm around her. "Be sure to listen to what they tell you to do, Anna. Remember, we'll do everything we can to get you back here with us. I hope you remember this is your new home, and we are your new parents."

Anna remained silent, so John pulled her close before standing up. Turning to leave, he paused, as if he were unsure if he would get a reply from her or if there was something else to be said. The hesitation was just that, his instinct was to leave before he started crying, this time for the loss of his best friend's daughter.

Erica was waiting by the foot of the stairs. When he reached her, she quickly grabbed his hand and squeezed it. "Have a good day, honey." He promptly disappeared out the back door. *That's okay,* Erica thought, *Judge Thorton's decision broke his heart too.*

Erica sat down next to Anna and was struck by how much Anna reminded her of Bridget. There was something in that silent, withdrawn posture and blank, emotionless face that caused her to pause for a moment. "We did everything we could to keep you here with us. You know that, don't you?"

Anna erupted in anger and quickly stood up. "Well, you didn't do enough, did you?"

Erica brushed off the sting of Anna's comment. She understood Anna was an orphan and a teenager who was losing everything she knew and loved. Now she was forced to adjust to a new life in a foreign-sounding place far away from home. "Come on sweetie, let's get your box downstairs and get you something to eat."

"I'm not hungry."

"I don't suppose you are. Maybe at least you'll have a little bit of your favorite cinnamon rolls with white icing."

"If you say so," Anna mumbled as she picked up a sweater and her sewing bag.

When they got downstairs, Peter was at the dining room table, eating a cinnamon roll. He'd gotten a friend to do his chores and was planning on going with his little sister to Helmhurst.

"I suppose you've been crying again," he teased.

"What's it to you? You don't have to go to some stupid place and be away from home."

"You're right. I was just teasing you. You're still broken up over Mom and Dad dying, then this happened. It's a lot for a little pip-squeak like you."

"Ha ha ha. Like you're some shining example of how to handle things. You still go out drinking every night? That's the way you handle it. At least I'm not some dead-end alcoholic, nobody like you."

"You two stop it right now."

Peter then got up and gave Anna a side hug and kissed her on the top of her head. "I'll miss you, Anna."

~ ~ ~

Joan Bridenbaugh arrived at the Dowd home an hour late, driving her five-year-old Packard. She stood by the car, primped, primed, and smiling the smile of victory. She honked her horn impatiently, signaling that Erica, Peter, and Anna were to come to the car. With faces grim, they silently and slowly walked out of the house. Peter was carrying the locker.

"I thought I told you one suitcase." Joan's voice sounded harsh and angry. "What's this wooden box?"

Erica shot back, "Pretend it's a suitcase Joan. Use your imagination for once."

"I know a suitcase when I see one, and this isn't a suitcase. The rules say one suitcase, not one box. Oh well, come, come. We're already late."

"You're the one who made us late. We've been waiting on you for an hour," snapped Anna.

"Well, it couldn't be helped. I had other things to do. Smarty mouth, little girls like you aren't my only concern."

Erica sat in front. Anna and Peter in the back. As the car pulled out the driveway, Anna laid her head back on the thick plush seat and, for a short while, gazed at the leaves overhead. They blanketed the streets of Grant Grove with serene, peaceful shade. Like the last two years of her life, they gradually became a blur. She soon closed her eyes. *I wonder what they'll do to me in that Helmhurst place?*

AUTHOR NOTES

In 1975 while serving as the Director of Professional Services at the Glacial Ridge Training Center in Wilmar, Minnesota, I met an extraordinary woman. Many years later, she became Anna Olson, one of the central characters in the novel you just finished reading.

Miss Olson had recently transferred to our facility for developmentally disabled individuals from another Minnesota institution. As a part of our intake evaluations, my psychologist administered the Weschler Adult Intelligence test to every new admission. She scored a 100, meaning she had "average" intelligence. This finding was a huge surprise because we knew that IQ scores go down the longer people are institutionalized. Anna had been in Minnesota institutions continuously for over 40 years! I thought she must be one strong-willed person to have survived all those years with her intellect intact!

For some reason, we found most of her files purged, except for a few basic facts. We knew she came from southern Minnesota, where she lived on a farm and had one older brother. She and her brother became orphans shortly before her admission. Her record showed she was committed because she had epilepsy. When she came to us, she was still on one seizure medication. But our blood workup showed the dosage amount far below the therapeutic level. She didn't have any seizures recorded in her medical records, let alone epilepsy.

I recall my first meeting with her and her treatment team. I informed her we had no legal basis for holding her, and she was free to leave any time she wished. Her retort was sharp, "Where am I going to go? I have no idea how to get along outside an institution! I don't know about money, have any money, or know how much things cost." She had a good point. She was finally free, but not free.

We worked with Anna in planning for her transfer to the next phase of her life. She wanted to go to Minneapolis to live. Fortunately, we found a transition program there that helped people like her move from institutional life to independent living.

For many years I thought Anna was unique. Which is why I wanted to write about what I thought her story might be. In researching this book, I learned about eugenics and the harmful things it did to many people. I learned that there were tens of thousands of Annas who, for even minor reasons, were committed to institutions. Many were kept there for decades, solely to work at menial but necessary jobs to keep those institutions operating. In the sequel to *American Genes*, I explore in detail what Anna's life would have been like inside the fictional "Helmhurst."

ACKNOWLEDGEMENTS

There are so many people who helped me along this journey. Thanks to all my friends in reading groups. Your ongoing support and encouragement moved me forward. I sincerely appreciate everyone who read drafts of the book, chapters, and short stories and taught me how to become a better writer. Tim Vargo, Katrina Karac, Charles O'Donnell, and Clayton Cormany are but a few.

My best friend, Ric Zaharia, put me on the writing path ten years ago. His persistent encouragement, guidance, and insights have been invaluable. This book would have never happened without him.

Finally, thank you to the love of my life, Cheryl. She read every line of every draft and served as my editor at home. Her suggestions and encouragement are the foundation upon which my work comes together.

ABOUT ATMOSPHERE PRESS

Atmosphere Press is an independent, full-service publisher for excellent books in all genres and for all audiences. Learn more about what we do at atmosphere-press.com.

We encourage you to check out some of Atmosphere's latest releases, which are available at Amazon.com and via order from your local bookstore:

The Hidden Life, a novel by Robert Castle
Big Beasts, a novel by Patrick Scott
Alvarado, a novel by John W. Horton III
Nothing to Get Nostalgic About, a novel by Eddie Brophy
GROW: A Jack and Lake Creek Book, novel by Chris S McGee
Home is Not This Body, a novel by Karahn Washington
Whose Mary Kate, a novel by Jane Leclere Doyle
Stuck and Drunk in Shadyside, a novel by M. Byerly
These Things Happen, a novel by Chris Caldwell
Vanity: Murder in the Name of Sin, a novel by Rhiannon Garrard
Blood of the True Believer, a novel by Brandann R. Hill-Mann
The Dark Secrets of Barth and Williams College: A Comedy in Two Semesters, a novel by Glen Weissenberger
The Glorious Between, a novel by Doug Reid
An Expectation of Plenty, a novel by Thomas Bazar
Sink or Swim, Brooklyn, a novel by Ron Kemper

ABOUT THE AUTHOR

Kirby Nielsen lives in Delaware, Ohio, where he writes novels and short stories. His research and subject matter is eugenics in America from 1900-1970.

After receiving his Master of Arts degree in Applied Behavior Analysis from Drake University, Mr. Nielsen became the Director of Professional Services at the Wilmar State Hospital in Wilmar, Minnesota. It was there he began a career that provided him with a rich background for his stories.

Mr. Nielsen hopes his work, although historical, will raise red flags for modern professionals so they may avoid the horrible mistakes of the past.